The Hunt for Jack Reacher Series

Don't Know Jack
Jack in the Box
Jack and Kill
Get Back Jack
Jack in the Green
Jack and Joe
Deep Cover Jack
Jack the Reaper
Black Jack
Ten Two Jack
Jack of Spades
Prepper Jack
Full Metal Jack
Jack Frost
Jack of Hearts
Straight Jack
Jack Knife
Lone Star Jack
Bulletproof Jack
Bet On Jack
Jack on a Wire

The Michael Flint Series

Blood Trails
Trace Evidence
Ground Truth
Hard Money

The Jess Kimball Thrillers

Fatal Enemy
Fatal Distraction
Fatal Demand
Fatal Error
Fatal Fall
Fatal Edge
Fatal Game
Fatal Bond
Fatal Past
Fatal Heat
Fatal Dawn
Fatal Shot

The Hunt for Justice Series

Due Justice
Twisted Justice
Secret Justice
Wasted Justice
Raw Justice
Mistaken Justice
Cold Justice
False Justice
Fair Justice
True Justice
Night Justice

Diane Capri

Trace Evidence

Published by: AugustBooks

http://www.AugustBooks.com

ISBN: 978-1-962769-31-0

Original cover design by: Cory Clubb

Published in the United States of America.

Visit the author website:

http://www.DianeCapri.com

Cast of Primary Characters

Michael Flint

Kathryn (Katie) Scarlett

Alonzo Drake

Veronica Beaumont

Jamison (Jamie) Beaumont

Josh Hallman

Mark Wilcox

Boyd Wilcox

Ruben Vega

Kevin Hayes

Sebastian (Baz) Shaw

Jasper Crane

Madeline (Maddy) Scarlett

and

Carlos Gaspar

For the readers who have supported me and enjoyed my books and asked for more.

I couldn't do this without you.

Thank you.

Trace Evidence

"It seemed to me that a careful examination of the room and the lawn might possibly reveal some traces of this mysterious individual. You know my methods, Watson. There was not one of them which I did not apply to the inquiry. And it ended by my discovering traces, but very different ones from those which I had expected."

—The Memoirs of Sherlock Holmes

Sherlock Holmes in "The Crooked Man"

Chapter One

Nassau, Bahamas
Friday

Michael Flint breathed evenly as he ignored muscle fatigue and the cold Atlantic Ocean pressing his body through his wetsuit like a taunting squeeze from an anaconda. He'd seen the sea do its worst. The ocean could surely squeeze a man to death more easily than the snake.

But he couldn't think about that now. It was too late to turn back.

He'd trained smart and hard for this mission. Reminded his body of lessons learned long ago and practiced but rarely employed these days. He was more fit than he'd been in years.

His combat dive training had guided his equipment choices, too. His wetsuit snugged like a second skin, allowing unrestricted range of motion. The diving knife strapped to his leg was easily within reach.

An untraceable standard Sig Sauer P226 was tucked into his suit. The pistol featured a waterproof chamber, which meant he could fire effectively underwater.

He wasn't expecting a gunfight before he reached **The Sea King**, but operations like these were unpredictable.

3 Trace Evidence

Around his waist were weights that countered his natural buoyancy and kept him effortlessly below the surface.

His lips and teeth held the mouthpiece for his rebreather system in place. The device recirculated a small volume of air, scrubbing away the harmful carbon dioxide before allowing the cleaned air back into his lungs.

The system was lightweight, which allowed freedom of movement, and eliminated exhaled bubbles that might otherwise announce his approach.

His exit strategy was just as sound. He wasn't worried. He lived, as always, in the moment. Alert. Oriented. Controlled.

He breathed evenly through the mouthpiece as he swam, large scuba fins propelling him steadily forward. He glanced at his watch. He'd been swimming below the surface for thirty-seven minutes from the drop-off point. His rebreather system functioned normally and guaranteed a healthy margin of error. No need to surface yet.

At his current rate of speed, he would arrive at the luxury superyacht precisely as planned.

The Sea King rested off the east coast of Nassau, Bahamas, relaxed and alone in the sunshine like a lazy lizard. The wind was slow, the waves gentle. The yacht was capable of remarkably high speed for its size. But speed wasn't its objective today.

5 Trace Evidence

Flint had studied every inch of **The Sea King** and its crew thoroughly for the past two weeks. As he completed his approach, another part of his brain ran through what he'd learned once more.

In the center, **The Sea King** rose three decks above the hull. The top deck was the owner's private preserve. The deck below was ringed with a continuous band of mirrored windows that deflected heat without obstructing the stunning views from inside. When not in use, the helipad at the bow was designed to serve as a sundeck, often occupied by nude sunbathers. But none lounged there today.

The Sea King was famous among a certain social set. If the decks and staterooms could only talk, Flint's client had said, scandalous secrets of internationally renowned masters of the universe would be revealed. To Flint, the depraved behavior of frivolous gadabouts was unimportant.

He wasn't here to party.

As his father had done before him, the yacht's current owner hosted a legendary card game each week. Participation was by invitation only, for men of a certain quality. A long list of potential players lusted after a seat at the table. Some worthy, some not, waited years for the chance. For more, the invitation would never come.

Flint was not welcome. Which was why his preparations had been especially thorough.

7 Trace Evidence

In a casino bar, he had befriended the ship's private chef. Plied with enough alcohol, the chef had confirmed **The Sea King**'s custom interior layout, which Flint had retrieved from the manufacturer's secret archives. With a high-powered telescope and secure military satellites, Flint had spent two weeks studying **The Sea King**'s activities.

The chef had drunkenly confirmed other details. The regular crew numbered ten, all weapons trained. Two were dedicated to security. The security team was identifiable by the black name tags they wore on their starched white uniforms. But it was their ruddy seaworn faces and bulging muscles that distinguished them as the ones most likely to win in close-quarters combat.

Flint had watched as wealthy visitors were ferried from the island to the helipad at **The Sea King**'s bow several times. Occasionally, women who didn't behave like wives were included. Up to twelve guests could be luxuriously accommodated overnight. Daytime visitor capacity was 120 souls.

He'd learned **The Sea King**'s systems and routines, charted its timetables, placed trackers on the ship's vehicles.

In short, over the past fourteen days, he'd identified, eliminated, and minimized risks until nothing but irreducible dangers remained.

Two hours before he entered the water, Flint had watched the helicopter deliver just five gamblers for the high-stakes poker game. With the crew and the owner, there were a total of sixteen people on board. Sixteen men. No girlfriends, no hookers, and certainly no wives or children.

Today's batch were longtime gamblers, but they were not the best of the best. Which was how the yacht's owner liked it. These players were the perfect patsies.

Just as Flint's client had been.

Should the patsies ever realize they'd been cheated, they'd have no legal recourse.

Not that his client wanted to make a legal claim for his losses. Far from it.

Attention to his plight from the courts or anyone else was the last thing he wanted. Which, in addition to extraordinary competence, was why he'd hired Flint. Discretion.

His client had lost a family heirloom. A not-so-small piece of jewelry. More specifically, an amber and gold pendant. The pendant was priceless because it had been a gift. From Nicholas II. The last Russian czar.

The client's great-grandmother had been a young violinist. In the dark months before the Russian Revolution, she had performed a private concert for the Romanovs and their guests.

Czar Nicholas II had been so moved by the performance, his own children so entranced by the girl's artistry, he had taken the pendant from his wife's neck and bestowed it upon the young musician.

Hers was the last concert ever performed for the czar's family. Months later, the Romanovs were executed in a grim stone cellar. The girl went on to become famous, for a time. She wore the Romanov pendant during every performance for the remainder of her career.

The pendant had been passed down through her family, until Flint's client inherited it. Because of its provenance, the pendant was appraised at eight million dollars, but it was not insured. Money could never replace the heirloom.

Flint patted the cheap replica stashed in the waterproof pouch in his wetsuit. The genuine Romanov pendant was resting inside the safe in **The Sea King**'s private office, deep within the owner's suite on the top deck.

All Flint had to do was exchange the fake pendant for the real one. When he thought of the mission like that, it seemed simple enough.

He kept up his rhythm, syncing his breathing to his power strokes with his arms and legs. **The Sea King**'s hull appeared dead ahead, relaxed and waiting in the sparkling water.

He glanced at his watch again. The first scheduled break in the poker game had ended fifteen minutes ago.

13 Trace Evidence

They should be well under way again in the glass-enclosed salon on the main deck.

Flint approached the yacht's aft, where the full-beam beach club featured a fold-down swim platform, deployed when guests were present. The platform was the easiest, fastest place to breach **The Sea King** from the ocean and the area least likely to be occupied during the intense poker game.

He stayed well below the surface and swam around the underside of the platform. There were no feet dangling in the water. He approached the platform's right side and slowly lifted his head from the water. The platform was unoccupied.

Rattan furniture with thick white cushions and ocean-blue pillows was arranged on the teak wood floor to provide seating for six. Two club chairs, a love seat, two end tables, and an ottoman in the center completed the grouping. All as expected.

Flint removed his fins and attached them to his belt. He dropped his weights into the ocean, then lifted himself out of the water and onto the swim platform, keeping out of sight of a closed-circuit security camera.

He backed against the hull and grabbed his gun. From the same waterproof pouch he pulled a towel and wiped down his wetsuit. The last thing he needed was a trail of wet prints leading anyone to him.

15 Trace Evidence

Satisfied, he tucked the towel under one of the cushions.

The owner's suite was on the upper deck, two decks above him. Careful to avoid the security cameras, he moved into the ship along a corridor and took the rear stairs to the main deck. He flattened himself against a pillar and peered around its edge into the giant glass-walled salon.

Views of the vast ocean through the mirrored windows were breathtaking, but the six poker players seated at arm's length around a circular table were intent on the game. Stacks of poker chips rested at each player's right arm. No one spoke.

The dealer was a man from Long Island, New York. Flint recognized him from his dossier. A man of loose morals and questionable business practices. The stack of chips at his elbow was taller than any of the others. His reputation for expert gambling seemed well displayed.

Flint silently continued to the next set of stairs and climbed to the upper deck. He adjusted his grip on the gun. **The Sea King**'s security crew relaxed procedures while the yacht was at sea, knowing they could easily hear any approaching conveyance, in the unlikely event one should arrive. As expected, the owner's suite entrance door was wide open.

Flint eased up to the side of the doorway. All he heard was an occasional exclamation from the gamblers below and the distant throb of the yacht's engines, idling to provide power for climate control, lighting, kitchen equipment, and the like.

He had to keep moving. The longer he spent on the ship, the greater the chance of discovery and failure. Timing was always everything.

Chapter Two

Flint looked around for threats and, seeing none, slipped carefully inside the owner's suite. So far, so good.

Every inch of the suite screamed wealth and privilege. **The Sea King**'s multimillion-dollar purchase price had paid for custom interiors well beyond what many seafaring monarchs could afford.

He ignored the grandeur and passed through the lounge area to a short corridor. Two doors led off to bedrooms, but at the far end was the office. He checked behind him and moved into the passageway.

19 Trace Evidence

His footsteps seemed loud to his hypersensitive ears inside the confined space. The gamblers were below him. He had to hope the yacht's builders had been generous with the sound deadening between decks.

Wood creaked ahead of him. A door popped open. A crew member in a white suit stepped out, a silver tray with the meal's remains held in both hands. His eyes widened at the same time Flint reversed his grip on the gun and threw a straight-arm punch.

The man's mouth had barely begun to open when Flint's knuckles hammered into his jaw. His head twisted sideways. His eyes rolled up and his body leaned backward.

Flint grabbed the tray with his free hand and shoved it against the collapsing man, pushing him to increase his backward momentum.

Flint quickly checked the room beyond the open door. The bed was unmade. He must have been cleaning the owner's suite.

Flint lowered the unconscious man to the floor. "Marco," according to his name tag. Flint placed the tray on the bed and dragged Marco into a closet. He closed and locked the door. Marco would be out for a while. By the time he regained consciousness, Flint planned to be long gone.

He listened hard. The players were still gambling and the engines were still rumbling. He heard no one headed in his direction.

21 Trace Evidence

Back in the corridor, he removed his tools from his pack and advanced toward the closed door. The office was the owner's exclusive domain, according to his chef. Entry was restricted to two people, the owner and his head of security. A biometric panel controlled the lock.

Flint grinned when he saw the setup. It was just as the drunk chef had described.

A retina scan was required to unlock the office. Retina scanning had an error rate of one in ten million. Impossible odds, even for those seeking vengeance against a cheating gambler. Thus, it could be relied on to thwart the average burglar.

But while retina scanners seemed cool in the movies, they were finicky technology. Simply put, they weren't reliable. Bright or inconsistent lighting, such as on this yacht, could cause malfunctions. If either the owner or his security chief developed any one of a number of eye conditions, the scanner would fail.

Which meant the retina scanner could lock the owner out of his own office as easily as it kept others out. Unacceptable.

The owner was wise enough to know the scanner's weaknesses. He would also know that tech-savvy governments now chose iris recognition instead of retina recognition for reliability.

23 Trace Evidence

All of which meant that sophisticated individuals clever enough to use a retina scanner for security locks also had a backup system.

Like an iris scanner coupled with a fingerprint or palm-print scanner.

Or, like **The Sea King**'s owner, all three.

Flint grinned again. With advance planning, these backup systems could be hacked. And he was nothing if not an advance planner.

His preparation time had been well spent. More than once in the past two weeks, he'd crossed paths with the yacht owner in the VIP men's lounge at the casino. He'd acquired samples of the owner's fingerprints and palm prints. He'd captured high-resolution images of both of the man's irises. He'd requested duplicates of all three biometrics from the lab. The entire process required a man with Flint's talents and connections, of course.

He shoved his weapon into his belt and reached into his tool bag again for his counterfeits.

First, he allowed the retina scanner to reject his retinas and engage the backup system.

Next, he used the duplicate fingerprints, palm prints, and iris scans in the proper order to release the lock.

He stepped inside, closed the door behind him, and reengaged the biometric scanners.

25 Trace Evidence

The safe was on the far wall. It was a high-quality item with an old-style combination lock. The owner was overly confident in his perimeter security. He didn't expect a burglar to get this far.

Flint attached a small box to the safe door and donned an earphone. He listened to the clicks as he rotated the dial. Five turns first, to completely unwind the mechanism. Then he reversed direction, listening and feeling the clicks. The change in sound was easy to find with the specially designed amplifier, yet it took a full minute to get the last number.

The safe's door popped open.

He heard footsteps. He brought the Sig up and aimed at the door. Flint strained to hear beyond the barrier.

"Marco," a man called out, his voice hushed. "Marco, where are you?"

Flint heard doors being gently tapped, and then footsteps leading away. He waited a moment longer before lowering his weapon and returning to the open safe.

He tucked the Romanov pendant securely into his waterproof pouch. He pulled out the documents and valuables, arranged them on the floor, and took photographs. As a billionaire once told him, every good businessman always keeps insurance.

27 Trace Evidence

He restacked the contents inside the safe.

Finally, he placed the fake pendant on the precise spot where the real one had been a few minutes before. His client needed time to receive the Romanov pendant and return it to his safety-deposit box before the yacht's owner realized it was missing. Satisfied the safe's contents were arranged exactly as he'd found them, he locked the safe.

Briefly, he scanned the office. Luxury emanated from every square inch of the place. Had Flint been a different sort of burglar, he could have a very nice haul. But he was there for a purpose, and he had achieved it. He left everything except the pendant precisely where he'd found it.

Eight minutes after he'd entered the office, he pressed the lock release to open the door, slipped into the suite, and pulled the door closed. He heard the lock click into place and the beeping sounds of the biometric alarm resetting.

Still well within his planned elapsed time for the mission. Only his extraction remained.

He opened the door and glanced into the stateroom with the unmade bed. The tray and its mess were still in place. Whoever had come looking for Marco had not done the job for him. Flint closed the door again and moved on.

His bare feet padded down the corridor into the opulent lounge.

29 Trace Evidence

Behind him, a loud bump. Flint spun, gun at the ready. The room was empty, and below, the gamblers were still talking. He breathed easy.

The door to the owner's bedroom crashed open. Marco stumbled into the corridor, still groggy, hand to his head, barely able to stand.

Marco was in no condition to fight, but his noise would summon more of the crew. Flint turned and ran.

When he reached the stairs, he saw the crew was quicker than he'd expected. One of the two security guards, Hewitt, stood on the bottom step, a tree-trunk-thick arm pointing a Glock 19 at Flint's chest. He gestured to Flint's gun. "Drop it."

Flint had been running, his arms pumping hard. He'd been preparing to take the stairs three at a time and keep going. The Sig was pointed upward. There was no way he could take aim before the guard fired.

Besides, he had come for an heirloom, not a killing spree.

Flint held his gun out, keeping it pointed toward the outside of the yacht. He heard footsteps behind him.

The groggy Marco arrived at his side. He shook his fist in Flint's face and glowered. "Ass—"

Flint grabbed Marco's arm before he could get the words out and launched him down the stairs. Flint followed behind, steering the man into Hewitt with his forearm.

The guard sidestepped. Flint launched a kick with his left leg into Hewitt's groin. The guard buckled but didn't collapse.

Flint shoved Marco in front of Hewitt and leapt toward the stairs to the lower level. Two more crewmen were climbing the steps. They were unarmed but could easily slow his progress until reinforcements arrived.

Flint veered around the stairs and ran toward the bow of the boat. Hewitt was back on his feet and closing fast.

Two shots rang out. Wood splintered from the low wall beside him. Flint dove for the floor. He was used to being shot at, and this bullet told him one thing. The first was a professionally placed warning but the next shot would hit him.

He ran behind the wall, doubled over to minimize his exposure. Hewitt appeared around the corner of the low wall. Aiming low, Flint fired once. Hewitt screamed and twisted sideways, tumbling out of view. Flint kept running.

He reached a stainless-steel ladder on his right. He threw himself onto the rungs, gripping the upright with one hand.

"Freeze," growled a voice at the bottom of the ladder. The second security guard, Gilbey, wielded another Glock.

Chapter Three

Flint paused. He didn't remove his hand from the side rail. He could easily drop the six-foot distance to the main deck without injury. At that point, he could run, but a bullet from Gilbey's weapon leveled at his abdomen would travel faster.

"Down," said Gilbey, waving one hand in that direction as if Flint might not understand the word.

Flint held his gun arm straight, the muzzle pointing out to sea, and moved down three rungs. Another crew member reached up to grab the Sig. Flint looked at the guy, then turned to stare Gilbey in the eyes, and back at the other man. Gilbey's gaze followed Flint's.

Flint lashed out with his right leg, punching his heel backward into Gilbey's face while firing a single shot over the crew member's shoulder. He lurched backward away from the Sig.

Flint threw himself at Gilbey, shoving him back and using a forearm to push his Glock away. Gilbey twisted to deflect Flint's weight and force.

Flint swept his Sig's grip onto Gilbey's temple. It was a solid blow expertly delivered, but Gilbey merely grunted and rammed a fist into Flint's stomach.

35 Trace Evidence

The pouch on the front of his wetsuit absorbed the brunt of Gilbey's strength, but the blow carried enough force to shove Flint's breath away.

Gilbey pounded a heavy fist into Flint's jaw. Stars danced in his vision. While he was recovering, Gilbey grabbed Flint's weapon and twisted the pistol out of his hand.

Flint drove a knee into Gilbey's groin.

He grunted, tossed the Sig away, and shoved Flint backward. Flint grabbed the guard's arm and rammed it through the ladder's rungs and let him go. Gilbey's own weight sent him tumbling to the deck.

He rolled flat on the deck, seeking enough space to push upright. Flint dropped to one knee and shoved the heel of his hand up hard against Gilbey's chin, knocking his head back against the deck. A satisfyingly hard but hollow thump sounded on the teak when the guard's head bounced. His eyes rolled back. His grip on his gun went slack. He was out cold.

Flint grabbed Gilbey's Glock. He fired over the heads of two crew members running toward him. They pulled back as he ran toward another ladder.

Hands on the outside of the rails, and feet never touching the rungs, he slid down and pushed away from the hull to free-fall the last five feet to the deck.

37 Trace Evidence

He landed in a narrow walkway that led toward the helipad on the bow of the yacht. Hewitt, the first guard, appeared at the aft end of the walkway. Flint raised the Glock. Hewitt did the same.

Flint had no intention of reenacting a Wild West shootout. He threw himself sideways into an alcove storing a full-size life raft. The raft hung from the ceiling on webbing arranged to make it easy to slide off the side of the yacht in the event of an emergency.

Flint grabbed his knife from its sheath on his thigh. The sharp tool easily hacked through the webbing. The raft was solid and heavy. As it fell, he shoved it into the corridor and wrenched the lever that inflated the buoyancy system. The self-contained gas bottle inflated the raft. It jerked and bounced, and in moments it filled the walkway.

The curve of the yacht's hull splayed outward below. He could jump, but the guard behind him would have a clear shot at short range and would make the most of the opportunity.

Flint heard shots followed by the hissing of air as the bright yellow raft began to deflate. Flint glanced over the side of the yacht. The surface of the Atlantic was a long way down.

He heard the raft being moved. Hewitt would be through the flimsy barrier in a moment.

39 Trace Evidence

Flint fired two shots over the heads of the two crewmen who had ventured toward him again, and they ducked back. He vaulted over the walkway's handrail, tucked and rolled when he hit the lower deck, and ran full out toward the side rail, gathering speed and momentum.

His neoprene wetsuit offered no friction and no resistance to gravity as he leapt over the rail and hurled himself toward the ocean, firing the Glock above his head until it was empty. He heard fire being returned, but his downward rush was the only thing that mattered.

He clamped his feet together and straightened his back before arrowing into the water.

The Atlantic stole his velocity. The great anaconda had him in its grasp again. He pulled his knees up to roll fast, got his head pointed down, and swam hard.

Straight white lines like silent spears traced their way into the water around him from the guns fired above. The automatic fire was blunted but not stopped by the water's relentless force.

He cupped his hands and worked with his legs. Full, complete strokes driving as fast and hard as he could. His lungs burned. He hadn't had time to oxygenate his blood, and diving without weights to pull him deeper consumed all his effort.

He fumbled until he found the rebreather mouthpiece and shoved it into his mouth. A white bullet line burst into life in front of him. Close. Too close.

He renewed his downward plunge, angling underneath **The Sea King** out of the line of fire.

The bullets stopped slicing through the water.

His ears complained at the change in pressure, but he rested to catch his breath. He glanced at his watch to check the time. He could wait here. He was safe from gunfire under the yacht.

Too briefly.

A deep growl reverberated through the water. A misty plume launched and grew at the rear of the ship. The screws were turning. **The Sea King** was under way.

He kept close enough to the side to use the yacht's hull for protection, and deep enough not to be caught in its churning wake. The yacht effortlessly pulled ahead. In a minute, he'd be exposed in the ocean behind the yacht.

The crew's gunfire would have a clean sight line.

He quickly donned his fins.

His only hope was speed and depth. He kicked with his legs. The big fins multiplied his efforts. He kept his head forward and down, to fight his body's natural buoyancy, and steered to the left of the screws.

43 Trace Evidence

Too quickly, the dark shadow of the yacht swept away.

But **The Sea King**'s speed worked to Flint's advantage, too, separating him from their guns faster than he could manage under his own power.

White bullet lines sliced around him again but stopped after a few rounds. Their guns were no match for the water's drag, and they were rapidly moving out of effective range.

Flint arced upward. In the crystal-clear water, the ship loomed large. It seemed as if it were still on top of him. An illusion. But he worked to move farther from the luxury monster before breaking the surface.

The rear deck of the yacht was filled with white-clad crew members sporting all manner of weapons. His heart pounded harder against his ribs when he saw that two of them appeared to be assembling a .50 caliber machine gun on a heavy tripod.

Once readied, he'd never escape its range under his own power.

Flint spun around, searching the horizon. A couple of hundred yards to his right, his hired jet skis bobbed in the water, waiting. The two drivers saw him as soon as he saw them. The engines screamed to life.

One machine headed straight for him while the other curved around closer to the rear of **The Sea King**. The second jet ski operator fired warning shots to keep his attackers occupied.

45 Trace Evidence

The white-clad figures on the yacht dove for cover.

The driver of the first jet ski tossed a boogie board into the water as it screamed past Flint. He caught the board. A bungee cord unfurled from the rear of the jet ski. Flint rolled onto the board and gripped the sides. The bungee reached its full length, and the energy stored in its stretched length was unleashed. The board shot forward while Flint hung on, rolling his weight from side to side to keep the board upright.

The jet ski's engine continued its scream unabated. Soon, Flint was speeding the same forty miles an hour as the machine, leaving **The Sea King** too slow to follow.

The second jet ski caught up. The driver gave Flint a thumbs-up as he passed by.

Flint patted the pouch. The pendant was still there.

He watched the yacht grow smaller in the distance. The extraction wasn't executed as precisely as he'd planned. But he had the Romanov pendant, and no one from **The Sea King** had followed.

He edged up onto his elbows as the board hammered against the waves, and watched the approaching coastline, enjoying the ride.

Mission accomplished.

Chapter Four

Houston, Texas
Sunday

Sunday in Houston was typically quiet and Flint was sleeping late. He rolled over in bed and slapped the bedside table until his fingers found his phone. The special ringtone assigned to Scarlett had been jiggling the phone periodically for the past hour. She wouldn't stop until he picked up. When Scarlett had a bee in her bonnet, she never gave up.

Without opening his eyes, he said, "What?" It came out a little more harshly than he'd intended.

"Michael," a peeved seven-year-old girl's voice demanded, "where are you?"

He groaned. He could ignore her mother, but Maddy Scarlett was another matter. He rolled over and held the phone to his ear. "How can I help you, Miss Scarlett?"

"You're late. You're never late. You promised to take me to the zoo today. Do you know what time it is?"

He pictured her small toe tapping and her arms folded over her chest. He opened one eye. She was right. He had been due to pick her up more than an hour ago, but he'd returned from **The Sea King** job after two a.m. and flopped into bed after four. He hadn't slept enough yet.

He groaned again. "How about if we do it tomorrow, instead?"

"I'm ready now. I need to go today." She stated the facts without whining.

"I'll throw in a trip to Daisy's. Would that be enough to sweeten the deal?"

She giggled in the way that displayed her dimples. Daisy's was the local ice cream joint. Maddy loved the place and her mother did not. Sneaking over to Daisy's for a cone was one of their secrets. Of course, her mother knew every time they went because Maddy couldn't eat her favorite chocolate ice cream without getting it all over her. But it thrilled Maddy to think that she had a secret date. Truth be told, he got a kick out of her delight.

Maddy said, “I can’t go to the zoo tomorrow.”

“Why not?”

“I have school, Michael.” Her tone was the same as if she’d said her beloved mini schnauzer, Whiskers, had four legs.

He grinned. “You do? What day is it?”

“It’s Sunday.” She sighed in that exaggerated way only seven-year-olds can. As if adults were so very clueless. “We can skip the zoo since it’s so late already. But you should take me to Daisy’s today.” She paused and whispered, “I have a favor I want to ask you.”

51 Trace Evidence

"A favor?" The statement made him uneasy. Maddy's favors were usually all about things her mother had forbidden. When he gave in to Maddy, as he always did, her mother's temper flared in extremely unpleasant ways. Instinctively, he rubbed the scar on his chest where her mother had accidently shot him with an arrow playing William Tell when he was eight. "What kind of favor?"

"I'll tell you when you get here," she said, giggling again.

He could almost see the joy on her face through the phone. He groaned. "Okay. You wore me down. Give me an hour."

"A whole hour?"

"And Maddy?"

"Yeah?"

"Don't tell your mom." Her infectious laugh as she hung up made him grin again despite his lingering exhaustion.

He'd planned some time off to relax and maybe focus on a personal matter that had been nagging him lately. Tomorrow would be soon enough to get started. He had returned the Romanov pendant to its rightful owner. The client had paid Flint's fee, half the appraised value plus expenses, and deposited the four million dollars directly into his numbered account in Grand Cayman. The case was closed. His bank account was healthy.

He drifted back to sleep.

He often wondered about Maddy's father. Whoever he'd been, Katie Scarlett would never speak of him, no matter how many ways Flint broached the subject. Flint was not much of a kid person, but how could any man be indifferent to such a delightful girl? Maddy was a perfect daughter. No man could do better. The man didn't know what he was missing. When Flint caught up with the jerk, he planned to make sure he understood what he'd lost.

His phone rang again. He opened one eye, groaned, and threw back the covers. "On my way," he said, before Maddy could chastise him again. "Headed to the shower now."

When Flint pulled up outside Scarlett's home, Maddy was waiting on the front porch. The door was open and her nanny was watching. She ran down the steps and along the sidewalk, brown curls bouncing, fairly dancing with impatience. Her joie de vivre was infectious. He was already laughing when she jumped inside the car and slammed the door. She pulled her seat belt across her slender body and folded her hands.

"Are you ready?" If he'd asked her mother such a question, Scarlett would have punched him.

"Yes, yes, yes, yes, yes!" Maddy giggled. "Let's go!"

"Yes, ma'am." He rolled away from the curb and entered the eastbound traffic at the intersection. “Should we stop at Matt’s Garden Center first? How about Joe’s Hardware?”

Maddy glowered at him. “Don’t tease me. You know where we’re going. Daisy’s.”

“Right. I forgot.” He nodded. “Tell me the best stuff you and Whiskers did this week.”

Flint had given Maddy the miniature schnauzer for her sixth birthday. Maddy had asked him for the puppy precisely because she’d known her mom wouldn’t buy it for her. Her mother had enough to do without taking care of a puppy, she’d said.

Flint had intended to ask Scarlett’s permission first, but he’d recently learned a valuable lesson about childhood. Other people's kids were for spoiling. Simple as that.

Besides, Whiskers was a great dog and Scarlett would have her housebroken eventually. Flint's plan was to stay scarce until that happened.

He parked in the lot at Daisy's, and they stood in the long line waiting to be served.

Maddy's chattering about everything from her mom to school to Whiskers and beyond washed over Flint while he nodded occasionally and tried to stay focused on the constantly changing world of a seven-year-old.

They took the ice cream outside to one of the picnic tables. Chocolate with chocolate sprinkles, as always, for Maddy. Flint had ordered black coffee.

"Okay, Maddy. Out with it. What's this big favor you got me out of bed on Sunday to handle?" It was autumn in Houston and still warm enough for summer clothes and ice cream. The leaves hadn't begun to turn, but the scent of fall was in the air.

Maddy pushed her ice cream cup aside and folded her hands on the table. Her expression became serious. "It's about my friend Jamie."

"Do I know Jamie?"

She shook her head. "He's new. He's sick a lot. So he's missed a lot of school. We have to help him catch up, our teacher said."

Flint nodded somberly, wondering where this story was headed.

"Jamie needs your help. I told him you were the best heir hunter in the world. I told him you could find anybody. He didn't believe me. But I've heard you say that's true." Her green eyes widened. "That is true, right, Michael?"

Flint nodded again. He promised his clients he could find anyone, anytime, anywhere—for a hefty fee. A boy in Maddy's second-grade class wasn't likely to present much of a challenge. "Who is Jamie trying to find?"

She shrugged. "I'm not sure who he is."

59 Trace Evidence

"I see." Flint tried to keep a serious expression on his face. "Well, can't Jamie's dad help?"

"Jamie doesn't know who his dad is." Maddy shook her head slowly, a sorrowful look on her face. "I don't know who my dad is. Neither do you. Jamie is like us."

Flint cocked his head. Already, the situation was more complicated than he'd hoped. "How about Jamie's mom? Surely she can find this fellow?"

"She's tried. And she's rich, too. She's hired people." Maddy shrugged again. "No one else can find him. Only you can do it."

Flint closed his eyes. He was tired. He'd taxed his body and his mind during **The Sea King** case. He wasn't ready to take on a new client just yet.

"I told Jamie you'd help. You will help him, won't you?" Before he could answer, she waved toward the other side of the parking lot and slipped away from the picnic table. Flint watched her approach a boy only slightly taller than she was, pale and reed thin. He had the sinking feeling that this was Jamie and the well-tended woman standing next to him was his rich mother.

Maddy, the little imp, had backed him into a corner. She was just like her mother in too many ways.

61 Trace Evidence

Before Flint could come up with a suitable excuse to escape, Maddy had returned, her friend in tow.

The woman looked vaguely familiar. She was dressed in navy slacks and a white sweater that could have come right off the runway this season, like a New York City fashion model, but not quite as emaciated.

Artificially red hair fell to her shoulders in that casual way that usually meant a thousand-dollar haircut. Perfect makeup. Brown eyes. She frowned and extended a well-manicured hand to meet his firm handshake.

"Veronica Beaumont. This is my son, Jamison. We call him Jamie. You are Michael Flint, correct?"

"I'm Flint, yes." He nodded. "Nice to meet you, Mrs. Beaumont."

"Ms. Beaumont." She stressed the title aggressively. "Call me Veronica." She glanced at the yellow picnic-table bench and remained standing. He figured her dry-cleaning bills were a sizable chunk of her weekly take-home pay.

Flint remained standing, too, to be polite. She acted as if he should know her, so he ran her name through his memory for a full five seconds and came up empty. Probably best not to mention that.

Maddy said, "Jamie is the boy I told you about. He needs your help. You're the only one who can do it, Michael. You have to try."

He smiled, sheepishly. "Maddy's opinion of my skills is flattering, Ms. Beaumont, but . . ."

"Veronica. Apparently I was misinformed about you, Mr. Flint. So you're not the best heir hunter in Houston, then?" Her challenge bordered on insult. In that moment, he realized who she was. Veronica Beaumont owned one of the hottest new tech companies in Texas.

"Houston isn't a very big pond, Ms. Beaumont." He squared his shoulders and met her eyes steadily. "Didn't Maddy tell you? I'm the best heir hunter in the world."

She narrowed her eyes. "Can you prove that?" The obnoxious challenge again. She didn't act like a woman who needed his help for anything. Nor was he much inclined to volunteer.

He smiled. Nodded. Curtly. Once. He felt a little sympathy for Jamie's missing dad. This woman was a bitch on wheels. Life was way too short to take crap from her. Or anyone else, for that matter.

But Maddy was watching. He wouldn't behave badly in front of her, even when provoked. He was the only male role model she had. As a boy who'd never had a father figure in his life, he felt the responsibility keenly. Maddy needed to know that not all men were assholes, even if behaving with grace under pressure was a challenge sometimes.

Besides, Veronica Beaumont was nothing to him. When he walked away, he need never speak to her again.

“It was good to meet you, Ms. Beaumont, Jamie.” He picked up Maddy’s ice cream cup and handed it to her. “Come on, Maddy. We need to get back.”

Maddy didn’t argue. Maybe she sensed his anger or something.

Whatever it was that went on in the heads of kids was way, way out of his wheelhouse. In fact, Maddy Scarlett was the only kid he knew, and he wasn’t sure what she was thinking most of the time.

Maddy took her ice cream cup from him and said, "Bye, Jamie. See you in school tomorrow."

Flint tossed his half-empty coffee cup into the trash on the way to the car. He opened the door for Maddy and walked around the car to get in on the driver's side.

Before he started the ignition, Maddy said, "She was rude, wasn't she?"

He clenched his jaw. "It's okay, Maddy. No worries. How's that ice cream?"

"It's good. But Michael?"

"Yes?"

She'd lowered her chin and he saw a single tear fall into her ice cream cup. Her voice was quiet. “Even if his mom was rude, Jamie still needs your help.”

He cocked his head, trying to understand the seven-year-old’s logic. “Why is this so important to you?”

Her chin quivered and she avoided his gaze. “Because Jamie’s sick. Our teacher said he might die. She said he knew it and we kids should know it, too. It’s sad.”

“And this man Jamie wants to find?”

Maddy shrugged. “I just know it’s important. Real important.”

Flint ran his palm over his head. He frowned, started the engine, and pulled out into traffic.

He could never refuse Maddy anything. He was stuck and he knew it.

Maybe the job would be easy and he could do it tomorrow. With luck, he could avoid talking to Veronica Beaumont more than twice.

Something niggled, though. It was odd that Maddy had come to him.

“Have you asked your mom to help Jamie?”

She and Maddy were usually pretty open with each other. Katie Scarlett was almost as good an investigator as Flint. And she had a team that worked with her, including Carlos Gaspar, who had skills far above the norm.

Scarlett could put boots on the ground and fingers on the keys and cover twice as much data in half the time. This job seemed like one she could knock out in half a day.

Maddy's face flushed bright red. She stammered, "I, I just want you to do it. Mom's too busy."

"Ah." **Man, you're slow on the uptake sometimes.** He smiled. "So you like Jamie, then? Is that it?"

Maddy's face flushed even more. Her hands flew to cover her mouth and she shook her head so rapidly that her curls bounced.

"Okay. Don't freak out on me." Flint reached over and patted her shoulder. Finally, he understood the problem. "I'll look into it. And we won't tell your mom. At least, for now."

The relief that flooded Maddy's face was almost comical.

Flint smiled. So Maddy had her first serious crush on a boy. How cute was that?

Chapter Five

Reno, Nevada
Six Years Ago

Josh Hallman waited impatiently at the private airstrip for his two college friends, Dan Shafer and Skip Evans. There was a storm coming in, and they were late. As usual.

He was packed and eager to get this last leg of the journey to Red Maple Lake completed. His fishing gear was stowed, and the party gear was within easy reach inside the Cessna Turbo 206. The Cessna was outfitted with amphibious floats, or pontoons, which meant several alterations to the aircraft, and all for the better as far as Josh was concerned.

A pilot was only as good as his equipment.

The three friends had been planning this trip for a long time. Back when they were fraternity brothers, they'd been inseparable. But now, more than ten years after college, they saw each other rarely. But the three amigos, as they'd called themselves, were bonded for life by those college experiences.

Dan and Skip were Josh's closest, best friends. He would do anything for them and he knew they felt the same.

Anything but exhibit some patience, apparently. He shook his head and grinned.

Dan and Skip had faith in him to fly the last leg of this trip. Could he do it? Hell, yes. Of course he could. That's what he'd said at the time. In the bar. After a few beers. When their women weren't around.

Which was not at all the same thing as standing out here in the cold mountain air preparing to fly two hundred miles to the middle of nowhere and land on a mountain lake colder than melted polar ice. Josh shivered just thinking about swimming today.

Sure, he liked a challenge. Of course, he'd done more difficult things in his life. Dumber things, too. He shook his head and inhaled deeply through his nose and filled his lungs with crisp fall oxygen.

A campfire burned nearby. He caught a whiff of it and smiled. Tonight, the three amigos would be lounging by a campfire, too. Sharing bullshit stories. Tall tales of derring-do, plied with beer and the sheer joy of being together. He was looking forward to it.

Everything would be okay. He'd fly the plane. They'd have the experience of a lifetime. Just like they'd planned. Josh was glad they'd scheduled the trip and followed through after that night in the bar. He needed a break.

75 Trace Evidence

Things had not been going well, but the trip would be a turning point for him. He could feel it in his gut.

He'd had some dark days this past couple of years. Lost his job in the most recent downsizing. Debts piled up faster than he could pay them. That mess with Veronica. Through it all, he'd lived for this five-day adventure with his closest friends in the world, as if they were his lifeline. Although they didn't know how desperate he'd become, they'd help him as soon as he explained things. No questions asked. He knew they would.

He glanced at his watch. Twenty minutes late already. Come on. Where are you guys? We're burning daylight here. Not to mention the time before that storm comes through.

He inspected the Cessna again. He had piloted floatplanes before, but each plane was a little different, with its own quirks. The yellow-and-white T206 was big. The floats were knee-high, and there was another step board to make it up into the cockpit. Sitting in the pilot's seat made him feel like he was king of the world, and the roar of the big Lycoming engine added to that feeling. God, he loved flying.

Red Maple Lake presented a few extra challenges for takeoff and landing, too. There was no landing strip out there, so the lake would be his runway. In principle, landing on water was no different from landing on solid ground, but principle and practice were always two different things. Everything was easier on paper than in execution.

The drag from the floats meant getting too slow on landing was a real danger. Despite the big engine, spooling it back up and gaining airspeed was a painfully slow process.

Fighter pilots said that speed was life, and he believed it. With enough airspeed he could handle any problem, and he wasn't going to be caught without enough. Not with Dan and Skip aboard. Hell, not ever.

His mechanic had checked the Cessna out thoroughly and he'd flown a bunch of touch-and-gos last week. He'd never been to Red Maple Lake, but he was confident he could land the plane when they got there and take off when they were ready to leave.

He checked his watch. He glanced at the sky. He tapped his foot. Impatience was his constant companion. Josh had two speeds, dead stop or full out. He seemed to have no way to throttle his energy. Maybe he should've been on meds or something, like Veronica said.

He cupped the back of his neck with his hand and rubbed the tension that settled there whenever he thought about Veronica. He'd liked her well enough, but he didn't love her and he wasn't interested in marrying her, for damned sure. She'd felt the same, he knew. She'd told him often. He wasn't devastated when she left him. No, he'd been relieved. Especially after the abortion.

Their relationship had not been the same carefree romp after they'd made the joint decision and terminated that pregnancy. Not that anything should have been the same after that. The decision wasn't made lightly. They'd spent days and nights fighting through it, hashing it out, coming eventually to the only real choice.

They didn't want to get married. They didn't want to be tied to each other forever, raising a child together. Hell, by the time everything was over, they weren't even speaking to each other. Josh realized it was because they both felt guilty. Ashamed. They'd accidently created the possibility of a new human life together. And they'd ended that possibility without giving the child a fighting chance to make it in the world.

How could any relationship be the same after something like that?

The whole situation had made him swear off women for a good long time. He'd had a few hookups here and there since Veronica. But no one he'd been remotely serious about. He found he liked it that way. He liked being single. At least, until the right woman came along. He never wanted to go through an experience like Veronica's abortion again as long as he lived. Once was more than enough.

81 Trace Evidence

And then he lost his job. The debts. Well, what did he have to offer a woman, anyway? He was glad he didn't have a child to support, too, even as he wondered what might have been with the baby that would never be.

Would that emptiness go away eventually? Sure it would. Lots of people had abortions without a second's remorse, didn't they?

His two college fraternity brothers were completely different. Dan and Skip had moved on with their lives. Grown up. Both were involved in serious relationships.

Dan was dating a woman he'd met in college, and they seemed serious enough. A destination wedding was planned for next year. Josh couldn't remember the location. Someplace exotic, no doubt, knowing Dan.

Skip was already married, with a baby. Cutest little girl on the planet and probably a genius, too, according to Skip. Debbie was pregnant with their second child. A boy this time. Skip loved them all like crazy and he seemed exceedingly happy with the whole arrangement.

But to Josh, Skip's life looked like a tight noose around his friend's neck with an anvil attached to the other end of the rope.

He shook his head. Nope. Josh just wasn't ready for family life. He thought he would be someday. Maybe. He shook off the melancholy. He had plenty of time for those decisions. Skip and Dan had made the leap too soon. They were only thirty.

A Toyota SUV appeared in the distance and turned onto the long driveway to the private airstrip, kicking up dust all the way. When the red beast approached, Dan was driving with Skip slouched in the passenger seat.

Josh grinned. Typical. Skip had been an amiable passenger, one way or another, for as long as the three friends had known each other.

Dan parked the big Toyota in the dirt parking lot, and the two began collecting their gear. Josh went over to help.

“Where the hell you guys been?” Grins and man hugs and

backslapping came next. Josh was a little surprised at how relieved and happy he was to see them. These two were like family to him, the only family he had since his parents died in a car wreck a few years ago.

“Yeah, yeah,” Dan said. He lifted the hatch and hauled out duffel bags and equipment. “Like you’ve been here more than ten minutes.”

“Sorry, my bad,” Skip said, laughing as he hauled his stuff out of the SUV. “Debbie was freaking out at the last minute, begging me to stay home. I swear, when she’s pregnant, she’s just a bundle of nerves. All worried about me and the kids. I keep telling her I can take care of myself, but—” He shrugged.

Josh slapped him on the shoulder and gave him another short, manly squeeze. “Good thing she didn’t know you in college. She’d have been freaked out every minute.”

“Like the time you bungee jumped off the clock tower on campus,” Dan chimed in.

“Or the time you chased those thugs that grabbed your wallet in Chicago,” Josh added.

“Yeah, yeah. Well, I’m a family man now. I have to be more careful.” Skip shook his head and frowned. His words were serious, but he joked, “Honestly, I don’t know what Debbie would do without me. How would she survive?”

"She'd find a decent guy like Josh here to take care of her," Dan replied, in the way of men whose insults were accepted as affection.

"Stop fooling around with a screwup like you." Skip laughed. "Yeah, like that would ever happen."

"What?" Josh said, his arms full of gear. "Debbie loves me better than you, anyway."

They had collected all the gear now and were headed toward the plane, docked on the other side of the grass landing strip. Josh had already checked everything out and prepared for takeoff. They wouldn't need to stop to refuel. They should reach Red Maple Lake well before nightfall, with enough fuel for the return trip.

The three friends continued to joke and tease each other while they loaded the Cessna and strapped themselves in, but Josh took his flying responsibilities seriously and they knew it. As he worked his way through his preflight checklist, they quieted down.

Before starting the engine, he buckled up. The harness didn't cinch all the way tight. The webbing slid off his shoulder. He shoved it back into place. He wasn't going to cancel the trip because the belt wouldn't tighten.

"Ready?" he said. He didn't wait for a reply before pushing the throttle forward. The roar swamped all other noise. The yoke shook in his hands. The big propeller fought the air. It was a battle the propeller was winning. A thousand feet later, he pulled back on the yoke and they were airborne.

Chapter Six

Houston, Texas
Sunday

After he dropped Maddy off, Flint was too restless to sleep, even though recuperation time was exactly what his sore muscles needed after **The Sea King** case. Underwater work was always tough, even when he was in great shape.

He should do it more often.

His stomach growled. He hadn't eaten anything for way too long. His body was still burning calories like a campfire gobbling dry kindling, but his refrigerator was as empty as his belly. A quick trip to the drive-thru diner solved his problem.

He carried his food and a liter bottle of water through to his desk and fired up his laptop. He started with basic online information searches about Veronica Beaumont. Google returned twenty-six million results in less than half a second. Impressive.

He inhaled the first hamburger as he perused the list of articles.

Beaumont had been named to several lists of wealthy CEOs since her first appearance five years ago, when her tech company went public and she became an instant millionaire. Before that, she had been named to **Houston's Top 40 Under 40.** A quick review of her list-mates revealed the usual suspects. Many of them were brats with rich daddies he knew personally.

Beaumont's tech success story was familiar by now to people who followed the industry. She was still in college in Chicago when she came up with her LookBook idea for a software program that focused on people in the fashion business. She developed the software program to connect her and her friends to the fashion icons she adored at the time.

Expansion had been exponential and fueled her growth.

Flint shook his head. She was a savvy businesswoman, but everything about her online persona proved she'd been shallow all her life.

Still, Beaumont was in the right place at the right time and her software took the fashion and social networking worlds by storm. These days, she was a powerhouse multi-millionaire on her way to becoming a billionaire. The more he read about her, the more convinced he became that she was everything he hated in a client.

Sure, she was rich. That didn't bother him. In fact, extreme wealth was a plus because he liked to get paid. He'd grown up in poverty and he'd escaped. He didn't intend to go back. The problem with Beaumont was that she was a demanding, cold female used to getting her own way and having everyone around her kowtow to her every wish.

None of that was going to work with him. Not even close.

He moved on to information about her private life as he gobbled the second hamburger.

Before relocating to Houston, where her son was born almost eight years ago, Beaumont had lived in Chicago. Flint found the official birth certificate for Jamison Beaumont. The boy's father was not listed on the birth certificate or anywhere else.

School records were sealed, which slowed his search. He'd finished his second burger, most of a large pack of fries, and the water before he found what little information existed in the school files.

93 Trace Evidence

At that point, Flint stopped prying. He didn't need to search for more data about Veronica and her son until after he talked to her, and maybe not even then. He saved his research and polished off the fries before he moved on to the work he had been planning to begin tomorrow. Work he had been avoiding for far too long.

A year ago, he had met a man who had claimed to know his mother. Within minutes of taunting him with that information, the man died.

Flint had ignored the claim, but it continued to nag him. The question popped into his dreams sometimes. When he was tired. Or idle for too long between jobs.

He wasn't interested in a new romance to fill his thoughts, so he handled the problem by taking on more work. Most days, he simply shook the unwelcome intrusions from his head.

He had lived thirty-three years without knowing his parents. His mother had abandoned him when he was an infant. For more than three decades, he'd had no desire to find her or to know who she was. That system had served him well enough. There were plenty of advantages to not being bogged down by family. Why mess with success?

He'd always believed he could find his parents, if he'd wanted to.

But he'd never felt the urge.

95 Trace Evidence

He was an heir hunter. The best in the business. He knew that people gave up their children for good reasons, and he respected that choice.

As for his own situation, he was happy enough. He wanted for nothing. If his parents had chosen to abandon him, he was better off without them.

He nodded, pushed away from the desk, and carried the trash from his meal into the kitchen where he stuffed it into the compactor. Nobody nagged him to eat off plates or do the dishes. Being alone had its advantages, particularly for a man in his line of work.

He was beholden to no one. And he liked it that way.

Felix Crane had changed all that when he'd taunted Flint on a cold and snowy mountaintop.

Crane had tried to hire Flint, but he'd refused the case. Crane didn't take it well.

"I knew your mother," Crane had said.

He was the first, last, and only person who had ever made such a claim in Flint's entire life. The moment he'd heard the words, he'd known he wouldn't be able to ignore them forever.

At the time, Flint had other things to worry about. He and Crane had faced off, weapons aimed. Big money was at stake and Crane would have said anything to win.

So Flint shrugged off the taunt.

That was then.

The claim had bugged him more than he let on.

Now, a year later, Crane's words rested in the back of his subconscious and refused to be forgotten.

I knew your mother. What did Crane mean by that? Were they lovers? Something else?

The obvious thing would be to follow up.

Obvious, but not possible since Crane was dead.

Flint was a man of many talents, but conversing with people beyond the grave was not a skill set he had managed to perfect. Unfortunately.

He found a crystal glass and poured a healthy four-finger portion of single-malt scotch. He added a couple of large ice cubes and returned to his desk.

He tapped his right knuckle against his teeth and looked at the laptop screen.

A man like Crane was easy to investigate. He had been in the public eye far too many times. Billionaires often were. Privacy was not possible and usually not even remotely desired.

Crane had fathered four children, according to Flint's quick research, three daughters and one son, all older than Flint. The daughters lived in Europe somewhere. Not completely untouchable, but not as easy to confront without a lot of travel hassle.

Flint wasn't especially interested in globetrotting to track down whatever connection Crane might have had with his mother, even assuming Crane's daughters would know. Which was a long shot, at best.

There was an easier option.

The son.

Jasper Melvin Crane.

What a hideous moniker for a kid, although it probably suited the adult fairly well.

Flint cocked his head and flipped through the images on the screen. Jasper's mother must have had some strong genes, because Jasper was a good-looking guy.

If you liked the lean and smarmy type.

Plenty of women did.

As he continued flipping through the images on the screen, he saw many such women on Jasper's arm at one event or another. He was taller than his father and, odds were, he was less controlling. Maybe that elevated him to chick-magnet status.

But probably it was the oil and gas business gushing money.

When a boy grew up in his father's long shadow, two outcomes were common. The boy could become aggressively violent or passively aggressive. Either would get him noticed by his dad, which was the only thing most boys wanted.

Approval was good, but attention was better.

Jasper looked like the kind of man who'd mastered the passive aggressive style long before his dad relayed the business baton to junior.

Flint curled his lip and held the scotch a while on his tongue.

He liked a man to behave like one. Stand up for himself. Take his licks for it if he lost the fight, but fight like a man in the first place.

Jasper didn't look like the fighting kind.

Flint shook his head. Hard to believe this was Felix Crane's kid. But he had seen the birth certificate. This effeminate dandy was Crane's son. No doubt about that.

Jasper was now the head of Crane's oil empire. He'd inherited everything when his father died. He was already living in the mansion and working for the company before he inherited it. But now he had what had eluded him all the years his father was alive. Control.

According to the financial news reports, Jasper wasn't doing such a great job. But the kid had only been in charge for a year. He still had plenty of time to turn into as lethal a snake as his father had proven to be.

Question was, did Jasper know anything about his old man that Flint couldn't discover through other means? Meaning, would talking to Jasper make Flint's search for his own mother easier and faster, or precisely the opposite?

A quick phone call to the man could elicit the information Flint wanted, if Jasper was inclined to share. But in Flint's experience, that kind of call never worked. He'd need to see Jasper in person and encourage him to tell what he knew.

Which had a slim chance of success.

Or he could find the information another way.

So, alternatives first. Leaving Jasper for later, if necessary. He might be able to avoid the man entirely.

Hope lightened his mood.

Flint eventually located the background data he was looking for on old man Crane.

Felix Crane had been born in Mount Warren, Texas, an oil boomtown back in the day. He'd grown up there in the rough-and-tumble way of such places. He'd cut his teeth on the oil business, living with his parents until he left for college.

When he graduated, he returned to Mount Warren to work in his father's oil company for several years afterward. He started his family there and took over the family business when his father died. Just like Jasper.

Flint leaned back in his chair and sipped the scotch. Given the time frame, if Crane actually had known Flint's mother, he could have known her in Mount Warren.

Or at least it was a reasonable place to start looking.

Flint had been to Mount Warren once. Booms and busts in the oil business had come and gone since Crane's time.

Now, it was a small, depressed town deep in West Texas.

Thirty-four years ago, when Flint was conceived, the town's permanent population had waned from the oil boom days. Small city, small population, not many women of childbearing age.

If Flint's mother had known Felix Crane in Mount Warren, finding her would be fairly easy.

Which presented an entirely new set of issues.

Flint stood and paced the room.

Briefly, he considered his uncharacteristic indecision.

His instincts were solid. He'd relied on them to keep him alive for a very long time. He thought of himself as a point-shoot-aim kind of guy.

His experience and training had provided him with everything he needed to solve the relatively minor puzzle of his mother's identity.

Hell, he could have done that years ago.

The problem was that he didn't know whether he wanted to solve that particular riddle. Everything kept coming back to that point.

He shook his head and drained the last of the scotch from the glass. As a kid, maybe he'd wondered about his parents. Maybe he'd wanted to find them. Maybe he'd harbored normal childhood fantasies about being reunited with his mother and father.

And maybe not.

If he'd had those desires and fantasies, he had no memory of them.

Not that he had amnesia or anything. He'd just never thought about it. Not even once.

His earliest memories were of living with his foster mother, Bette Maxwell, at the Lazy M Ranch and Boarding School. It was the only home he'd ever known.

Like most kids, he remembered very little of anything before the age of four or so. But as far as Flint was concerned, his life began when he was eight.

That was the year he met Katie Scarlett.

She had arrived at the Lazy M when she was ten. She was already a holy terror, just like Flint. They became inseparable almost immediately.

That's when his world began to take shape. Everything before that was muddy and irrelevant.

Flint and Scarlett had been glued to the TV set, watching old Westerns every night, during that first year. He grinned just thinking about those old shows.

He held out his left hand and looked at the scar on his palm where Scarlett had sliced it with one of Bette's sharp kitchen knives she'd stolen that morning. He remembered how serious her face looked. Scarlett had the idea, but he hadn't needed persuading. He was always up for anything remotely exciting.

The cut had hurt like hell. He'd screamed out when she did it, and she'd told him not to be such a baby. She cut her own left palm and barely winced.

When they held their hands together and commingled their blood, Scarlett seriously intoned that they were now blood brothers, because she resisted her femininity fiercely, both then and now.

Scarlett had always acted more like a boy than a girl. He couldn't imagine a better male role model than the one she had been for his eight-year-old self.

They'd remained closer than family all these years, which was fine with Flint. She and her seven-year-old daughter were the only family he had, and he liked it that way.

Or at least they had been his only family.

Until he met up with Bette Maxwell again.

Until she told him what little she knew about his mother.

Until Crane taunted him at gunpoint.

Flint learned from Bette Maxwell that his mother had been a teacher in West Texas. He suspected she must have lived and worked in Mount Warren because Crane had lived there.

And now that he knew these facts, what was he going to do about them?

Mount Warren was an easy flight from Houston. He could go down there tomorrow. He could find his mother in a couple of hours. He could talk to her.

And say what? Ask what? Did he want to know why she had abandoned him? Some secrets were better left buried.

Bette Maxwell had said he was an illegitimate child. His mother was a schoolteacher and the conventions at the time made keeping her son impossible. Okay. He could accept that.

What had sparked his curiosity was why she never came back.

Never. In all those years.

Bette had tried to make him feel better about his mother's abandonment by invoking the closed adoption process. Closed adoption records were sealed. No one could unseal them, even if they'd wanted to. Not the bio mom or the adoptive parents or even the kid.

But Flint had never been adopted.

His mother had left her young son with Bette and simply never tried to find him again.

People who gave up their children had the right to make those decisions. That's what he told his clients, and he believed it.

Now was the time to take his own good advice. To let this go.

If she had wanted to find him, any halfway decent investigator could have done it.

His mother had never made the effort.

Still, the open issue nagged.

He could ask Carlos Gaspar to complete the research. Gaspar had joined Scarlett's agency a while back. He brought with him years of experience and excellent army and FBI training. Gaspar was talented, too. He could find things other people missed.

But searching for his birth mother was not something he was ready to reveal to Gaspar or Scarlett or anyone else. Not until he knew more.

Before he could rationalize away the urge, he sent a quick request to one of his sources. No explanation. Just the questions. She would search government, public, and private databases. She'd send him what she found.

He'd know what to do when he had more facts.

He closed the laptop, carried his glass into the den, and poured another. He wasn't going anywhere tonight. Might as well get buzzed. He did some of his best thinking that way.

He plopped down into his favorite chair, put up his feet and closed his eyes, and leaned his head back. He pushed a button on the remote to change the music to something quieter so he could think. Classic country music usually did the trick.

Did he want to find his mother? How about his father? What if Crane had meant his taunt literally? That he had **known** Flint's mother in the biblical sense.

Was Felix Crane his father?

Did Flint really want to know that, assuming it was true?

Definitely not.

Flint heard the back door open. He didn't move. He'd been expecting her.

"It's a bad sign when you're drinking alone in the dark, listening to Haggard and Jones," Scarlett said as she walked into the room. He opened one eye and watched her fill the glass she'd collected in the kitchen on her way through. "You're not gonna cry or start a fight or anything, are you?"

He grinned and opened his other eye and lifted his glass to her in a silent hello.

She plopped down on the sofa across from him and propped her feet up on the coffee table. She slouched and sipped and finally said, “So what’s up? What am I doing here in the middle of the night?”

He grinned again. She always exaggerated everything. “It’s not the middle of the night.”

“It is for me. You have any idea what time a seven-year-old gets out of bed to go to school?” She sipped again. “You enticed me over here with the scotch, which is excellent. But I can’t stay long. What do you want?”

He took a deep breath. He wasn’t really sure what he wanted.

He knew that as soon as he told her about his mother, his problems would multiply. He wanted to put that off a bit longer and maybe forever.

So he chose a different subject.

“Tell me what you know about Veronica Beaumont.”

Scarlett stared at him as if he’d sprouted two heads.

“What?” he said, grinning. It was so easy to wind her up.

“Tell me you’re not dating that woman,” Scarlett demanded in the same way she had demanded his complete compliance with everything she’d ever said since the first day they met.

He didn't know how real sisters behaved, but he'd always imagined any sister would act exactly like Scarlett toward a younger brother.

She stared him down. "Because if you are dating Veronica Beaumont, you're in big trouble. That woman is a barracuda. She will eat you alive."

He grinned again and sipped the Scotch. "You don't think I can take care of myself?"

Scarlett cocked her head and narrowed her brown eyes. When they were kids, that look preceded a quick kick or sharp punch, but she was across the room and couldn't reach him right now. He imagined her shooting lasers from those green eyes that pierced his throat and almost laughed out loud.

"I've known Veronica Beaumont for years. I've seen her go through one man after another, usually leaving them in a crumpled heap by the curb. She's taken down much stronger dudes than you." She pointed down the corridor, toward his bedroom. "Definitely don't be bringing her back to your place. She's like a black widow or something. You don't want that bad karma in your house."

This time he did laugh before he let her off the hook. "Don't worry. I met the woman only once and she is definitely not my type."

Scarlett's face contorted into something much more fierce than a frown, but she said nothing. She would get him back for teasing her.

But she'd do it when he was least expecting it. More effective that way.

He made a mental note to stay on his toes around her for a few days.

"What's your professional opinion of her? She wants me to find a guy," Flint said.

Scarlett leaned back and relaxed a bit. She was always comfortable when discussing business. Like Flint, she was one of the best investigators around, and she could handle herself.

Service for Uncle Sam had prepared them both well for this line of work. They made a good team, although they didn't work together much these days.

"Veronica can definitely afford your fees. No worries on that score." Scarlett paused. "She'll be a pain in the ass to work with, but so are you."

He laughed again and she lifted her glass in a mock toast. "What else?"

Scarlett pursed her lips and shook her head. "I've met the boy. Veronica's son. He goes to Maddy's school. He's very sick. Some kind of leukemia, I think. The rumor is that he needs a bone marrow transplant and they can't find a donor. Is that the problem she's asking you to solve?"

Flint hadn't actually talked to Veronica about the case yet, but that was a good guess.

"A mother will do almost anything to save her kid. I can't even imagine how I would handle that. If Maddy was as sick as Veronica's boy." Scarlett paused and bowed her head a moment. "If it's the father she wants you to find, that makes sense. See if he's a match. Why can't she just call the guy and ask?"

"I suspect she doesn't know where he is. Maybe not even who he is." Flint arched his eyebrows and Scarlett returned a knowing look. "We both know that relatives are eligible bone marrow donors only about seventy percent of the time, though."

"What about a public appeal? Or is that too much negative publicity for the queen of fashion?"

He shrugged. “She’s got enough money to hire anyone she wants. She’s tried to find the guy and came up empty, I gather, from what little I know so far.”

“So she’s turned to you because she thinks you can do what no one else can.” Scarlett shook her head and drained her glass and rolled it between her palms. “Well, the problem is, we all know you can do it.”

Flint laughed. “How is that a problem, exactly?”

Scarlett stood. “We’ve had this conversation a hundred times. Just because you **can** do something doesn’t mean you **should.**”

Flint was pretty sure she was talking about more than finding Veronica Beaumont's ex. And he knew she was right.

He'd been wrestling with a similar question before she arrived. He **could** find his mother. But **should** he?

"So if I take this on, can you help me out or not?"

She sighed, but she didn't say no. "What do you need?"

"I'm not sure yet. After I meet with Beaumont, I'll have a better idea."

"You know where to find me." She left her empty glass in the kitchen on her way out.

Chapter Seven

Red Maple Lake, California
Six Years Ago

Josh was using visual flight rules and traveled below radar. He hadn't filed a flight plan because it wasn't required and he'd seen no need to do so.

All of which meant he wasn't communicating with air control towers, even if there were any out here, which he figured there weren't.

Ahead of the storm, it was a beautiful day for flying. Visibility was sufficient to see and avoid obstacles and other aircraft below eighteen thousand feet. They needed to get up over the mountains, but they didn't need to cruise higher than ten thousand feet to reach Red Maple Lake.

They spent the flight time catching up on their lives since they'd seen each other last. Josh didn't mention Veronica or the abortion because he knew they wouldn't approve. Hell, he didn't approve. But he'd seen no other way, then or now.

As he listened to Dan and Skip share stories about their families, he wondered if he'd been wrong. Would he have made a decent father to Veronica's baby?

He shook the thought from his mind. Regrets were useless. The decision had been made a while back and it was not changeable now.

Still, he wouldn't tell his friends. Nothing to be served by feeling their judgment at this point.

He laughed at Skip's stories of his daughter's cute shenanigans, and he whistled at Dan's exaggerated tales of sexy nights with his fiancée. But Josh had searched his soul and could find no lost love in his heart for Veronica.

Half an hour from Red Maple Lake, a weather front moved in quickly from the northeast. Rain ran in streams across the windshield. He flipped on the screen heater to keep humidity from condensing on the glass.

The storm drove the plane sideways. He couldn't hold it on the rudder, so he resorted to rolling back onto course after each barrage. The same went for the pockets of air that momentarily stole the lift from the wings. The plane dropped a few feet each time. The fall shoved his stomach into his mouth. It must have done the same to the others because the conversation inside the cabin all but stopped. He was glad they'd arrive soon and get out of the weather.

The sun was low on the western horizon as they approached. They'd passed the beautiful and enormous Lake Tahoe a while back and continued south. Fallen Leaf Lake was behind them now, too. According to the maps, Red Maple Lake would be coming up soon.

“I hope this clears up by tomorrow. I can’t wait to fish the lake,” Dan said. “My buddy who told me about the place? Showed me some amazing pictures when we did that fly-in last year up in Canada.”

“Any chance we can do some water sports while we’re here? I brought my wetsuit just in case,” Skip said, sounding like the big kid he actually resembled in every way.

“If this rain doesn’t let up, you’ll need the wetsuit just to use the outhouse,” Josh said.

“What outhouse? I thought this was a luxury resort,” Skip whined.

Dan laughed.

Winds buffeted the wings and tossed the Cessna in a stomach sickening thrill ride.

Josh circled the lake so he could get a visual of the landing site. The lake was a reasonable size and he could land the floatplane in a relatively short distance, but the water looked rough. No whitecaps but lots of chop. The lake was ringed by mountains, so he would have to drop fast and level off over the water before touching down.

The crosswind had picked up. Turbulence lifted the nose of the plane. Rain pelted the windshield.

During the circle recon flight, Dan pointed out the posh campground they had booked for the week, barely visible where it was set back from the lake amid the trees. "Looks like that's it. I thought it would be bigger, though. Weren't there more outbuildings in the brochures? Where's the heated swimming pool?"

They had considered other lodges and facilities, but the smaller, more remote, exclusive Red Maple Lake Resort was primo, according to Dan's friend. In the planning stages, they'd all seen the appeal of time spent in the wilderness, away from all modern civilization.

"Man, this is gonna be sweet!" Dan said, rubbing his hands together like a gleeful munchkin. "That hot tub. At night, after fishing all day, the cold mountain air, a cold beer. The very definition of man heaven, isn't it?"

Skip laughed. “Having a wife and kid around to make you feel loved is great. Don’t get me wrong. But I am really looking forward to some peace and quiet and something to talk about besides domestic stuff.”

“Zip it, guys. I need to concentrate,” Josh said. He glanced toward Dan in the copilot seat. “Everybody snug up your harness. It’s choppy down there. We could be in for a few bumps.”

“You got it,” Dan said. Josh saw him make the adjustments through his peripheral vision.

Josh pulled on his own harness. It flopped off his shoulder. Dan saw his problem and looped the belt around the winder mechanism, shortening the belt. Josh nodded. “Thanks.”

Skip should have been seated behind Josh, but he had been out of his seat and taking pictures throughout the trip and as they'd circled.

"All belted in back there?" After a couple of beats, Josh said, "Skip? Got your harness snugged up?"

"I'm on it," he replied, but his voice seemed to come from Dan's side of the cabin.

"Skip. This is important. Get into your seat and get your harness on. Now."

Josh's tone was harsher than he'd intended. He wasn't exactly worried. He was a good pilot. He'd trained in flight school while Dan and Skip were working their way up the civilian corporate ladder. He'd had some of the best training in the world and he'd flown for years. But a new landing zone always presented some wrinkles, and this landing was going to be as wrinkled as an elephant. He took a deep breath. He could do this. No problem.

He took one more circuit of the lake. The easiest way in, between the mountains, would put him sideways into the wind. The alternative was to fly straight into the wind so he didn't have to account for the crosswind, but that would mean dropping like a stone from above the peak dominating that side of the lake. He chose the lesser of two evils and headed for the easiest way. **Between the mountains it is.**

He was still facing a few-hundred-foot drop to the lake, followed by leveling out and landing. He took a deep breath and crested the mountain at eighty knots and less than fifty feet above its craggy summit.

He pushed the yoke forward, plunging the aircraft. Dan groaned at the unnatural drop.

A recorded voice calmly announced, "Gear up for water landing." Josh nodded. Roger that. The wheels were up, floats were down. So far, so good.

The plane's speed accelerated in the descent. He resisted the temptation to back off the throttle. Speed was life, he reminded himself.

Below the level of the mountains, the crosswind changed direction. Some effect of the bowl shape of the lake, probably. He leaned the plane to the right as he pulled back on the yoke to level out the aircraft.

The Cessna's wings rocked. He kept pulling back on the yoke. Slowing their descent was harder than he'd envisaged.

The ground whipped away under him. The lake stretched in front. The nose of the aircraft was still too low for the lake's choppy horizontal surface. He pulled hard, his fingers gripping the yoke and both arms straining.

The nose climbed slowly. The lake was broad and wide and long.

Too late, he realized his eyes had deceived him.

The last moments of any landing went by in a dizzying blur. He'd heard it explained with trigonometry, but all pilots knew it as ground rush. He glanced at his airspeed. The water below him wasn't solid ground, but at ninety-three knots, the surface would feel as hard as iron.

And it was sweeping up too fast.

He jerked the yoke right to bring the wings level and kicked in some rudder to counter the crosswind.

With the load on the wings, the plane reacted slowly. Too slowly.

The right pontoon hit the water. The shockwave traveled through the aircraft structure and almost ripped the yoke from his hands. He bounced back in his seat, and his harness spilled over his shoulder.

The impact had been hard and level. The pontoon had been almost horizontal. The force pushed the aircraft back up, out of the water. Like a stone skimming across a river.

He fought the yoke. If he could keep the aircraft level he had another chance, but it rolled sickeningly to the left.

The water below him seemed to slow.

He rammed the throttle full forward. The impact with the water had stolen all his speed.

There was no way he was going to get airborne again.

The next few moments seemed to pass simultaneously with sickening speed and excruciating slowness—the zone where the world whipped by but his thoughts couldn't keep up—like a slo-mo film.

He twisted the yoke and hung on. He was a passenger now. Like Dan and Skip. The plane was no longer flying. It was a ballistic projectile and it would suffer the same fate as all ballistic projectiles.

Terminal impact.

The left pontoon slammed the water. The pontoon was almost level, but the plane was leaning ten degrees.

The asymmetric force sheared off the float.

The left side of the plane dropped. The wing dug into the water.

The noise was deafening. White spray was everywhere. A pounding force rammed Josh's face into the yoke.

The engine died.

The nose of the aircraft dove down into the water.

The plane cartwheeled.

Without a tight harness to hold him in place, the force shoved Josh into the instruments.

Something heavy snapped behind him. It sounded like a tree limb, but the screaming that followed told him the snap was something else.

The aircraft lurched to a halt.

It pushed down into the water and surged back up.

The Cessna tipped forward again. The engine was the heaviest component of the plane and the Cessna's nose began to sink, lifting its tail in the air.

The weight of the water was forcing the air out of the cabin.

Dan was still strapped into the copilot's seat. He groaned between gasps. Skip cried out with pain from somewhere in the back.

Josh felt the adrenaline running through his body and recognized it for what it was. His limbs felt energized. His heart pounded hard against his sternum. All senses were on full alert. Except for a few scrapes and bruises, he was unharmed.

Normal time returned.

He unlatched his harness and heaved himself out of his seat. He had to open the rear door. If they sank, opening the door would be all but impossible underwater. They'd never get out. He wasn't quite ready for a watery grave.

The left pontoon had been sheared, which meant the left side of the Cessna would sink first. The right side would stay out of the water a bit longer. The doors were on the right side.

He steadied himself as well as possible, found the latch, and leaned his shoulder into the door. He pushed it open. Water would soon begin to flood the cabin.

Chapter Eight

Houston, Texas
Monday

Veronica Beaumont's offices dominated the section of Houston where all the trendy, successful businesses battled for attention. Flint approached the front entrance like a man headed for the guillotine. He walked through the revolving door and felt it suck shut behind him with a whoosh, as if he might not keep going without a shove.

"Ms. Beaumont is expecting you, sir," the man at the security desk said as he handed Flint a temporary visitor's badge to pin on his lapel. “Take the executive elevator all the way to the top. Someone will meet you there.”

Flint’s boot heels punctuated his walk along the granite tile. Another security guard stood by the elevator door. He pushed a special release button and the door slid silently open. Flint stepped inside and the elevator shot to the top, leaving his stomach on the ground floor. The elevator opened onto a reception area. A fashionably emaciated-looking woman greeted him with a wide smile created by expert cosmetic dentistry framed by fat lips courtesy of Houston’s best plastic surgeons.

“Mr. Flint?” she asked as she pushed back from her desk. Her legs ran all the way to her neck and her skirt barely covered her ass. "Right this way. Ms. Beaumont is expecting you."

He liked his women with a little meat on their bones and natural body parts. He wondered what kind of man would be attracted to a woman like her as he followed the receptionist down a series of corridors to a door that opened into a private conference room. The rectangular conference table filled most of the space. There were shades covering the floor-to-ceiling windows and the lighting was dim. A seventy-inch television screen was mounted on the wall.

Veronica Beaumont was sitting at one end of the table holding a small remote control. She did not stand up.

“Thank you for coming.” She waved to a chair on her left. “Have a seat.”

Flint might have remained standing simply as a gesture of defiance, but it seemed rather childish. He pulled the chair away from the table and sat, ankle resting on his opposite knee, hands clasped in his lap. But his temperature was rising, so he said nothing. Doing a favor for Maddy was one thing, taking orders from Veronica Beaumont was something else altogether.

“I have something to show you and we’ll talk after that,” Beaumont said. She pushed a button on the remote and the TV screen came to life. A recorded television news program, with a date line from almost seven years ago, began.

Images of an idyllic alpine lake reminiscent of Lake Tahoe filled the screen. Craggy mountains thick with pines, aspens, and other high-altitude trees surrounded a basin filled with sparkling blue water. In several places, the tree line reached the water's edge. On the south and west edges, rocky beaches extended fifty feet or more from the waterline.

Flint had been to Lake Tahoe, Crater Lake, and other alpine lakes many times. The water was always clear and beautiful, but much too cold. He preferred the warm water of the Caribbean for water sports.

The news reporter said that a small Cessna Turbo 206 floatplane carrying three passengers had crashed six weeks before. He said the three men aboard, a pilot and two passengers, had been traveling to the Red Maple Lake Resort but never arrived. It wasn't until they failed to return home at the end of their planned weeklong fishing trip that their families became alarmed and contacted authorities in the area. The Cessna had not filed a flight plan, and search-and-rescue operators couldn't find the plane right away. The crash site was ten miles west of the resort, as the crow flies.

As news stories generally do, this one seemed to develop over time. The first report ended and a second began. The second story aired three days after the first. Deepwater search-and-rescue divers had found the plane resting on the bottom of Red Maple Lake. The plane was hauled out of the water by a helicopter.

The Cessna T206 was severely damaged, the reporter said, as if the images on the screen were not self-explanatory. The left float had been sheared off and was missing. The left wing had been torn almost in half. The back door was open and the cabin was flooded. No bodies were found inside. The three men remained missing. One of the divers said, “Red Maple Lake filled this valley when the glaciers passed. The bottom is as deep and as jagged as the mountaintops. Bodies may float to the surface. If they don’t, we may never find them.”

Flint glanced at Beaumont. If the idea of three drowned men floating up from the depths bothered her at all, she didn't show it.

The video continued.

The next dateline was two years later. A reporter narrated while a montage of video played. He said deepwater search-and-rescue organizations had approached the area with cadaver dogs. The reporter explained how cadaver dogs could locate a body below the surface. Cadaver dogs had been used to retrieve drowning victims in Red Maple Lake before, but none had found the three men from the Cessna. Until this time.

Next was a short interview. One of the divers, still dressed in his underwater gear, said they had retrieved two bodies trapped on the bottom of the lake. The bodies were remarkably well preserved, probably by the extremely cold water temperatures.

Made sense to Flint. Alpine lake water would function like a liquid deep freeze.

The brief pictures of the recovery operation, obviously filmed from a distance, were chilling. Glimpses of portions of the bodies looked almost as if the men had been lost the day before.

"The two men were identified as Dan Shafer and Skip Evans," the reporter said, showing headshots of each man in happier times. He asked the diver, "What about the pilot?"

The diver wiped a palm over his face. "We looked everywhere we could. We didn't find him."

"Will you be going down again?"

The diver cleared his throat. "If we get another lead, we will go back. For now—" He shook his head.

The reporter closed with an eerie reminder that seemed to stretch the facts. "The divers have assured us they will not give up the effort to find Josh Hallman."

When the story ended, Beaumont clicked off the screen and pushed another button on the remote to raise the window shades. Diffuse sunlight flooded the room, causing momentary blindness.

"I need to find Jamie's father." She nodded toward the screen. "He was the pilot on that plane."

"It's an underwater search-and-rescue operation. You need someone with equipment and skills in that line of work."

Beaumont sighed. "I don't believe Josh Hallman is at the bottom of that lake. I think he escaped the fate of the others."

"What makes you say that?"

"I know Josh. Let's just leave it at that." She didn't sound the least bit sad.

"Let's say you're right. It takes more than instinct to find a man. Have you ever tried it?" Flint cocked his head and leaned a little farther back in his chair. "If a man is simply missing, the authorities do a pretty good job of locating him, usually in the first forty-eight hours. If he stays missing longer than that, things get tricky. After what? Six plus years? Nobody's looking anymore. Know why? Because it's usually pretty pointless."

"So I hear. You're not the first investigator I've contacted." Beaumont nodded. "But I'm told you are the heir hunter of last resort for people like me. And I'm at the end of the line here, Flint. If you can't find Josh Hallman, then . . ." Her voice trailed off and she shrugged.

"Then what?"

"Then I don't know what happens to Jamie." Beaumont folded her hands on the table. Her nails were short and well manicured and without polish. She bowed her head for a moment and then raised it to look at Flint again. "Maddy must've told you that Jamie is very sick. Now the doctors say he needs a bone marrow transplant."

That had been Scarlett's guess. "And you think his father could be a donor match?"

She shrugged. "No guarantees from the doctors, but I hope he is. We've tried everything else. Jamie is in the database and hoping for a match that way, but if we could find Josh .

. ." Her voice trailed off again. She took a deep breath. "It might be a waste of time. Or not. Do you have kids, Mr. Flint?"

He shook his head. "In my line of work, I've seen a lot of dysfunctional families. I'm in no hurry to jump into that situation myself."

"Jamie has been special to me from the moment he was conceived." Her voice grew low and it softened her features. She seemed less like a ballbuster and more like a mom all of a sudden, and he liked her a little better, even though he suspected the transformation was temporary.

"He's a wonderful child. He has his father's ways."

"What does that mean?"

"Do you know what an alpha male is, Mr. Flint?" He nodded. The epithet had been hurled his way a few times, usually by angry women on the way out the door. Not that he disagreed with the label. He was as alpha as a man could possibly be. He didn't consider that a bad thing, but Beaumont obviously did.

"Imagine the opposite. Josh Hallman is all man, but he has a deep feminine side and a lot of emotional intelligence." She cocked her head and gave him a steady stare. "You don't find that in very many guys. Jamie's like that now. Imagine what he'll be like at thirty."

Pushed around by a woman like his mother, probably. Flint nodded again because he didn't know what else to do. "I'm not sure what you're asking of me, exactly."

"I think Josh Hallman is alive." She leaned forward on the table. "Before you ask me, no, I can't prove it. But they didn't find his body when they found the others. And, sometimes, a mother simply knows things."

"So what you want me to do is find Jamie's dad, dead or alive?"

"Yes," she said slowly. "I guess that's it. But I really don't believe he's dead and I don't think you should make that assumption. And frankly, he won't be of much use to me if he's dead, so I'd rather not go with that right off the bat."

They could go around in circles on the point for hours, so instead he asked, "Did you know the other two guys he was with?"

"I did. They didn't like me and I wasn't crazy about them, either." She wasn't apologizing for anything. He might be able to like her a little for the strength of her convictions, at least.

She reached into her pocket and pulled out a small data storage device. She put it on the table and pushed it toward him. "Everything you need to know is there. All the information I have. I'm sure you have access to records and databases and things that I don't have, but I've hired investigators before, as I said. They've been very thorough. This will save you some time. And there's a video of Jamie. Show it to Josh when you find him. It will help."

"You seem to like him well enough. Why did you two split up?" The last thing Flint needed was a nasty domestic situation on his hands.

She shrugged. "Our relationship was a fling. Never intended to be permanent. It ended. That's all."

"What about Jamie? Hasn't he ever seen his son?"

She pursed her lips and narrowed her eyes. "No." She offered nothing further on that score.

It was Flint's turn to shrug. As long as the ex didn't try to shoot him, he didn't really care why they broke up.

"Do you have a deadline of some sort?"

"I thought I told you?" She blinked. Maybe she was a little glassy-eyed, but the sunlight was still strong in the room. "Jamie's doctors say he needs the transplant now. They can't keep him alive indefinitely. Sooner is better."

Flint felt himself being drawn into a deep quagmire from which he might never extricate himself. Like quicksand tugging on his ankles. The truth was that most people were not that hard to find. There weren't many places to hide in the modern world. Most average Joes and Janes couldn't manage the feat.

Death and witness protection were the two most obvious answers when a missing person couldn't be located with a few hundred keystrokes and a dozen phone calls. After that, Flint concluded that the missing were making an active effort not to be found. Usually for valid reasons. Which made the hunt exponentially more difficult.

Assuming Josh Hallman wasn't dead, which was a big assumption, he had managed to stay unfindable for almost seven years. Which required some serious motivation, and Flint wondered what his motive was.

Flint picked up the thumb drive from the table and slid it into his pocket. "I will look at this stuff and let you know whether I can help you. But it's likely Josh Hallman's body is at the bottom of Red Maple Lake. Because of the temperature down there, his body should be well preserved. You might be able to get bone marrow for the transplant from the cadaver."

Beaumont was shaking her head before he finished. "I know Josh is not dead. I feel it. My instincts have carried me a long way in this world, Mr. Flint. Keep an open mind."

He shrugged, but he didn't believe her. Beaumont wasn't the kind of woman who operated on instinct. She knew something. He couldn't refuse the job and move on. He'd promised Maddy that he'd try to help her friend. "It's your money."

“I’m well aware of your fees. I’ll deposit the first five million dollars today. I’ll pay the rest when you find Josh.”

“Plus expenses. Which will be hefty. You can count on it.”

She nodded. “No problem. Another five million to start, and more if you need it. Will that be enough?”

“I’ll let you know.” He paused until he felt he had her full attention. “Have you considered that he might not agree to the transplant, even if he is alive and even if we do find him?” He picked up the business card she’d laid before him and handed her one of his own containing the information she’d need to deposit the funds into his Cayman Islands account.

"I know this is a long shot, Mr. Flint. But it's the only one I have and I have to take it." Beaumont stood and he followed her to the elevator. She pushed the call button, and when the doors opened he stepped inside. "Keep me posted. Let me know if you need more money."

On the way down, Flint sketched out a quick plan in his head.

He tossed his visitor badge on the security desk, and as he left the building, he made the first call.

Chapter Nine

His contact picked up the call immediately. Flint had spent years in the service of Uncle Sam. Everything from combat to covert ops. He kept his former colleagues close. Even did a bit of business with them now and then. Mutual back-scratching was the only form of payment they required.

"How can I help you?" she asked. He could hear keys clicking in the background and she seemed distracted.

"I need intel on a person."

"Full name and date of birth?" He gave her the information. "Got a social security number?"

"Not on me. But last known address was probably Chicago." He heard more keys clicking, and enough time passed for him to reach his car and open his laptop. He shoved the thumb drive into the port and opened the data. "Okay. Here's his social." He gave her the number.

A few more clicks and then she said, "This guy looks pretty normal. The only odd thing is I've got no data in the past six years. Which I gather means he is missing?"

"Roger that. Anybody been looking for him?"

"Not lately. There was activity from creditors and the like for a while. Nothing in the last couple of years. But there may be trigger traps installed, if anybody's looking for your guy. They'd send out an alert when he accesses any of this stuff."

"So they'll get an alert because you're looking at the files now?"

"Pretty much. Assuming they still care enough to bother looking."

"Got it. What else?"

"It's like he fell off the face of the earth six years ago. I've got birth records, school records, employment records, military records. Credit cards." She paused while she scanned the data. "If he's alive, he has not filed a tax return in six years. Uncle Sam takes a dim view of shenanigans like that. If he shows up, he might find himself staring through bars."

"Roger that. What else?"

"He hasn't paid any property taxes. In fact, it looks like his home was foreclosed and sold a few years back. Credit card balances sent to collection a while ago, probably written off."

Flint nodded, even though she couldn't see him. Pretty much what he expected.

She kept talking as if she was looking at lists on a screen, which she probably was.

"Driver's license is expired. Passport expired."

"Death certificate?"

"I don't see any. Did he have family? Because usually family makes the report and requests the certificates."

"I'm still chasing that down." He fingered the thumb drive.

"One thing, though. He had a couple of bank accounts at small community banks. Untouched for the same six years as everything else. Looks like they're flagged to turn over to the government for inactivity. One has a balance of more than fifty thousand dollars."

Flint whistled quietly through his teeth. "That's a lot of money for most folks to walk away from."

"I'll say. If he doesn't want it, maybe he'll give it to me."

"Maybe he will. When I find him, I'll ask."

She laughed. "You do that. But you'll need to be quick about it. He's got to claim the money by the end of the month."

"Okay. Send me everything you have on those accounts. Any parents or siblings in the files?"

"It'll take me a bit to find, if we have it, and I'm in the middle of something else at the moment. Can I call you back?"

"Yeah. And upload whatever you've got to my secure server for me. I'm traveling to an area with limited cell service. I'll take a satellite phone, but you may not be able to reach me right away."

"Got it." She disconnected.

He spent about half a second thinking about what she'd said before he started his car. He did a quick search on his laptop for Red Maple Lake and the exclusive resort mentioned in the newscast.

Locating Red Maple Lake Resort online was pretty simple. Like everyone else these days, they had a website. Originally built decades earlier as a private lodge by some Hollywood types with money to burn for a place to play away from the prying eyes of media and fans. To say the place was remote was like saying the ocean was wet.

While it was not possible to drive directly to the resort itself, the website explained, vehicles were secured in a nearby parking lot where visitors would be collected by the resort valet and driven to the main lodge in an off-road vehicle.

Problem was, traveling from civilization to the resort parking lot was tricky, too. The closest commercial airport was Reno, Nevada, which supported regional jets with limited service. The resort was an eight-hour drive from there because of road conditions.

The easiest way to reach the resort was exactly what Josh Hallman and his friends had tried to do. Bush pilots could land a floatplane on the lake. If they landed close enough to the resort, the ORV could pick them up from there.

Flint had flown just about every kind of airborne vehicle at one time or another, but he knew when to call in a specialized professional. He pressed the number three speed dial button on his phone.

The closest thing Flint had to a sidekick, Alonzo Drake, picked up immediately. “What’s up?”

“I’m working on a new case. I don’t think it should take very long, but you never know how these things will go. I need to travel from here to a place called Red Maple Lake Resort in California, tomorrow.”

“Anybody going to be shooting at me?” He sounded a little cranky. Even back in their military days, Drake didn’t crave the excitement of combat.

“Possible.” Flint grinned. “But not likely.”

“Because I’m tired of getting shot at. And for that matter, I’m too old for bar fights.”

“Quit whining. It’s conduct unbecoming.” Flint grinned again and he knew Drake could hear the humor in his voice.

“Reno has a pretty good airport. You could fly in there and get a car.”

“I could, but I don’t want to spend the next two days in the wilderness.

What I need is a good bush pilot. You used to be one of the best. Still got your skills?"

"Once a bush pilot, always a bush pilot," Drake said. "But I don't like the sound of this. You wouldn't need me if you were going somewhere normal."

"If heir hunting were easy, anybody could do it. Clients wouldn't need high-priced talent like us now, would they?" Flint grinned.

He felt energized. He loved the challenge of his work.

Drake, not so much. He didn't reply.

"The guy I'm looking for was last seen at a private airfield outside of Reno." Flint put the transmission in gear and pulled out of the parking lot. “He rented a floatplane.”

“I’m looking at this place online right now. That lake is surrounded by mountains on all sides. It’s a basin like Tahoe, but it’s a lot smaller. You can get some nasty crosscurrents going in a place like that. Landing’s tricky, too. There’s only one way to come at it and have enough distance to set down.”

“Yeah, I noticed that.” He wound around Houston’s surface streets, moving toward home. “This guy didn’t have those skills, apparently.”

“He crashed his plane into that lake?”

“Something like that.”

“What happened to him?”

“He had two passengers. Their bodies were found a couple of years after the crash. They never found the pilot. He’s the guy we’re looking for.”

“So you’re hiring deep water rescue? That’s not my thing. And even if it were, you’re gonna need guys down there with special equipment, which I don’t have.” Drake’s tone changed, his voice deepened. “There’re a lot of stories about the number of bodies on the bottom of Lake Tahoe. I’ve seen some photographs. It can be nasty, deep in those mountain lakes.”

“We’re not doing any of that.” Flint ran a hand over his hair and cupped the back of his neck. He let out a long stream of air as he exhaled and pulled his car into his garage. “The woman who hired me doesn’t think he’s at the bottom of the lake. She says divers already looked and his body has never been found. She thinks he survived.”

“How does she know?”

This was the part that troubled Flint, too. “Dunno.”

“Who’s the client?”

Flint hesitated before he replied, “Veronica Beaumont.”

Drake whistled long and low. “So this is a guy who went out for a pack of cigarettes and never came back? Because if I was hooked up with her, that’s what I’d want to do every minute of every day.”

Flint collected his laptop and left the car on his way to the house.

"So are you in or not?"

"Life is too short, man." Drake paused and Flint let the silence linger for a long time. Drake finally said, "I take it there's a big payday at the end of this."

"There always is. I wouldn't take the case otherwise. Especially not for a woman like Veronica Beaumont." Flint was starting to think this job might not be as bad as it looked at first, though.

"When do you need to go?" Drake asked. "I've got to arrange some things and rearrange some others."

"As soon as you can be ready."

"I'll call you back." Drake ended the call.

Flint was inside now. He dropped his car keys on the kitchen counter, grabbed a cold bottle of water, took the laptop into the den, and went back to his research while he waited.

One thing he'd learned a long time ago was that he could never be overprepared.

Almost a full hour passed before Drake called back. "Okay. Fastest thing to do is exactly what your guy did. Fly commercial to Reno and rent a floatplane at the same airfield where he rented his."

Flint nodded. He figured that would be the answer. Josh Hallman was looking like a worthy challenge. At least he'd done his homework on the front end.

After reviewing all the material on the thumb drive, he still felt uneasy about Beaumont in many ways. He had honed his instincts over time into quick reflexes that triggered faster than his brain could work through the facts.

Instincts had saved his ass more than once. He wasn't about to ignore them now.

But if Beaumont was as desperate as she claimed, why not tell him everything? What the hell was she hiding?

Flint said, “I’m not sure where all this is headed, and I don’t want to be dependent on commercial air travel. Let’s take the Pilatus. It will give us the flexibility we need.”

The Pilatus claimed to be the world’s first super-versatile jet. It was designed to operate from short paved or unpaved surfaces and remote fields. Flexibility was key. The PC-24 could land in well under two thousand feet, and Drake had access to the jets.

Drake replied, “Flexibility? For what? How long do you think we’ll be gone?”

“You know how this goes. One thing leads to another. Field conditions change,” Flint said. “I hope we’ll be back in less than twenty-four hours, but I never make plans based on assumptions."

Drake paused a few seconds longer this time before he said, "I'll make some calls."

"Great." Flint disconnected.

It was highly likely that Josh Hallman's body was at the bottom of Red Maple Lake.

He understood why Beaumont didn't want to believe Hallman had died, but the reality was staring him in the face. Flint didn't really want the job and he didn't need the money.

He'd promised Maddy.

Otherwise he'd give this up now and turn his time to something that was likely to be more successful.

He tossed a few clothes and supplies into a bag. After that, he ordered a pizza and settled in for the night. He thoroughly reviewed everything Beaumont had supplied, noted the missing pieces, and then moved on to more research of his own.

By the time he'd consumed the pizza, he'd formed a fairly complete picture of Beaumont and Hallman. He'd also researched Jamie's medical condition and the bone marrow transplant procedures.

Everything he found pointed toward a watery grave for Josh Hallman. And a sad outcome for Jamie Beaumont.

Flint thought long and hard about Maddy. Would she be satisfied if he found Hallman dead and her friend was no better off than before Flint had taken on the hunt?

Not only no, but **hell** no.

Maddy believed Flint could do anything. She was seven. Until now, he'd never let her down. But the facts here simply did not look promising.

He opened a beer and paced, thinking about the situation, as well as he knew the facts. One thing didn't seem to fit.

Veronica Beaumont was a smart and successful bitch. Would she pay him five million dollars in advance, and another five when he found Hallman, if it was more than likely that the man was lying at the bottom of that lake somewhere?

She would not.

Which meant Veronica Beaumont had something more than a Ouija board telling her that Hallman was still alive. She was that kind of woman. She kept secrets.

Screw that. He would do the job, but he wouldn't leave Houston without full intel.

He glanced at the clock. It was late, after midnight. He called Beaumont's cell phone. "I'm on my way over. I have a couple of questions before I head out tomorrow morning."

“I’ll be available for thirty minutes,” she said, and hung up.

He pressed the disconnect button and dropped the phone into his pocket, shaking his head. What a piece of work.

If he hadn’t promised Maddy, he’d give Beaumont walking papers right now and move on. He had better things to do.

He poured the half-full bottle of beer down the drain, snagged his keys off the kitchen counter, and headed out the back door to his car.

Chapter Ten

Red Maple Lake, California
Six Years Ago

After Josh opened the door, he moved deeper inside the Cessna's cabin. They had to get out of the plane. Otherwise, they were headed for a watery grave for sure.

Both Dan and Skip had been injured in the crash. Dan's scalp was bleeding from what looked like a laceration inside the hairline above his left ear. Josh wasn't a doctor but he'd been trained in basic field first aid. He'd rarely had to use that training before, but he knew from experience that scalp wounds produced a lot of blood, even if they were not serious. He needed the first aid kit, which was in the back.

“Skip? Hand me the first aid kit. It’s on the floor behind the seat.” Skip moaned in response. There was very little room inside the cabin. It was difficult to see behind the co-pilot’s seat, where Josh had been tending to Dan. The left side of the plane was sinking. Water seemed to enter the cabin much too fast. Dan had to get out of that co-pilot’s seat or he’d soon be submerged.

Skip groaned again, louder. Dan’s blood had begun to coagulate.
The flow from his scalp laceration slowed, but he seemed dazed. Not quite with it. Josh checked his vital signs quickly and he seemed okay, considering.

He patted Dan's shoulder and removed his harness. "Come on. You've got to move." He tugged on Dan's right arm, reinforcing the message.

Josh contorted his body to move into the back of the plane again. Instantly, he saw why Skip was moaning in pain. He had not been secure in his seat at the time of the crash, and now he was sprawled on the left side of the plane, half on the passenger seat and half floating near the floor in the rising water.

Skip's face was pale. His eyes vacant. His lips opened to moan.

Both of Skip's hands were holding his right thigh.

His blood-soaked cargo pants were ripped, and the jagged edge of his femur poked through a broad gash in the fabric about four inches above his knee. Blood was pulsing from the open wound around Skip's hands, even as he tried to slow the volume.

Josh felt bile rise in his throat when he saw the gaping wound. He clamped his jaws together and swallowed to stop his gag reflex from bringing up his lunch. Nothing he'd learned about rendering emergency medical care had prepared him for something like Skip's open femur break. But there was no way to call a doctor and Dan wasn't much help.

The only one Josh could rely on right now was himself.

Carefully, he moved Skip around to sit closer to the right side of the plane. He lifted Skip's leg onto the slanting passenger seat, steeling himself against Skip's screams and the icy rising water.

Josh remembered the advice that returning the damaged leg to a position that was at least closer to normal could alleviate some of the pain. How could he do that under these conditions? Elevating the leg slowed the blood flow somewhat simply by thwarting gravity, but that was no help with Skip's pain.

He found a cold, wet towel on the floor and wrung it out as well as he could. He folded it and covered the blood pulsing from the gash, pressing hard. Even as he applied pressure to the wound and felt the blood slow, he knew it wouldn't stop. Skip could die from blood loss before they had a chance for rescue.

Josh found Skip's bag and used it as a weight to hold the towel in place. He maneuvered around his friend's splayed body until he found the first aid kit. He opened it. No medical tourniquet. And nothing else inside the kit was a suitable substitute to encircle Skip's heavily muscled right thigh. He'd need to improvise.

He climbed over Skip and rooted around quickly, sorting through the fishing equipment they'd brought on board until he found a leather belt in Dan's gear. He did his best to apply the makeshift tourniquet to Skip's leg and to ignore his friend's excruciating screams of pain.

The belt worked to slow the bleeding, but not to stop it.

Josh glanced at Dan. His eyes were unfocused, as if he'd zoned out or something. Nothing would matter if they all drowned. And Josh couldn't get the three of them to shore alone.

He rummaged quickly through the first aid kit until he found the smelling salts and reached up to wave them as close to Dan's nose as he could. Whether he was close enough or whether Dan was already coming around, Josh couldn't say. Dan coughed and moved his head and pushed the smelling salts away.

"Skip? Can you hear me?" Josh pressed a palm to Skip's clammy forehead. He was sweating and his skin was pale and cold. He was breathing rapidly but seemed confused, as if he didn't understand where he was or what was happening to him. He continued moaning and crying out. Josh recognized the signs of shock.

Dan groaned from the front seat. He raised his fingers to the gooey mess above his ear and pulled his hand away to look at the blood. "What the hell?"

Josh's relief escaped in a shout. "Dan! Get the hell back here. I need help."

Dan seemed groggy and slow to react, which was probably due to the head trauma, or maybe he was suffering from shock, too. But when he turned around, he saw Skip. His eyes widened. His mouth flopped open like the largemouth bass he'd planned to catch in Red Maple Lake.

He fumbled out of his seat and stumbled toward Josh.

"Tell me what to do," he said, his voice shaky. At least he was trying.

Josh shook his head. He didn't really know what to do. He only knew they couldn't stay in the plane. The water was midcalf now, and the left side was almost totally submerged. They had to get out and get help. And Skip could not swim in his present condition.

The floatplane had tilted sharply to the left side now. Soon, it would flip over onto its roof. Josh looked out of the windshield. The shore was at least fifty yards to port. The mountain water temperature was probably well below sixty degrees.

Skip had said he'd packed his wetsuit. "That's stupid, Josh," he said quietly to himself. He couldn't have stuffed Skip into the suit under the best of circumstances. And he'd only brought one suit. No. They couldn't swim to shore from here without protection. Hypothermia would set in quickly once they entered the water.

There were life vests in the plane. And he'd seen an inflatable life raft in the cargo area of the Cessna.

The weight of the engine pulled the plane down, but with momentum and one buoyant pontoon, the aircraft rolled over and tumbled upside down. The roof became the floor.

Skip flailed to keep his head above water as he was twisted and lifted, flopping onto the roof.

Dan and Josh held on to whatever was closest as the plane rolled over.

Water poured in through the open door at an alarming rate as the dark curtain of icy water crept relentlessly over the windows beneath them.

The world outside grew still and silent.

In mere moments, Josh knew, the only thing that could possibly be seen from the shore was the faint white bottom of one pontoon, holding them afloat.

Rapid thoughts ran through Josh's mind. The plane was already partially submersed and going down. The damaged pontoon wouldn't hold much longer. He'd managed to slow Skip's bleeding but not stop it. Dan's head injury was probably mild, but Josh had no idea how either of them would be affected by submersion in cold water.

He could leave them both and go for help, but how long would it take and where would he find it and would they be dead already by the time help arrived?

He ran through the rescue possibilities in his head as quickly as he could and found no good answers. He knew he had to do something and do it fast. He just didn't know what that something was.

"Josh?" Dan's panicked question broke through. He was holding Skip's head above water with both arms clasped around Skip's chest.

"What?" Josh forced himself to sound calm even though he was the furthest thing from it.

"Skip's not breathing. He's not breathing. Here." Dan grabbed Josh's fingers and placed them against Skip's carotid artery. "Feel that? Nothing. No pulse."

Josh pushed his fingers deeper into Skip's neck. He felt something. Faint and weak but present. How long could Skip last? He'd lost a lot of blood. He was in a lot of pain. The mountain lake water was like taking a bath in an arctic ocean.

Josh hadn't called in a Mayday on the way down, but had anyone seen the plane crash? Was help on the way? He didn't know, but he knew they couldn't wait anymore. He had to do something and do it now.

He scrambled around until he found one of the life vests and put it on. Dan watched as if he was deeply puzzled and didn't quite comprehend. Josh found a second life vest and put it on Dan. He found a third and put it on Skip.

He'd found the plane's life raft when he'd searched for the tourniquet. The raft would inflate automatically, and with Dan's help, they might be able to get Skip into it and drag themselves to shore. Or they might all drown in the process.

"We have to get help. We can't wait here. There's a life raft. It may or may not work for us," Josh said. "Looks like you've had a pretty sharp blow to your head and you seem like you're not quite with it. What do you think, Dan? Can you swim from here to shore, if we need to?"

"I don't know. I don't feel right. I don't know if I can swim or not."

Josh looked at him, as if he could see straight through to his brain, and explained as simply as he could, hoping Dan would understand him. "I'm not gonna lie to you. I'm not sure Skip will make it no matter what we do. I just know that if we do nothing, he's going to die right here. This plane is sinking. We might survive until help comes, but he'll drown if his injuries don't kill him first. If we get to shore, we may have a better chance. But I don't know that, either."

Dan nodded as if he was processing Josh's words at half speed but did not reply. His teeth were chattering. The water was above his waist now.

Josh wasn't sure whether Dan understood the seriousness of the situation or the hopelessness of their choices. Either way, he could spend no more time trying to talk.

He secured Dan's life vest as tightly around his waist as possible. He did the same with Skip's and his own.

He found a coiled rope, enough to tie the three of them together, which he knew might be stupid. They could weigh each other down if they fell into the water. They might all drown. But at least he wouldn't lose them. He was a strong swimmer. He might be able to pull them all to shore, if it came to that. Which he prayed it wouldn't.

He pushed the plane's door fully open and struggled to move the heavy life raft from the back. He tied the soft valise's rope securely to the plane to prevent it from drifting away on the choppy water after it inflated. He heaved the valise out of the wide doors. The valise plopped into the lake and bobbed like a fishing lure.

Josh yanked hard on the rope to trigger inflation, and the raft's air cartridges deployed as they were meant to do. The black-and-orange raft filled with air and was in position to board in less than ten seconds.

Josh heaved himself up and climbed out of the plane. He braced his feet on the Cessna's slippery surface and shouted to be heard over the wind. "Dan, lift Skip up and I'll grab him. Let the water's buoyancy help you."

Dan was smaller than Skip, but somehow he managed to lift him and get his head and shoulders out of the plane's door. Josh reached in to pull Skip the rest of the way out.

Josh tried to set Skip gently onto the raft's floor, but he couldn't manage it. The sinking plane, the choppy lake, the bouncing raft, the sharp, cold wind, and Skip's heavy body combined to defeat Josh's efforts. Skip fell hard into the raft and landed oddly and screamed.

The rope tied around Skip's waist pulled Josh into the icy lake. He went under the surface briefly, feeling the cold grip on his lungs, before the rope pulled him back up. He clambered aboard the raft and fell on top of Skip.

The other end of the rope, tied to Dan's waist, pulled taut, cutting painfully into Josh's stomach. He yelled, "Dan! Come on!"

Dan waited at the Cessna's doorway as if he didn't understand or couldn't bring himself to move toward the lake. Josh was already cold and shivering. He pulled on the rope in an effort to tug Dan forward. But Dan put his hands on either side of the doorway and resisted, vigorously shaking his head.

“Dan. Buddy. You’ve got to jump in. We have to get to shore.” Dan’s eyes were the size of saucers and he shook his head even more rapidly. Dan had always been afraid of the water. His lips were already blue and his whole body shook. Whether from cold or terror, Josh couldn’t say.

Josh found an oar inside the raft and paddled to keep as close to the door as he could while floundering in the rough, cold lake. But if Dan didn’t get into the raft, he’d pull them all down as the plane sank.

Josh stopped paddling, reached around, and grabbed the rope connecting him to Dan and yanked as hard as possible from his seated position. By a miracle or adrenaline or something else, he pulled Dan out of the plane and into the water. Dan began to kick reflexively toward the raft. He knew how to swim, he was simply petrified.

Josh pulled Dan into the raft and released the anchor rope. The raft began to drift. Josh handed Dan the second paddle and pointed toward the shore. They paddled in sloppy unison against the strong wind, and the raft began to move slowly in the right direction as the Cessna dropped lower into the water.

Somehow, by the grace of God, they made it to shore. Josh's muscles were screaming with fatigue and tension. His body shook with cold. Dan jumped out of the raft at the water's edge and Josh followed.

Chapter Eleven

Houston, Texas
Monday

Veronica Beaumont lived about ten miles and ten million dollars from Flint's neighborhood.

He drove the familiar streets easily and stayed within the speed limit. His blood alcohol level was well within legal limits, but he didn't need the hassle of dealing with the local cops tonight.

He reached Beaumont's gated community in less than fifteen minutes. At the guard station, he gave his name and was waved through, although the security cameras at the station recorded his entry.

Six minutes later, he pulled into Beaumont's driveway, parked, and walked up to ring the doorbell. He stood on the porch, hands stuffed into the front pockets of his jeans.

She'd been waiting. She opened the door only slightly and peered out, as if she was worried about who might be standing there. She was dressed in the same expensive, fashion-model-casual style she had sported at the ice cream shop. Full makeup and five-inch heels.

Flint lived in a mostly male world, but none of the women he knew spent evenings at home alone dressed like

Beaumont. Maybe she had a live-in lover or something.

“May I come in?” Flint asked, hoping she’d say no and save him a lot of trouble.

She opened the door, waved him inside, and closed the door behind him.

“We can talk in here,” she said as she led the way to a private study.

The house was as expensively furnished and spacious as he had expected. She didn’t offer him any refreshments of any kind. Whether she didn’t approve of him or simply wanted him to get to the point, he didn’t know and didn’t care.

Whatever her reasons, the arrangement suited him fine.

He sat down. She wasn't going to rush him through this and she should know that right off the bat.

"I've looked at everything you gave me on Josh Hallman and his plane crash. I've also done a little digging on my own. The guy has been totally off the grid for six-plus years since that plane went down," Flint said. "There's no reason to believe that he is still alive. I've checked government records, private investigation files, even witness protection because I have contacts in that arena. No dice. Not one mention. In six years."

"If Josh could have been found by a record search, I wouldn't need you." Veronica remained standing, like she wasn't going to get comfortable. "I was told you had additional skills."

"I do." Flint nodded. "But before I deploy those skills, I insist that my clients tell me everything they know. And you are holding back on me, Ms. Beaumont."

"Why would I do that? I've already told you what the stakes are here. Why wouldn't I want to do everything possible to save my child?"

Her response was huffy and offended. Flint didn't buy it.

"Good question. I think you're worried about something you know." He leaned forward, forearms on his thighs. "Why do you think Josh Hallman is still alive? There is absolutely nothing I can find to support that idea."

"I already answered that question."

"Let me put it this way, Ms. Beaumont." He leaned back in his seat. "You can tell me why you think Hallman survived that plane crash when his two passengers did not. Or get yourself another guy. I won't put my team in harm's way for you without knowing what we're getting into."

She looked at him steadily for a while before she turned and walked to a drink cart in the corner and poured herself a glass of vodka.

Straight.

No ice.

"Anything for you?"

"Single malt if you have it."

She poured his scotch and carried both glasses back. She handed one to him and sipped her own. Still, she did not sit.

She paced the room awhile. Flint waited. He could wait for her to work out whatever her problem was.

But he wouldn't wait forever.

He finished his scotch and set the glass on a table.

He stood. "I'm sorry. I will not be able to help you, Ms. Beaumont. I'm not in the habit of disappointing my niece and I don't appreciate that you've put me in this position. Don't call me again."

He turned to leave. He'd walked all the way to the front entrance and his hand was on the doorknob before she called him back.

For more than half a second, he considered leaving anyway.

He turned and stood in the foyer. He wasn't walking back in there.

She could damned well walk to him this time.

Her voice was low. "After the plane crash, a man came to see me. I was living somewhere else at the time, somewhere with less security." She held the vodka glass with both hands. "He knocked on my door without warning. When I opened it, he pushed his way in."

Flint waited.

She drained the glass. “He had a gun. He was looking for Josh. He said he knew Josh had survived.”

“What else did he say?”

“Can we sit down again? I don’t want Jamie to overhear.” Before he answered, she turned and walked back into the study.

He followed her and closed the door. She poured herself another drink and offered the bottle to him. He shook his head.

“What else did he say?” Flint repeated his question because she seemed to be ignoring it.

She took a big swallow of the booze.

“He said he would find Josh. He said if Josh contacted me, he would know.” She drained the glass and refilled it again.

Flint cocked his head. She seemed genuinely scared. “What else?”

“He said he knew Josh was Jamie’s dad. No one knows that, Flint. Not even Josh or Jamie. I’ve never revealed Jamie’s father to a living soul before you. I don’t know how he found out, but he had resources of some kind.” Her hands were shaking now. “He told me never to tell anyone that he’d been here.”

Flint watched and said nothing.

“Look, I’m a businesswoman and a single mom. That’s it. I don’t travel in those kinds of circles. No one has ever threatened me like that before. This guy was absolutely terrifying." She sat in a chair across from Flint and took a deep breath. "The message I got was pretty clear: if I told anyone about him, he'd come back and—do something to Jamie."

Flint nodded. He could see she was still frightened, after all this time.

Maybe the guy threatened her back then and maybe he could have followed through. But whether he was dangerous or not, Veronica Beaumont had clearly believed him.

It seemed she still did.

"I never told anybody about him before." She drained her glass again. Her speech was slurred. He wondered how much she'd had to drink before he arrived. She'd have a hell of a hangover tomorrow. "I wouldn't be telling you now except I'm desperate to do whatever I can for my boy. I know you don't have kids, but surely you can understand that."

"I do, actually," Flint nodded. "But I can't do this job for you if I don't know everything you know. Describe this guy for me."

"He was about your size, I guess. A little heavier. A little older." She closed her eyes as if she were attempting to visualize him clearly. "Medium height and medium build. Brown hair, brown eyes. He didn't have an accent, but I had the impression that he was Hispanic."

"You mean Mexican? We have plenty of Mexican Americans around here."

"To be honest, I was so terrified of his gun and everything about him that I didn't spend a lot of time trying to memorize what he looked like."

"Was he alone?"

"I was so shaken . . ." Her voice trailed off and she seemed to think about the question for a bit. "But now that you ask, I think there was someone else in the car with him. Another man. I heard him say, 'Let's go,' as he approached the car when he left."

Flint nodded again to encourage her.

He'd questioned hundreds of witnesses. They had usually

observed more than they realized. If he kept asking specific questions, he could learn the rest.

“What was he wearing?”

She closed her eyes again. “He was well dressed. Casual khaki slacks, a pressed shirt, a leather blazer. He wore expensive shoes.”

She opened her eyes and grimaced. “I always notice the shoes. His were fine leather loafers with leather soles. No socks.”

She’d described half the men at any country club in the world. “How old was he?”

She thought about it. “Maybe mid-forties? Not old. But not a young punk, either.”

"What can you tell me about the gun?"

"Not much. I'm not that familiar with guns."

"Was it a handgun or a long gun?"

"A handgun."

He pulled his Glock from his waistband and showed it to her. "Did it look like this?"

She shook her head.

"Was it bigger or smaller?"

"Bigger. At least, it seemed bigger to me at the time."

"Okay. Good." He nodded and returned the gun to his belt. "Tell me again what happened, one step at a time. Use his exact words, if you can remember them."

"He rang the bell. I answered and foolishly opened the door. There was an SUV in the driveway. A black one. Fairly new. Expensive." Flint nodded to keep her going. "He was clean-shaven. He had the gun out when I opened the door, and he pushed the door open and came inside. I was petrified. I didn't know what to do."

"What was the first thing he told you?"

She closed her eyes again, almost trance-like. "He said, 'I'm looking for Josh Hallman. Is he here?' And I was shocked. I hadn't seen Josh since before I left Chicago. Before Jamie was born. So I said, 'No. Why?'"

"What did he say?"

She swallowed hard before she continued. "He said Josh had piloted a small plane that crashed. He said Josh survived the crash and ran away. He demanded to search my house." She swallowed again. "The house was small. It didn't take long. He went into every room and opened every door. He even looked under the beds. He went into the garage and looked in the car."

"Was Jamie home at the time?"

"No, thank God. He was in day care." She clasped her hands together as if she might say a prayer of thanks. "After he didn't find Josh, that's when he said he'd be watching me. He said he'd know if Josh contacted me."

"Do you have any indications that he has been watching you?"

Her eyes widened as if the thought hadn't occurred to her. "I don't know. I guess I just figured he'd watched for a while to confirm that I'm not in contact with Josh. Would he still be watching? After all this time?"

She'd be easy to monitor. It could be done remotely. Her home was a fortress, but her security was electronic. Watching her without her knowledge would be a relatively simple matter.

Flint assumed she was being watched.

Which meant he'd be on the guy's radar now, too.

"What did he ask you to do if you heard from Josh?"

She shook her head. "He said he'd know. I took that to mean that he'd be using whatever high-tech stuff people use to spy on people these days."

"Did you have CCTV at your house?"

She shook her head again. "Not then. I had it installed the next day."

"What was your address? I may be able to get video from nearby cameras." He said that, but he had little hope of finding any video. Surveillance systems back then were not what they were now.

But Flint had access to sources most civilians couldn't tap into.

She wrote the address down on a piece of paper and handed it to him. He knew the neighborhood. She was right. The chances of video cameras capturing something unexpected over in that residential section of Houston were slim.

“Tell me about the driver.”

She said, “He was about the same age as the first guy, I guess. He stayed in the car. I couldn’t see him very well.”

Flint nodded again.

“You agree with me now, don’t you?” She raised her head and stared directly into Flint’s eyes. “You think Josh is alive.”

"Maybe." Flint sighed. "He may have survived the crash. But it was six years ago. Whether he's still alive is a totally different question."

"What do you mean?"

"Your guy with the gun seemed to make it pretty clear that he would find Josh and deal with him. It's too bad you didn't report that visit to the police when it happened."

Veronica buried her face in her hands and began to weep. It was the most normal human reaction he'd seen from her since they'd met.

"I'll do what I can." Flint stood up again. "But these guys sound like thugs to me. If they found him, it's not likely they simply let him go."

Veronica nodded. “I understand.”

Flint wondered if she really did. By not reporting the threat when it happened, she’d effectively eliminated any chance that Hallman could have been forewarned and hired protection.

The poor sap had been on his own, and his basic military training would not have equipped him to defend himself from two determined killers.

Not only that, but finding Hallman had just become even more difficult.

He wasn’t simply missing anymore. He was actively hiding.

And he was good at it.

Totally different gig.

Chapter Twelve

Red Maple Lake, California
Six Years Ago

Dan and Josh pulled Skip and the life raft as far from the shoreline as possible. Josh collapsed on the rocky beach, breathing hard, sucking air into his lungs. His arms and legs felt like the Gumby rubber doll he'd played with as a kid.

Dan flopped onto the rocks, shivering, teeth chattering, gasping. Dan was in good physical condition, but the crash and his head injury and the hard paddling had pushed him beyond his limits.

Josh crawled over to the raft. He put a palm on Skip's face. Skip was chilled and shivering and his face was contorted with pain. But he was still alive.

How long could the three of them possibly remain that way? Everything they owned was soaking wet. The sun had settled behind the mountains and the wind was cold. His own teeth were chattering. His skin felt as clammy as a fish. The struggle had pushed the limits of his physical conditioning, too.

How could they survive when the temperature dropped tonight?

They had no food. No fire. Both Dan and Skip were injured.

One thing at a time.

That was the only answer that popped into his head.

One thing at a time.

Josh looked back at the Cessna. Only its tail section poked above the waterline and was barely visible from the shore. The weather continued to deteriorate. Stiff, steady wind blew in from the north. Sleet pelted his skin where he lay on the rocky beach. Skip had passed out or something. Josh feared the moment when his breathing would stop, too.

Josh was exhausted. His breath came in ragged chunks. Dan had manned up enough to paddle the distance, and somehow they had managed to reach dry land. Dan collapsed on the cold beach stones and pulled Josh down, too. They were still connected by the ropes he'd found inside the plane.

Skip was moaning, even though he wasn't conscious. Pain and blood loss were probably to blame. Josh patted his pockets until he found his waterproof phone. He pulled it out and pressed the power button. The phone powered up, but found no cell signal. Figures.

With stiff, cold fingers Josh fumbled to untie himself from his two friends and struggled to push himself up to stand. His legs felt wobbly and weak. He turned to look back at the plane, which was upside down. The only thing visible was the bottom of the right pontoon and even that was almost totally submerged now.

Dan was conscious and breathing hard. His lips were blue from the cold. His teeth chattered. But he was alive. They all were. To stay that way, they needed help.

They had seen the resort as they approached from the air. But Josh was disoriented now. Had Red Maple Lake Resort been east or west of here? And how far away? He shook his head. He didn't know.

He rubbed his hands over his biceps and moved his legs in place in a fruitless attempt to warm up. He closed his eyes to visualize the Cessna's circling approach again.

The tallest of the mountains was on the lake's north side, but the terrain was elevated all around the alpine lake basin. The way he remembered it, the rocky coastline ran up from the water and disappeared quickly into the treeline.

He frowned and thought hard. His brain seemed muddled and foggy, but as he concentrated and visualized he thought, maybe, when he was circling above the landing area, he'd seen the rooftops of Red Maple Lake Resort across the lake from the highest peak and to the east.

He opened his eyes. The sun had already dipped behind the mountains to his right, which should mean the resort was to his left. East of where they'd come ashore.

The more he thought about it, the more he believed he was right. East. He'd seen those rooftops to the east. Definitely. No question.

But how far? Could he walk there? Maybe not. His legs wobbled with tension when he tried to stand. But really, what choice did he have? If he didn't go for help, they'd all die of exposure or dehydration. Or something worse. Bears and cougars and who knew what other carnivores prowled in these mountains. Predators that would see Skip as an easy meal.

He shook his head. Staying here and waiting for rescue was not an option.

He approached Dan, still lying on the rocks, eyes closed, shivering with cold. Josh knelt beside him and put a hand on his shoulder. Dan's eyes popped open but he didn't move. Josh felt his carotid pulse, which was erratic but present. His skin was cold.

"Dan, you can hear me, right?" Josh lowered his voice. He didn't want to alarm Skip, assuming his friend could hear anything at all.

Dan's voice was dry and weak. "Yeah."

"Skip is in a bad way, man. We've got to get him out of here and find a doctor. Can you stay with him while I go look for help?"

"Yeah." Dan's eyes widened and darted wildly, as if the idea of staying with Skip frightened him beyond anything they'd endured so far. Josh understood. Skip might very well die before Josh got back.

"Look, Dan, we both love Skip like a brother. We've got to do everything we can." Dan's wild-eyed terror seemed to grow with every word Josh said. "We can't leave him alone. And you're in no shape to go for help."

Josh didn't say that if they all stayed here, Skip would probably die and they might die, too. Dan shook his head rapidly. His nostrils flared. The more Josh thought about it, the more frightening his imaginings seemed to become. But Dan would have to get himself together. He couldn't see any other way. He had to go for help. It was their best chance.

Josh patted Dan on the shoulder and pushed himself upright. He staggered a few steps and steadied his weight evenly. Cold gooseflesh covered his skin. His body began to shake. He needed to move. To warm up.

He had to go now. While he still had some daylight. He dug through and found four flashlights in the life raft. He checked them to be sure they were working and handed two to Dan. He searched for matches and found a lighter. They had nothing to burn for a fire. Dan would have to take care of that much.

“When it gets dark, turn on one of these flashlights. I’ll be back as soon as I can. I’ll bring help. Look around in the raft for something you can use to start a fire. Maybe some blankets that didn't get wet and some kind of dried food or something, too." He'd been scanning the tree line for a path into the woods and he didn't see one. The trek through the thick forest wouldn't be easy in daylight. It might be impossible after full dark. "Stay here so I can find you again. I'll be back as soon as I can."

Dan nodded and said nothing more. Maybe he was still dazed from his head trauma. Or maybe his reaction right now was caused by pure fright. Either way, there was nothing more Josh could do to assuage Dan's fears. He felt the same things himself.

Josh started off toward the east looking for some sign of civilization. Or even a cell phone signal.

He began a slow jog to cover ground more quickly and to warm up a bit. He stayed on the rocky shore, traveling east, until he found a reasonable break in the trees. Not a trail, but an opening.

Now he was headed southeast. The going was slower here. His feet landed awkwardly on rocky and uneven ground, even as the dense forest protected him from the sharp wind and the stinging sleet. He was forced to slow down, to dodge the undergrowth and maneuver around the big pines and aspens and other trees and bushes he couldn't identify.

Inside the woods, it was darker. He pulled out one of the flashlights and turned it on and held the beam directed to the ground in front of him. His stomach growled with hunger a few times and he considered that a good sign. It felt normal. He hadn't eaten anything for several hours. Of course, he was hungry. Made sense. Josh liked things that made sense.

He'd traveled maybe two miles, give or take, when he heard voices ahead. He paused to listen. Three voices, he thought. All males. Campers, maybe. Or guests at Red Maple Lake Resort, if he was lucky. He hadn't been lucky in a long time. Maybe his luck was about to change.

"Hello!" he called out before he could see them clearly.

"Hello!" one of the men called back.

Relief washed over him like a long, hot shower. He'd found help. Maybe Dan and Skip would be okay. Maybe they all would. He judged the distance and direction of the voices and jogged closer.

Chapter Thirteen

Houston, Texas
Tuesday

Flint met Drake at the private airfield in Houston. Drake had the Pilatus out of the hangar and ready to go. Flint parked his car and grabbed his bag.

He hustled over to the jet and climbed aboard. As he settled into the co-pilot seat, Drake's attention was focused on his pre-flight checklist.

After takeoff, Flint brought Drake up to speed on his visit to Beaumont, filling him in on the rest of the conversation and the research he had done to date. Drake was one of the best wingmen on the planet, and Flint wouldn't send him into the situation uninformed.

"So I guess that's progress. At least we know we're not chasing a dead man to the bottom of that lake," Drake said.

"What we know is that Hallman probably didn't die in the crash. At this point, we don't know what happened to him afterward. If those guys found him, he could be dead now."

Flint had loaded his laptop with satellite imagery of Red Maple Lake and the surrounding area.

The lake was south and east of Lake Tahoe. Flight time to Reno on a commercial airliner was just under six hours with at least an hour layover. In the Pilatus, they should be able to shave off the travel time.

Drake would land at the private airfield outside of Reno where he had reserved the floatplane.

"What kind of plane did you get?"

"Same one Hallman used. Cessna T206. It was the best choice and I'm familiar with it. The weather is forecast as calm and clear. With luck, we won't run into any crosswinds or downdrafts as we try to land on that lake, like Hallman did."

"You researched the FAA files on the crash." Flint glanced over to see

Drake nod. “Was there a definitive cause determined?”

“The official conclusion was pilot error. It looked like he came in too fast and off course, particularly for the weather conditions. There’s only one good way to land on that lake and he missed the coordinates. The crosswind tilted the plane so that it didn’t land flat on both floats.” Drake shrugged. “After that, the bird was unstable. He couldn’t manage the plane.”

“Any estimate on how long it took for the Cessna to go down in the lake?”

“They had plenty of time to conduct a water evacuation, if that’s what you’re asking. The plane had an inflatable life raft in it. Assuming they were conscious when they landed, there would have been time to get ashore."

Flint found his laptop and opened it. He looked at the videos that he'd seen in Veronica Beaumont's office again. He slowed the video to take a closer look at each frame.

As they had pulled Hallman's plane out of the water, it only had one damaged float still attached on the right side. According to the FAA report, the left float had been sheared off on landing.

The left wing was also severely damaged, probably by contact with the water. That would have made the left side of the plane sink first.

But the exit doors were on the right side of the cabin, as was the pilot seat. Josh was the pilot. He'd have had the best chance. If the two passengers were in the co-pilot seat and the back left seat, they'd have taken the brunt of the force.

The engine pulled the plane's nose underwater and the plane flipped over, but if the passengers had their harnesses on properly, they should have survived the crash.

And then, as Drake said, they'd have had enough time to deploy the inflatable life raft before the plane sank into the lake. They should have been able to get to shore.

"Was there something wrong with the raft?"

Drake shook his head. “Hard to say, since no one ever found it. Under the conditions out there, they won’t keep looking for pieces of a life raft. Even if they were still around. We’ll never know what happened to that raft.”

“That’s not the only odd thing about the situation, though.” Flint clicked a few keys on his laptop. “The videos Veronica gave me from the body retrieval were pretty damned odd, too.”

“In what way?”

“Took a while, but I got the autopsies on the two passengers early this morning. Beaumont didn’t have them. Autopsies say cause of death was not drowning. One of the men, Skip Evans, had a serious compound fracture of his right femur, which must've hurt like hell. He might have died from blood loss or a host of other things related to the crash. But his cause of death was listed as morphine overdose." Flint pulled up the two headshots he'd found for the deceased men and showed them to Drake. "The other guy, Dan Shafer, would have survived his crash injuries, the autopsy says."

"Why didn't he live then?"

"Cause of death is stated as gunshot wound. Two gunshot holes from a handgun. One in the back of his head."

Drake's eyes widened and he shook his head slowly, probably running the same set of variables through his mind that Flint had covered. "Not looking good for Hallman, is it?"

"Question is whether Hallman delivered those gunshots and somehow got away afterward."

Drake cocked his head. "Which leads to the question of why he'd want to do that."

Flint nodded. "Or were the guys who threatened Beaumont the ones who killed Shafer and Evans?"

"If so, Hallman's probably dead now, too," Drake said.

"We haven't found any paper trail to suggest otherwise."

"Nothing? For six years?" Drake shrugged. "Not good."

When they landed in Reno, Drake refueled and tied down the Pilatus before they moved their gear into the Cessna.

They were expected at Red Maple Lake Resort before nightfall. Flint had made reservations and confirmed they would be picked up at the landing site. He'd been reminded that the resort had no cell service. This could be his last chance to check with his contacts and download any updates. He left Drake to inspect the Cessna and headed into the terminal.

He logged on to his private server and checked his deposits. He found and downloaded three new files from his contact. He bought two black coffees and returned to the Cessna and climbed into the copilot's seat.

The flight over the mountains toward Red Maple Lake was nothing short of breathtaking. Snowy peaks capped greenery below the tree line. As they approached the basin, Red Maple Lake glittered in the sunlight like a thousand fairy lights winking on and off.

When Drake approached the lake for landing, Flint said, “Take a couple of circles. I want to see what’s down there.”

“You won’t see much from here,” Drake replied. “The satellite photos were mostly dense forest. No way to get in there except maybe on horseback.”

On the first pass, Flint identified the rooftops of the resort to the east.

The resort was all but engulfed by the greenery that separated it from rocky beach closer to the lake. But even from the air, the resort looked luxurious.

Drake pointed westward. “There’s another set of rooftops down there. Smoke coming from the chimney. See it?”

Flint pulled out the binoculars for a better look. “It’s a smaller cluster of buildings. More secluded.”

“Closer to the crash site, too. Probably a private residence.”

“Someone at the resort will know who owns it.” Flint continued to scan the area through the binoculars but saw no other buildings.

Drake circled the lake again, positioning for the best approach and landing. He began his descent and landed the Cessna smoothly on the surface of the lake, without mishap. He taxied the plane to the shore and shut down the engine. By the time they tied up at the dock, anchored, and collected their bags, the resort's off-road utility vehicle was waiting for them.

The driver had parked the red Polaris Ranger Crew XP 1000 on the rocks. Before they'd finished with the Cessna, he approached and extended his hand. "Glad to see you made it. I'm Neville. Red Maple Lake Resort."

"Flint, and Drake."

“How was your flight?” Neville stowed their bags and they climbed into the Ranger.

“Perfect. Beautiful spot you’ve got here,” Drake said from the back

seat.

“I’ve been coming here since I was a boy.” Neville grinned as he started the engine. “The views never get old.”

“How many homes are there on this lake?” Flint asked.

“Not very many. Four or five. Too tough to get in here for most people.” He patted the dashboard on the Polaris. “This ORV is essential for us. Not the most comfortable ride, but it gets the job done.”

"There's no road in and out of here at all?"

"Yeah, about three miles west of here and up the mountain, there's a two-lane highway that runs up to Tahoe. But that's a long, hard way to lug groceries and stuff. We think of our remoteness as a selling point here. Unspoiled nature is a big draw for our guests. Particularly for fishermen and hunters."

"I thought I saw another rooftop west of here as we were flying in," Flint said.

"That would've been Boyd Wilcox's place. You know, the billionaire? His family's owned that property longer than I've been alive." He kept up a running travelogue as he turned the Polaris and drove over the rough terrain into the trees and they bounced along the hard ground.

A knot formed in Flint's gut. He had nothing against billionaires. They were likely to be his best clients, given the fees he charged. But Wilcox was another story.

"How far to the resort?" Flint almost bit his tongue when one of the heavy-duty tractor tires hit a hole and rebounded midsentence.

"Couple of miles, give or take. Feels farther because the trail washes out and switches back so much. Takes a while to go anywhere."

"Seems like a strange place for a luxury resort, doesn't it?"

Drake asked. "You'd get a lot more customers if the place was accessible, wouldn't you?"

"Possibly. Believe it or not, we're more accessible now than when Great Lodges of America bought the place. Added this trail and the pick-up service and the parking lot between the resort and the highway.

But yeah, only a certain kind of guy comes out here."

"What kind of guy is that?"

"Outdoorsy types. Hunters, fishermen, hikers, and nature lovers who don't want to tent camp." He turned the oversize steering wheel to follow an almost invisible route east. "We're not that far from Tahoe.

People who love Tahoe but don't love the crowds sometimes venture down this way."

"How long have you been working here?"

Neville grinned and glanced toward Drake. "Seems like all my life. My dad owned the place when I was a kid. We came here on vacations. He sold out when I was a teenager. I took this job during college and it just seemed to stick for me. Been here five years, I guess."

"There's the resort." He pointed straight ahead, through to a clearing in the trees. "Let's get you guys checked in. You'll want to wash up before dinner."

The main building was rustic but huge. It looked like a newer version of Yellowstone's Old Faithful Lodge, in much better condition. Flint wondered how they managed to get the materials in to do the construction in the first place and, now, supplies for guests. There was a lawn out front big enough for a helicopter. Maybe that's how they did it.

Neville pulled up to the front door along the big circular driveway, and a young man came out to greet them. He wore a uniform and his name tag said "Jeffrey." He picked up the bags. "Welcome to Red Maple Lake Resort. Follow me."

Jeffrey led the way. Flint and Drake followed. Neville pulled the Polaris around the building and Flint wondered where he was going.

They trudged up the exterior stairs to the wide wood porch and into the main lobby. A huge fireplace in the corner heated the room well enough for the season, but Flint figured they needed a lot more heat during the cold winters. The lobby was decorated with Mission-style furniture, and a few guests were relaxing here and there. Like Neville had said, mostly men dressed in outerwear.

At the reception desk, another young man completed their registrations and gave them keys to adjoining rooms.

Before darkness settled in, Flint wanted a good look around. “Can we rent one of your ORVs for a couple of hours?”

“Oh, sure. We’ll pull it up out front for you. Be careful to stay close to the lake, though. You’re equipped with GPS, but if you get too deep inside the forest, you might not find your way back by nightfall.” He glanced at the big clock on the wall behind him. “It’ll be dark here in about three hours. Once the sun goes behind the mountains, it gets cold quickly. You’ll want to return before then.”

Flint authorized the charges to his credit card and, after rummaging through to find his satellite phone, left their bags with Jeffrey for delivery to the rooms. He and Drake walked back to the porch and down the wide steps.

Neville arrived with a smaller, two-seater black Polaris Ranger.

“How far is it over to the Wilcox place?” Flint asked.

“If you stay near the lake, follow the shoreline until you come to a driveway, maybe ten miles or so.” Neville cocked his head. “Do you know Mr. Wilcox?”

“We’ve met a couple of times,” Flint said. Which was true enough, if Neville should check. But the times they’d met were large public affairs, and Boyd Wilcox would neither remember Flint nor care to. It was Wilcox’s brother, Mark, who would remember Flint all too well.

Neville nodded. After a few operating instructions, they were belted in and headed back down to the lake, Flint behind the wheel.

Chapter Fourteen

Red Maple Lake, California
Six Years Ago

Josh moved deeper into the woods toward the voices, but he didn't see them in the darkness until they were only ten feet ahead. Three average-looking guys dressed for hiking. Mid-forties, maybe a decade older than Josh. Their hiking equipment was of the weekend warrior variety rather than paramilitary or survivalist or something frightening like that. Totally normal.

Josh staggered when his foot tripped on a thick root and he nearly lost his balance. But he reached for a tree trunk and kept upright. His luck was changing. Maybe things were going to work out after all.

He hurried over to the three hikers and held out his hand. "I'm Josh Hallman."

One of the guys said, "I'm Ruben." He pointed to the other two. "This is Mark. That's Kevin."

They seemed wary, Josh thought. But he must have looked scary as hell, appearing out of nowhere, clothes wet and dirty, cuts and bruises on his face and neck. Hair plastered to his head. He shook hands all around and nodded and tried to look friendly so they wouldn't feel threatened. "We were flying in to go fishing at Red Maple Lake Resort and our plane went down. My two buddies were hurt. We need a doctor."

The three men looked at each other and some sort of meaning passed between them. Josh didn't blame them for being skeptical, if that's what they were. The situation seemed surreal to him, too. But they seemed to believe him. Maybe they'd heard the Cessna before it hit the water. It was certainly loud enough to be heard for miles.

"Dr. Kevin Hayes. I'm a pediatrician." One of the men nodded. He must have seen the relief on Josh's face. He frowned and his tone was somber. "Believe it or not, dispensing vaccines and treating kids for colds and flu is not the same medical skill set as adult trauma care. But maybe I can help. Where are they?"

"This way." Josh led the way back to the shore, covering ground as quickly as he could. He answered their questions about the crash and the injuries his friends had suffered. They seemed to get more comfortable with him as his story unfolded. At least, they didn't seem to be as cautious about him.

He thought he might have lost his sense of direction, but when they emerged from the trees onto the rocky beach, Josh looked westward down the shoreline and saw Dan's flashlight, shining weakly in the distance.

“There,” Josh said, and trotted toward the beam. The three men followed.

It was full dark by the time they reached the pair. Dan was lying on the rocks, exactly where Josh had left him. Skip was still semiconscious and moaning in the life raft.

But Josh had made it back. And he’d brought help. Something like hysteria was probably responsible for the stupid grin he felt as it consumed his face.

Kevin immediately began to triage the injuries. He checked Dan first. “Get this guy up and warmed. His scalp wound is probably superficial. We can stitch it up when we get back.”

Josh already knew Skip's injuries were severe. He didn't need to see the expression on Kevin's face to confirm his fears.

"We'll have to carry him," Kevin said.

Josh nodded. "He needs a hospital. Can we get him airlifted out of here?"

Ruben, Mark, and Kevin exchanged glances again. The silence lasted longer than it should have before Ruben shrugged. "Weather's coming in. We're guests at a private lodge not far from where we met you. Let's get back and figure out how to get your friend some help."

Ruben and Mark lifted Dan to his feet and encouraged him to stand. He yelped and lifted his left foot, in obvious pain.

Kevin knelt down and examined his leg. He glanced up at the others. “It looks like he’s got a bad sprain on that left ankle, too. He shouldn’t be walking, but there’s no way we can carry both of them.”

“I can manage,” Dan said, but his voice was weak.

They organized a makeshift stretcher out of the deflated life raft to carry Skip. Each of the four men took a corner and heaved the raft into the air. They struggled to keep Skip flat in the canvas bottom.

Skip was heavier than he looked, or maybe Josh’s muscles were already too fatigued. Either way, the third trek along the rocks threatened to overwhelm his meager energy reserves.

Dan followed along behind, hobbling on his sprained left ankle, but there was nothing more anyone could do for him now.

They stayed on the shore until they reached the break in the trees Josh had used before. When they ducked into the darkness of the woods, the terrain seemed impossible.

They trudged forward, making slow but steady progress. After a while, Josh saw a clearing ahead and a long dirt driveway. About halfway along the drive, a split-rail fence encircled the grounds surrounding a large luxury log cabin. An archway made of logs joined each side of the fence.

At first he thought this was Red Maple Lake Resort, where they'd been expected to check in a few hours ago for their six-day fishing vacation. Then he saw the sign above the entrance drive. "Wilcox Lodge," it said. On the fence was a "No Trespassing" sign, and Josh wondered who would possibly travel all the way out here to trespass.

"This is the place," Ruben said, as he led the way to the front of the big house. Josh's body began to shake with relief.

Chapter Fifteen

Red Maple Lake, California
Tuesday

Flint was at the wheel of the smaller two-seater Polaris, which drove exactly like a tractor. He and Drake were buckled into the front seats and headed east, the setting sun behind them. The rock beach was not particularly comfortable for long-distance riding, but Flint preferred to be doing something, even if it turned out to be the wrong thing.

“This feels like a lead,” Drake said.

Flint scowled. “It feels like a setup.”

Drake glanced across the Polaris. "How so?"

"Certain wealthy businessmen travel in packs, like wolves. Hallman wasn't one of the pack. How would he be involved with Wilcox?"

"He wouldn't," Drake said. "But the Wilcox place sits between Hallman's crash site and the resort he was trying to reach. He might have noticed it from the air, like we did. It makes sense that he would have gone there first, assuming he could find it."

Flint shrugged. His instincts said the connection was something else.

"Floatplanes are loud. Out here, it's quiet. Mountains keep the noise inside the basin. Wilcox could easily have heard the Cessna flying in. Could have heard the crash."

The Polaris moved faster now that they'd emerged from the forest, but the ride was still too rough to pick up speed. "Wilcox might have gone out to help. Brought Hallman back to his place."

Drake said, "I've never met Boyd Wilcox and you have. Does he seem like the good Samaritan type to you?"

Flint laughed. "Not in the slightest."

"So if he did go out to check on the crash, you're thinking he'd do what?"

"There aren't many options, given this location. And the weather was bad that day. Cold, sleet turning to ice during the night. He'd probably have taken Hallman and his passengers in overnight. Planned to go out in the morning."

"Right. The FAA report's final conclusion on Hallman's crash was pilot error. But he would probably have landed okay in the absence of the storm conditions."

The Polaris bounced and groaned over the rocky terrain. "This is a pretty hard slog, if Hallman was injured."

Drake pulled up the preloaded GPS tracker. "Looks like about two miles from the crash site to the Wilcox place. Then, if you knew where you were going, about ten miles to the

Red Maple Resort. But if Hallman tried to make it to the resort without GPS or even a map, he could wander around for a long time."

Flint glanced at the GPS briefly and returned his full attention to the treacherous drive. "There's no trail or road or anything he could have reached?"

"Farther up the mountain there's a road, like Neville said." Drake pointed to the road on the GPS screen. "Not likely he'd have made it that far, but if he did, he could have hitched a ride, maybe."

"To where?"

"Closest real town is Tahoe to the north. Southbound, it depends on which way he went." Drake moved the GPS images around, zooming in and out on the screen. “The highway, if you want to call it that, splits about twenty miles south. He could have continued south or taken either offshoot, west or east. Looks like there’s three options, all about the same distance from where the highway splits.”

“Any of them have airports, train stations, bus stops, car rentals?”

“Hard to say. Bus stops, maybe, in all three of those towns. No indication of a train station. The closest commercial airport is Reno, which is north and east. But that’s quite a hike from here.”

Drake held out the map on the GPS screen. Flint glanced at it. The flashing blue dot was their location. The Wilcox place was another three miles away, inside the forest and up the mountainside. Nothing that looked like a clear path between the trees to get there.

He drove into a small opening that might have been a path at one time, maneuvering the Polaris in a zigzag pattern, roughly headed toward the red dot that should be the Wilcox compound.

"What do you know about Boyd Wilcox?" Drake asked.

"He's an eccentric, but a wealthy one." The Polaris landed hard in a hole and climbed out again. "Like other wealthy eccentrics. You know, Bill Gates and Warren Buffet types."

"Guys with more money than God, you mean."

"Yeah, but not only that. Wilcox is probably on the autism spectrum, if I had to guess. A genius at some things and totally inept at others. Socially awkward, to say the least." Flint steered the Polaris around a fallen tree trunk. "And he's always the most important man in the room."

"How do you know?"

Flint frowned. "I had a case a while back."

"What kind of case?"

"Missing person. His brother's wife. She was kidnapped down in Las Vegas. A twenty-million-dollar ransom was demanded. The husband, Mark Wilcox, hired me to find her, but in the end, it was Boyd who paid my bill."

"Did you find her?"

"Not exactly." Flint scowled and steered the Polaris around a thick branch on the ground. "I found her severed head."

Drake's eyes widened. "Say what?"

"It was staged to look like an honor killing." He jerked the wheel hard to the right to avoid a deep rut. "She was Saudi. Her family was against the marriage. They had another husband in mind."

"Jesus." Drake swiped a palm over his face. "I saw some beheadings during my service in Iraq. Grisly stuff. Why do you say this one was staged?"

"She was killed first—strangled—then beheaded later, according to the medical examiner. The head was frozen for a while." Flint shook his head again, eyes straight, fighting the uneven ground. "A few weeks after she disappeared, her severed head was found in a dumpster in a Las Vegas neighborhood near where she was last seen."

"Kidnappers ever found?"

"No."

"What about the ransom?"

"Boyd Wilcox paid it. His brother didn't have the money, but it was loose change to Boyd."

"Something like that could really make a man crazy." Drake shook his head. "How'd the husband take it?"

"About as well as you'd expect. He blamed me. He said I should have found her before they killed her. It was one of my first cases, and let's just say I didn't handle it as well as I would now. The situation was pretty ugly for a while. But after a year or so, he created a foundation to fund efforts to find kidnap victims like her. He's made quite a crusade out of it. Got a reality TV show and everything." Flint glanced over toward Drake for a moment before he focused again on the driving. Speed was slower than five miles an hour. "You've never watched **The First Two Days**? It showcases unsolved murders and kidnappings and the like? That's Mark Wilcox's life now."

Drake whistled. "Powerful enemy, that guy."

"Two powerful enemies instead of just one, now that Mark is a worldwide celebrity like his brother. Hasn't been a problem because we've steered clear of each other." Flint shrugged. "But yeah, let's just say that I don't expect them to invite me to dinner anytime soon."

He struggled with the steering wheel in a losing effort to keep the Polaris flat on the ground. He tugged the wheel to avoid trees and boulders. Every now and then, the big tires hit a hole and struggled to climb out. It was slow going.

The blue light on the GPS beeped a couple of times and veered farther west.

"This would have been treacherous walking, if Hallman came this way," Drake said. "Maybe he had a good flashlight. Maybe he wasn't injured. Maybe he had some idea which direction to head."

"Hard to guess how he'd have made it out of here on his own." Flint's gaze didn't leave the windshield, but the view was the same in every direction. Nothing but tree trunks and rocky outcrops and thick vegetation blocking the daylight. "If that's what happened."

Before the words left his mouth, the unmistakable roar of a helicopter's rotors filled the quiet. The tree canopy was dense. He couldn't see the helicopter overhead, but he heard it pass. The noise increased as the helo's altitude dropped for landing.

Drake looked at Flint and raised his eyebrows.

So the best way into the Wilcox compound was to fly. And there must be a helipad nearby.

He continued to struggle with the Polaris, but he headed toward the deafening roar of the helo. Only about two more miles, according to the GPS. Without the GPS, he'd have been lost for weeks. He could see nothing but forest in all directions.

The helo landed and the engines shut down. Now it was the quiet that deafened him.

The GPS said another mile, straight ahead. Flint felt like his entire body had been viciously pummeled. After the return trip, he'd be sore for days.

Drake pointed to the right. Flint squinted through the darkness. He saw a fenced area where the trees had been cleared, creating a large green space. A gravel driveway led to a substantial log house. "The Wilcox compound, no doubt."

The GPS showed that the fence enclosed several buildings. The helipad must be located behind the house because the helicopter was not visible from the front.

Ten more minutes to maneuver the Polaris to the driveway. Flint drove through the archway and up to the house, parked the Polaris, and shut the engine off. When his feet hit the ground, his legs felt wobbly. He stretched the kinks out of his body and glanced around the premises.

Drake was doing his own stretching on the other side of the vehicle. No one came out of the house to greet them, which was odd.

“Wait here.” Flint took the steps two at a time and reached the front door with his fist raised, poised to knock. Before he had the chance, the door opened.

“How can we help you?” The man sounded friendly enough. He was probably about fifty, Flint guessed. Dark hair, gray at the temples. His body suggested regular use of a good gym. Well dressed, in the kind of bespoke outdoor casual clothes that city fashion magazines advertised and no real outdoorsman would ever wear. Only his boots were practical, designed to cover the uneven ground outside of the fence.

“I’m Michael Flint.” He extended his hand and the man shook it but didn’t offer his own name in return. Flint gestured toward the Polaris. “This is Drake. We drove over from Red Maple Lake Resort. We understand Boyd Wilcox lives here.”

The man neither admitted nor denied it. Nor did he invite them inside.

“I’d like to speak with him.”

“Wait here.” He closed the door. His boots echoed along wood floors toward the back of the house.

Flint walked the length of the porch and looked around the property as well as he could from this vantage point. On the west side of the house, beyond the green space was nothing but thick forest. The front drive continued about a hundred feet beyond the archway and then turned east, away from Red Maple Lake Resort. There were outbuildings on the east side of the main house.

Perhaps the only way in and out of this place was by helicopter. But then, why have a driveway at all? No, it was more likely that the driveway hooked up with another gravel trail of some kind on the east side.

Five minutes passed before the front door opened again. Mark Wilcox stood there, tall and solid and frowning. “What do you want, Flint?”

He held his temper. Clients were rarely satisfied when Flint found missing loved ones only after they’d been murdered. How could family be satisfied with that result? Flint promised to find people dead or alive. But dead was rarely anyone’s first choice. And Aludra Wilcox’s murder had been particularly gruesome. She and Mark were newlyweds. The sick bastard who killed her remained at large, despite all of Mark’s considerable efforts to find him. No reason why Mark Wilcox would have any lingering affection for Flint. None at all. And the feeling was mutual. If he'd known Wilcox was involved with Hallman, he'd have refused Beaumont's pleas right from the start.

"Any chance you've got a place to sit and a cup of coffee?" Flint asked. "This one's a long story."

"I'm not really interested in your story." Mark Wilcox scowled. "I don't have anything to say that you'd be interested in, either. And Boyd isn't here."

"Do you know where I can find him?"

"Call his office. His assistant can help you." Wilcox pushed the door and Flint put his booted foot between the door and the jamb and pushed back hard with his shoulder.

Wilcox wasn't expecting the move. He stumbled backward. Flint pushed the door all the way open and stepped inside. Drake dashed up the steps and followed.

Wilcox's surprise vanished and a deep scowl replaced it. "Get the hell out of my house."

"It's your brother's house." Flint settled his weight, prepared to fight.

Before Wilcox's anger could boil over, the first man returned, entering from a doorway on the right. "What's going on, Mark?"

Another man followed close behind the first. He might have been the helo pilot. Hell, he could have been anybody. Flint was past caring at the moment. He was willing to give Mark Wilcox a wide berth, but he wouldn't be pushed around.

"No problem, Kevin," Wilcox growled and waved the first guy away. "Flint and his friend are looking for someone. That's what he does. But he's not very good at it."

"We have no visitors with us," the third man said. His voice was low and a little gravelly. He looked vaguely menacing, as if his role in this trio was hired muscle. "Who are you looking for?"

"Let's sit at that table there. You can give me some coffee. And we'll talk," Flint said without relaxing his guard. He didn't expect Wilcox to start a fistfight, but he wouldn't mind. The man was an ass. Always had been. Always would be. There was unfinished business between them. Today was a fine day to settle it as far as Flint was concerned.

Wilcox shrugged. He turned and led the way to the dining table. All five men pulled chairs and sat.

"Let's start with names. As I said, I'm Michael Flint. This is Alonzo Drake. We know Wilcox. Who are you?"

"Kevin Hayes," the first man said. "Ruben Vega," the second one replied.

Flint nodded. “I’m a private investigator. I’m looking for a man who disappeared from this area. Josh Hallman. He was the pilot of a Cessna T206 that crashed in the lake six years ago. This is the closest dwelling to the crash site.”

The three men looked at each other. Something Flint couldn’t decipher passed between them. Ruben was the one who responded. “Boyd allows us to use the place. For fishing, hiking. Maybe once or twice a year.”

“So you’re saying you weren’t here at the time of the crash?”

“Not likely,” Kevin said, which wasn’t exactly an answer.

“There were three men in that plane. Three men with families.” Flint looked at Wilcox longer than the others. “You know how this goes, Mark. Wives and kids are looking for these guys. I’ve promised to find them.”

“Yeah, I know how you work,” Wilcox replied, a sour expression on his face. “If they crashed, they probably died. Finding the bodies isn’t going to make anyone feel better. We handle situations like this on my show all the time. The family is never happy with anything other than a happy ending.”

Kevin said, “Exactly how do you two know each other?”

Mark’s permanent scowl had left deep lines on his face that aged him beyond his years. “I hired Flint to find Aludra when she was kidnapped. We all know how that turned out.” Kevin nodded. Ruben stared.

They must have known that Wilcox had turned his personal tragedy into an empire based on a worldwide television audience. In the past few years, he’d assisted the FBI with cold cases and public manhunts on a massive scale. He was instantly recognizable and, some would say, enjoyed a reputation that bordered on hero worship among his viewers.

Flint looked from one to another. “Who uses this place besides you?”

Wilcox shrugged. “It’s my brother’s house. I don’t know who uses it. You’ll have to ask him.”

"I'll do that. But since I'm here, show me around. Could help me find Hallman." He pushed his chair back and stood. Drake followed suit.

"The place isn't that big. Won't take long." Kevin stood, too. "Let's take a quick tour of the house and grounds. You need to get back to the resort. It's easy to get lost in those woods in the dark and you don't have much daylight left."

Kevin led the way down a long, wide corridor with several closed doors on either side. "These are bedrooms. Eight. All furnished the same." He opened one door and allowed Flint and Drake to step inside. The room was furnished like a rustic hotel. Two beds. Dressers. Chairs.

An en suite bathroom.

Flint glanced around. "No telephone? No television?"

Kevin shrugged. "We don't have phone or internet service here and we come to this place to escape technology."

Flint and Drake left the room and closed the door behind them. They followed Kevin into a large open kitchen, decked out as if a hobby chef with too much money had furnished it. The kitchen, like everything else he'd seen so far, was sparse and expensively appointed and excessively tidy. Not a speck of dust or anything else could be seen on the gleaming granite countertops or the stainless steel appliances.

"Who does the cooking when you're here?" Drake asked. "And where do the supplies come from?"

"We take turns. We bring food with us in the helo."

Kevin led the way through the kitchen and out the back door to an open yard and large paved patio area that seemed newer than the buildings. A hot tub was nestled into a cozy corner. The helicopter rested idle and quiet on the helipad, a few feet beyond the hot tub. A couple of outbuildings flanked the side of the main house. "What's in those buildings?"

He pointed toward the farthest of the two. "A propane generator for electricity. A couple of freezers for supplies. Gardening equipment.

Things like that."

"Where's your pilot?" Drake asked.

"He's in the cabin over there," Kevin pointed to the first outbuilding. A light was burning inside.

Flint walked toward the cabin. "What's his name?"

Kevin raised his eyebrows again, before he followed along behind. "Larry Cole."

At the door, Kevin rapped firmly. A tall, rugged man opened. "Larry, this is Michael Flint and Alonzo Drake. They are looking for a missing man."

"Missing from where?"

"A plane crash in the lake."

"I didn't hear anything. Didn't see anything flying in, either."

"The plane went down six years ago."

Cole shrugged. "Before my time. I've only been flying out here for a few years."

"Who flew the helo before you?"

Kevin said, "Mark was our pilot until Larry took over the job."

"Sorry I can't help you," Cole said.

"Me, too," Flint replied.

Chapter Sixteen

Red Maple Lake, California
Tuesday

Kevin led them around the house toward the driveway. Drake walked behind. Flint was between the two. He felt like several pairs of eyes were following them, but the feeling was based on nothing. The only sounds he heard were the soles of their boots landing on the ground.

When Flint reached the Polaris, he stopped near the passenger door while Drake walked around and climbed behind the wheel. "What are you guys doing out here, Kevin?"

"Like Mark said. Fishing. A little hiking. Poker. Man talk." Kevin shrugged. He bowed his head and kicked at the stones in the dirt. "You know how it is."

"Where do you live?" Flint's internal radar was up on all of these guys. He'd already had a bad experience with Mark Wilcox. Wilcox's friends were likely to be no better than he was and might be worse. No reason to trust any of them.

"I'm in San Diego. Ruben travels. You already know about Mark and Boyd."

"What line of work are you in?"

"I'm a pediatrician."

Flint raised his eyebrows. “And Ruben?”

“He works with Boyd.”

Flint cocked his head. He’d been lied to many times in his life, but so far Kevin had seemed honest enough. Which probably meant he’d been asking the wrong questions. “One of Josh Hallman’s friends suffered a compound femur fracture in the crash. When they pulled his body out of the lake, the autopsy report stated that someone had tried to stabilize the fracture. They also found morphine in his system.”

“He must have been in a lot of pain.” Kevin looked down and kicked at the ground with his boot again.

"I'm thinking that someone with at least a strong knowledge of field first aid must have found him." Flint waited a moment. "Maybe even a doctor. It's not like there are pharmacies to get morphine out here. Someone must have carried the morphine and other supplies in from somewhere."

Kevin did not reply.

"When pediatricians leave their offices, even for a few days' vacation, people know. Staff. Insurance companies. Patients." Flint paused again, but Kevin still said nothing.

He heard footsteps crunching on the gravel behind him. He glanced around to see Ruben near the side of the house, headed toward them.

“We’d offer to fly you out, but there’s nowhere to land the helo over at the resort.” Kevin looked over his shoulder and turned back to Flint. “You can make it back before nightfall in your Polaris, but you need to get going.”

Flint nodded. “We’ll be on our way then.”

“The fastest route is to take the driveway and stay on it until it connects with a rougher path that leads almost straight up, toward the road.” Kevin waved in the general direction away from the Red Maple Lake Resort. “Then head west once you get to the road. You’ll see a sign for the resort after about an hour.”

“Thanks,” Drake said.

Flint shook hands with Kevin. “Until we meet again, Dr. Hayes.”

Kevin looked a little green, like a kid who had been told to eat spinach.

He’d find Dr. Hayes again. Kevin was a doctor. A healer. He was the weakest link in the chain of whatever was going on out here. Flint was sure these three knew more than they were telling. What he didn’t know was why they were being so secretive about events that had happened so many years ago. But he would find out.

Flint belted into the passenger seat, and Drake rolled away from the house down the driveway.

With Drake's driving skills and Kevin's directions, they soon reached the connecting path and headed up, away from the lake.

"So you figure Kevin Hayes was the doc who worked on Hallman's friend, Skip," Drake said, once they reached the connecting path.

"Doesn't take a genius to figure out he was here. When I confront him next time, I'll have more data."

Drake nodded, but his full attention was focused on driving. The path was barely marked and even with the headlights on, it was difficult to stay between the ditches. The ride was rough and the bouncing Polaris was no more comfortable now than it had been on the way to the Wilcox place.

After a while, Drake asked, “You figure Ruben Vega was the one who threatened Beaumont?”

“He fits her general description well enough, and he looks like the type who would do something like that.” Flint nodded. “He’s a little bit older than the man she described, but six years have passed. I’d put money on him.”

“Vega could be an executive instead of a thug.”

“Yeah.” Flint nodded again. “But that’s not likely. And there was definitely something going on back there. They know more than they’re telling.”

The Polaris was moving almost straight up now. Flint and Drake were pushed back in their seats by gravity. The Polaris strained to pull up the mountainside. Drake had the steering wheel to hold onto, but Flint was bounced around like a kid without a car seat.

Drake said, “One thing for sure. It wouldn’t be easy to walk anywhere to get to or away from that house. Josh Hallman must have been one hell of an outdoorsman.”

“Maybe.”

“So Hallman crashed the plane, killed one friend, drugged the other one, got to the Wilcox place, and no one was there. So he broke in. He stole the equipment he needed and hiked out." Drake seemed to be trying the theory on for size, as if it would make more sense if he said it aloud. But he shook his head. "Nope. Doesn't track."

Flint agreed. "More likely that he and his friends made it out of the plane and up to the Wilcox place. Someone was there. Probably Dr. Kevin Hayes, at least, given Skip's injuries."

"But then what happened? Wilcox has a helicopter. They could have flown up to Tahoe to the hospital. Gotten medical care. Still be alive."

"But they didn't. His friends died. We think Hallman got away."

Flint murmured to himself, “Where did Hallman go?”

“Why did he go anywhere at all?”

“What?”

“If he didn’t kill his two friends, why didn’t he stick around? Was he running from something or toward something?” Drake glanced at Flint briefly before the Polaris bounced into a deep rut, forcing him to pay more attention to the drive.

Now that he’d seen the situation firsthand, Flint had been thinking the problem through.

Suppose Hallman’s friends had been killed and he ran from the killers. It was a reasonable hypothesis.

Hallman had military training, so he was somewhat experienced in wilderness survival. He might have had enough equipment and food to carry him through the journey.

But most of his stuff had gone down with the Cessna. So where did he get the gear he needed to walk away from the Wilcox lodge, if that's what actually happened?

And escape would have been more complicated if he'd been injured, as his friends were. He could have died out here in this forest. If he'd wandered off the path, his body might never be found.

The Polaris struggled to crest the last rocky outcrop before they reached the road. When Drake pulled onto the shoulder of the winding two-lane, Flint almost cheered.

A few seconds later, Flint's satellite phone chimed to notify him he'd received a message. He pulled out the phone. The message was from his source. **File #4 delivered. Extremely time sensitive.**

He typed, **Roger that** and pushed the "Send" button, but the temporary signal had already vanished. He dropped the phone into his pocket. The message would go out the next time it found a signal.

The Polaris wasn't equipped for road driving, but Drake kept on the road anyway. They traveled eleven miles before they saw the turn to the Red Maple Lake Resort. They never encountered another vehicle or another person.

"Now what?" Drake asked.

"We get some food and some sleep. Tomorrow, we'll go to the crash site and check out the nearest houses along this road. I'll get Scarlett to dig up background on those guys. We'll take another run at them. How do you feel about San Diego?"

"Lovely city this time of year." Drake drove down the steep grade along the lane past the parking lot where three SUVs were parked and continued down to the resort.

When they reached the front entrance, Flint glanced at his watch.

Two hours to drive the fourteen miles from the Wilcox place. Again, he wondered how long it would have taken Hallman to hike the same route. In the dark. Without benefit of the GPS. And maybe injured.

He'd find out. But first he wanted a meal followed by a good long soak in that hot tub, an excellent scotch, and a long night's sleep.

He had a bottle of scotch in his bag. The resort was set up to supply the rest.

"I'm planning a quick shower and a nap before dinner," Drake said when they reached the door to his room. "I'll come to your room when I'm ready to eat."

"Works for me." Flint nodded and kept walking. He closed the door behind him, found the Scotch, and poured a shot into a water glass he found in the bathroom. He opened his laptop to check the three new files he'd downloaded from his secure server back at the Reno airstrip.

The fourth file, the one marked "time sensitive," had automatically downloaded during the flight before they left satellite range. All were from the source he'd queried about his mother.

He stared at the list on the screen for a while. He drank the scotch and poured another. He took a deep breath and released it slowly.

"Okay. Let's do this."

Chapter Seventeen

Red Maple Lake, California
Tuesday

Flint opened the laptop and found the fourth file, marked "Urgent." It contained only one sentence.

James Arthur Preston. Scheduled to die by lethal injection at Huntsville, Texas. Thursday.

He'd never heard of James Preston. His source had marked the file urgent and sent him a text to make sure he saw it. Her reasons were probably contained in the other three files.

Did he want to read them now? No.

He hadn't made up his mind about whether he ever wanted to read them at all, but he definitely hadn't planned to do it tonight. He'd lived his entire life without knowing. Why fix things that weren't broken?

He poured another shot. He downed the scotch and stared at the words on the laptop screen.

Who was James Preston? What had he done to deserve death? Why had Flint's contact believed he should know about the execution?

He'd requested an objective search for an unidentified woman, based on the limited information he'd found.

His source had known Flint a long time. Worked with him in the past.

She knew what he needed to do the job. Sometimes, she could anticipate his needs, and her search had led her to James Preston.

But she couldn't read his heart. Right at the moment, even he couldn't say whether he really wanted to know anything she'd discovered.

His first assumption was that his original birth record had been sealed. He had the means to unseal the record, but he had to find it first. He'd tasked his source with that project, supplying the limited information he had and what he could logically piece together.

His foster mother at the Lazy M Boarding School, Bette Maxwell, had told him all she knew about the distraught young woman who had abandoned him. She'd claimed to be a schoolteacher in West Texas. She'd claimed the father was unknown.

Which was a whole different thing from unknowable.

The young woman's story might have been true. Or not. He'd asked his source to check it both ways.

Bette Maxwell said no documents related to his origins existed at the Lazy M, and none were stored in any of the state's files. Again, his source would confirm.

The sketchy data was a challenge, not an impenetrable wall.

Every complicated heir hunting job started with seemingly insurmountable obstacles. What he needed was a single thread that he could use to pull the secrets apart.

In this case, Felix Crane was the obvious first thread to jerk because he'd said, "I knew your mother."

Flint used what he knew about Crane to find a way inside his bio mom's life.

Crane had been a man of the world. He had traveled extensively and, of course, many women had passed through Texas back then.

All of which meant that Flint's mother could have been anyone and he could have been conceived anywhere and he might have been born anywhere, too.

An average heir hunter would have stopped there, declaring the search too overwhelmingly huge. That's when they'd call Flint. After the others had failed.

He'd begun by looking for Crane's whereabouts during the relevant year. That's when he got lucky.

According to his tax returns, Crane had lived that year in the West Texas town where he'd been born, Mount Warren. If Crane actually had known Flint's mother, and if she'd told Bette Maxwell the truth about living in West Texas, they could have crossed paths there.

The first file his source provided was the result of her deep dive on public records that left no room for error. He scanned the file quickly.

Birth records for local hospitals near Mount Warren reported ten live births, and half were female. The five males were easily traced. She had checked them all.

None of those five boys grew up to be Michael Flint.

She had found twenty reported miscarriages and stillbirths as well. Doctors sometimes fudged the records at the mother's request to cover up the birth of an unwanted child. That didn't happen here. All the mothers were easily traced and none were likely to be Flint's mother.

Nor was Felix Crane listed as the father or next of kin on any of these records.

His source had narrowed the options to three.

He might have been born in a hospital outside of Mount Warren.

Or, he was not born in a hospital at all, but a legal birth record was created.

The third option was that no birth certificate existed.

Flint's original birth certificate had never been located, and the amended one he carried was contained in the official records. He had used it to acquire his social security number and his passport. It passed muster with Uncle Sam.

But it wasn't good enough for his purposes now.

Final conclusion? Obligatory record search completed. Results negative.

He nodded his approval. He hadn't expected her to find any answers in the official records. He'd have found those himself, if they existed.

The point of the exercise had been to rule out all of the alternatives and move to the next level.

Flint refilled his scotch before he opened the second file, labeled "Mother's Name."

The total list of women of childbearing age in Mount Warren back then was the starting point.

His source had eliminated females under the age of twelve and over the age of fifty-five, which isolated more than a thousand names.

He closed his eyes and steepled his fingers. He conjured an image of Felix Crane in his mind and thought about what kind of woman the dashing young wildcatter might have felt something for back then.

When he found his bio mom, would she resemble the image he'd conjured? Only one way to find out.

By all accounts, Crane had been something of a ladies' man in his youth, his source said. She guessed that he'd have been attracted to women younger than himself. She reduced her search to women over sixteen and under thirty years old.

Flint approved. If the woman who dropped her baby off at the Lazy M had been a schoolteacher, under Texas state law, she had to be a college graduate.

The list was narrowed to women between twenty-one and thirty.

She'd sorted by occupation. The sorted list contained three hundred names, mostly housewives. Fifty-three listed their occupation as teachers.

The number surprised him. It must have puzzled his source, too. The population of Mount Warren didn't seem large enough to require fifty-three teachers. The place must have been crowded with big families.

To verify her list, she had located one high school, one junior high school, and ten elementary schools in Mount Warren.

After that, she'd pulled up the faculty rosters and matched them to the list of fifty-three teachers. By the time she'd finished, she had produced a list of ten women who could have been his mother or, at least, might have known his mother.

Flint grinned. He'd trained her to use his methods well. She'd almost begun to think exactly like he did. He felt a little proud of her.

Next in the file was a comparison of those ten women who might have been or might have known Flint's mother, matched to their driver's license data, including ten drivers' license photos.

He clicked over to the next screen. He stared at the photo array.

None of the photos sent chills through his spine or anything corny like that. He'd looked at similar photo groups for clients dozens of times. They were just faces. Nothing more. So far.

He leaned forward and studied the ten images on the screen for a bit before he checked her list of death records. Two of the ten were deceased.

"And then there were eight. Who's my mommy?" he murmured as he stared at the faces. "None of you look like me. Perhaps I resemble my unknown father, huh?"

He enlarged and studied the pictures one at a time.

Each of the eight women continued to live in Mount Warren. They had all married at one time or another. Married names appeared on their driver's licenses and marriage licenses were included in the file.

One was a widow. Two were divorced. None were still teaching after all these years.

He felt nothing for any of them.

He returned his attention to the two teachers who had died.

One passed last year of a massive heart attack, according to her death certificate. She was survived by her husband and three sons who still lived in Mount Warren.

“Possible,” he said, as he flipped to the next screen.

“Hello, Mom,” Flint whispered.

It was this last one that riveted his attention. The one who had died thirty-three years ago.

More specifically, she had been murdered.

“Well, well.” His voice sounded dry in his own ears. He looked at the photo on the screen as if he expected her to answer his questions. She said nothing.

He closed the file and swallowed the last of his scotch.

The third file was labeled “Marilyn Baker.”

He’d been sitting on the bed, leaning against the headboard, legs stretched out. He picked up the glass and realized it was empty. How long had he been sitting here? He hadn’t noticed that darkness had engulfed the room and the world beyond.

His stomach growled with hunger. Where was Drake?

He pushed the laptop aside and stood to stretch. He flipped the lights on. The scotch glass was still in his hand. For a moment, he considered another drink. But his stomach felt too empty. He wasn't looking to get drunk tonight or be hungover tomorrow.

He put the glass down and walked down the hallway. He rapped on the heavy wood door of Drake's room. No response. He rapped again, louder, and waited.

He raised his hand to knock one last time. Drake pulled the door open while his fist was still in the air.

"You don't need to hit me, Flint," Drake grinned. "Sorry, man. Lost track of time."

Flint shrugged. "After a quick shower, I'm going downstairs to eat. Any interest?"

"Give me ten minutes." Drake closed the door again.

Flint walked back to his room and turned the shower on. He pulled clean clothes out of his bag and tossed them on the bed. The laptop waited there.

Flint plopped down and opened the third file while he waited for the hot water to come up.

Inside were several local newspaper articles about Marilyn Baker's death.

The story was sordid. The murder unsolved. If Marilyn Baker was his birth mother, this certainly explained why she never returned to him.

Chapter Eighteen

Red Maple Lake, California
Six Years Ago

When they finally reached the front door of the Wilcox lodge, Josh and the others lifted Skip carefully out of the life raft, carried him inside, and placed him on a large dining room table. Josh tried to reassure him, but he was moaning and writhing in pain. He mumbled words, but they made no sense.

Kevin immediately began working on Skip. He sent Mark to find the first aid kit and his medical bag, which he carried everywhere.

"Dan, sit there and elevate that foot until I can get a look at it." Kevin pointed to a straight chair. Dan, at least, was capable of following directions. "Ruben, can you get some water? These guys are severely dehydrated."

"Don't worry. Kevin has patched up our injuries out here before," Ruben said as he left the room. He returned with two large water bottles, one for Josh and one for Dan.

"Thanks." Josh downed the water like a man who had spent a decade in the desert. Dan did the same.

Mark brought Kevin's medical bag and stood on the other side of the table as Kevin dealt with Skip.

“We need to contact the hospital,” Josh said. “Is there a phone or radio or something we can use to call out?”

Ruben stuffed his hands in his back pockets and shook his head. “This place is pretty remote. That’s the reason we like it. We need a break now and then so we come here precisely because no one can reach us.”

Josh wondered briefly why these three would want to be out of contact with all civilization. It seemed dangerous, if nothing else. What if someone were to come down with appendicitis or something? “Do you have transportation we can use to get Skip to the hospital?”

"We have a helicopter. Mark is our pilot. He can fly your buddy up to Tahoe," Ruben said.

"But we can't do it tonight," Mark said. "Weather's already bad out there and worse coming in. Can't risk it."

Ruben looked over at Kevin. "Can you get him stabilized until this weather passes?"

Kevin shrugged and frowned, preoccupied with whatever he was doing to Skip on the table. "I've given him some morphine to help with the pain. Let's move him into the back, get him into bed. I'll see what I can do about his leg."

"He needs surgery, doesn't he?" Josh asked.

“I can’t do surgery here, even if I was qualified to handle something like this, which I’m not,” Kevin replied. “He’s lost a lot of blood. Lucky you put that tourniquet in place, but I can’t take it off.” He paused, glanced at the ground, and cleared his throat. “He should pull through this, but he may very well lose that leg.”

Kevin’s words hit Josh like a hard punch to his gut. It was his fault. All of it. Skip had wanted to book a commercial flight to Costa Rica. They should’ve done that. Dan had been open for anything when they were doing the planning, but Josh was the one who had pushed for Red Maple Resort after Dan brought it up.

Beyond that, Josh was the one who crashed the plane. Totally his fault.

Simple as that. He'd never forgive himself if Skip lost that leg. And Skip's wife would never forgive Josh, either. He knew it the way he knew the sun would rise tomorrow. Debbie didn't like Josh anyway. This would give her a perfect excuse to cut Josh from Skip's world. Permanently. Skip would go along with her. He always did. And Josh couldn't really blame either of them.

"Josh? We need a hand here," Mark said. Ruben and Mark were at Skip's head. Kevin placed both hands under Skip's mutilated right leg, holding the leg together. The blood-saturated pant leg flopped down from his waist where Kevin had cut the fabric away to treat his injured leg.

Josh put his arms under Skip's left side and the four men moved slowly, in concert, toward a bedroom in the back of the house. They passed several closed doors along the way, which Josh assumed were more bedrooms.

The morphine must've kicked in because Skip had finally stopped the constant moaning.

The setup was a normal guest room. A dresser, a private bath, a couple of chairs. Two twin beds, but both were higher off the floor than normal, as if they were made for an exceptionally tall person. Not quite hospital-bed height, but serviceable enough.

They settled Skip on one of the beds and moved out of Kevin's way. Josh stood by helplessly while Kevin worked. He put an IV in Skip's arm and attached the bag to the bedpost to allow gravity to do its work.

Kevin spent a few minutes working on Skip's leg wound, but the open femur fracture would require surgery. No question. Josh wasn't a doctor and he'd known that much when he'd first seen the break. Kevin shook his head sorrowfully from time to time, as if he already knew Skip would lose the leg. Josh felt the truth twist in his stomach.

"We need to stay with him around the clock," Kevin said when he had done everything he could do for the time being. "Mark, can you take the first shift here? I'll deal with Dan's foot and ankle. And then I'll be back to check on Skip. Call me if anything changes."

Mark replied, “Will do.” He pulled a straight chair closer to the bed and leaned forward, forearms on thighs, watching for something. Josh had no idea what he was looking for, but he was glad to have him there with Skip, acting as if he knew what to do.

Kevin nodded and left the room. Ruben clapped Josh on the shoulder.

Josh hadn’t really looked at Ruben before. His features were unremarkable, but his vibe was controlling and strong somehow. As if he was used to giving orders and expected them to be followed. Briefly, Josh wondered what line of work the guy was in, but he didn’t ask. Josh had other things on his mind.

"Go with Kevin. Let him clean you up, too," Ruben said. "The last thing you need right now is even a minor infection, right?"

Josh looked at his hands as if for the first time. He saw cuts and scrapes he hadn't noticed before. He glanced in the mirror above the dresser and barely recognized his face. Grime and dried blood marred his features. At least one deep cut on his jaw had dripped blood onto his shirt. He didn't remember receiving any of his wounds at all.

He nodded toward Ruben and followed Kevin to the main living area of the house, where Dan was still sitting with his foot elevated.

"He's had some kind of concussion or something, too," Josh said, while they were out of Dan's hearing range. "He was kind of dazed right after we crashed, and he hasn't been acting right since then."

"Got it." Kevin knelt down to deal with Dan's sprained ankle. He managed to get Dan's boot off the swollen foot and removed his wet, filthy sock. He cut the pant leg up from the ankle to the knee and used both hands to feel Dan's injury, probably looking for fractures or something. Then he moved on to the rest of his exam.

When he'd finished, Kevin said, "Dan, you've probably sustained a mild concussion. You should be okay. But concussions are unpredictable. We'll need to watch for symptoms."

Josh nodded, feeling worse by the minute. He'd really screwed up here and his friends were the ones paying for it. "What kind of symptoms?"

"Headache, dizziness, fatigue. Some patients display irritability, concentration, and memory problems. Insomnia." Kevin listed the symptoms automatically, like a pediatrician who had treated his share of schoolyard injuries. "The bigger problem at the moment is this sprained ankle because he shouldn't be walking around on it. It could be fractured, too. I can't rule it out. He needs an x-ray."

Dan said, "We'll be able to do that tomorrow, right? The x-ray?"

"Yeah. Over in Tahoe, they've had a lot of experience with sports injuries because of all the resorts and tourism they get." Kevin nodded. "In the meantime, both of you need a shower and some dry clothes and something to eat, followed by sleep. You've got another long day tomorrow."

"How far are we from Red Maple Lake Resort?" Josh asked. "Maybe they have a doctor there who could do more for Skip tonight."

Before Kevin responded, a fourth man Josh had not seen before entered from somewhere in the back of the house and overheard the question. He was tall and well groomed. His clothes were expensive and fit him like they'd been made specifically for his body, which they probably had. He was older than the others, maybe about fifty. The family resemblance to Mark was unmistakable.

"I'm afraid you landed quite a distance from the resort. You are maybe ten miles west, and the terrain between here and there is pretty rough. If the weather improves, you might be able to drive the off-road vehicle over there. But it would take at least a couple of hours, even in good weather. It's slow going. And it's a bumpy ride. Your friend's leg wouldn't be the better for the trip."

Josh stood and extended his hand. "I'm Josh Hallman."

"Boyd Wilcox. Mark's brother. I'm sorry for your troubles." He shook hands with Josh. "Kevin here will do what he can for now. Mark will fly you out to Tahoe in the morning, weather permitting. In the meantime, we'll get you set up with bunks for the night."

"Thank you." Josh's stomach growled and Boyd Wilcox smiled.

"Maybe we should feed you, too. Wash up and meet us back here for dinner. Kevin will show you to your room." When Josh nodded, Boyd Wilcox turned and left.

Josh cocked his head. "He looks familiar to me. Should I know him?"

"Depends." Kevin helped Dan up and put an arm around his body to keep the weight off his sprained ankle. The hallway was wide, but not wide enough for three men to walk abreast. Josh followed behind them. “Boyd is not a celebrity. CEO of StellarSoft. The tech company. You’ve probably seen his photo in the financial press.”

Josh whistled. Of course he knew StellarSoft. Everyone did. One of the most successful privately held companies in the tech world. Hell, in any world. StellarSoft operating system powered half the gadgets on the planet. Including those used by governments and industry.

Boyd Wilcox. The tech genius who named his company after his great passion, stargazing. The guy was at least as passionate about astronomy as he was about tech. Maybe more so.

Boyd Wilcox. Out here in the middle of nowhere. How crazy was that? Josh shook his head.

Kevin had stopped walking. “Can you open that door? We’ll put you both in here.”

Josh reached around and turned the doorknob and pushed the door open. Kevin walked and Dan hopped into the room and Josh followed. This bedroom was a copy of the one where they’d put Skip. Kevin helped Dan to sit on one of the twin beds.

Kevin pointed to the bathroom. “You can get a shower in there. I’ll find you both some clothes and bring them back here. You look to be about my size, Josh. Dan, maybe something I have will fit you, too. And we’ll have dinner in about an hour. Meet back in the dining room when you're ready."

When he turned to leave, Josh said, "Kevin?"

"Yes?"

"Thank you. I don't know what we'd have done out there if you guys hadn't come along." Josh felt tears in his eyes and he blinked hard.

"No problem. Doctors are supposed to help people. It's what we do, right?" Kevin left the room, closing the door behind him, without another word.

Chapter Nineteen

Red Maple Lake, California
Tuesday

Flint read the file through very quickly. Marilyn Baker died on June 18. Which meant she'd died not too long after she'd left him with Bette Maxwell. He'd have been about two years old.

Baker was a second-grade teacher. She taught indigent students at a Catholic elementary school on the south side of Mount Warren. According to the newspaper accounts, Baker's friends described her as extremely shy. She took her faith very seriously. She'd attended mass and communion every day, her friends said.

"Were you always so devout? Or did you develop that habit after you gave up your child?" He said aloud, barely hearing the water running in the shower now as he scanned the rest of the file.

Baker lived with her parents, who were described as loving but protective.

"Meaning they were smothering," he mumbled.

On the day she died, Baker told her parents she was going to confession at St. Michael's Church, where she was also a Sunday school teacher.

"Is that why you named your son Michael? Because of the church?" He continued to ask questions aimed at the pretty young woman's photo, but she didn't answer.

She had been the homecoming queen at Mount Warren High School. Another friend interviewed for the newspaper article said that Baker was strikingly pretty.

Baker's photos suggested her friend had a gift for understatement. Baker wasn't simply pretty. Her beauty was overwhelming.

She looked angelic. Even the old grainy photo showed off her spectacular appeal.

When Baker's parents did not hear from her that long-ago evening they thought she had stayed at church for midnight mass, which she often did.

But she never came home that night.

The next morning, they reported her missing to the local police department.

Later that day, kids riding bicycles outside of town found an odd trail of evidence stretching several hundred yards down the road. They found her purse, one of her shoes, and one of her gloves.

Police and volunteers searched for her, and two days later, her body was found face down in a canal several miles away.

According to the autopsy report, Baker died of suffocation. She had not been raped or beaten. Any physical evidence that might have identified her attacker, such as blood or semen or hair samples, was presumed washed away during the time the body was in the canal.

Flint shook his head. These days, forensics might have found trace evidence on the body. But years ago, evidence collection and evaluation techniques were not what they were now.

Law enforcement questioned known sex offenders, family members, coworkers, friends, and ex-boyfriends, the newspaper said. No one was able to supply helpful evidence.

The next line popped out as if it had a life of its own.

His eyes widened as he read the sentence aloud.

"Felix Crane and Sebastian Shaw, and several other local businessmen who knew Marilyn Baker, offered a $10,000 reward for information about Baker's death."

Flint swiped his palm down his face and groaned.

Crane.

He was on the right track.

Shaw.

He shook his head.

He'd come back to Shaw.

He continued to skim the materials.

Another article in the local paper three days later reported that the priest who heard Baker's last confession, Father James Preston, was under suspicion in the Marilyn Baker case.

Flint's gut tensed.

The priest had been serving at the church since completing seminary training. Church members said Father Preston's confession line moved slowly that night, and he was away from the sanctuary for long periods of time.

Fellow priests had noticed scratch marks on his hands the next day, and they'd said it was irregular for him to have taken Baker to the rectory to hear her confession. The police administered a polygraph test, which was inconclusive.

Father Preston was not charged in the case, which remained unsolved.

Flint nodded. This was the logical end to the Baker report.

But his source had included more. He flipped to the next screen.

Four years later, another young woman was similarly kidnapped and murdered in another Catholic church in another town where Father Preston was serving as a visiting priest. The second young woman, unlike Marilyn Baker, had been raped.

Eventually, Father Preston was arrested, tried, and convicted for the crime. The jury unanimously sentenced him to death and the long appellate process began.

Flint's source said she could find nothing else about the Marilyn Baker murder. The case was stone cold. It seemed the world had forgotten Marilyn Baker entirely.

But his source had included what she'd learned about James Preston.

Last year, Father Preston was once again in the news. He had exhausted his appeals and his execution had been scheduled. When he received the news, he had requested his priest for confession.

After the priest left Preston, a television reporter asked him whether Preston had admitted to the murder of Marilyn Baker.

The video of that interview was attached.

Flint watched it quickly.

The priest refused to violate the sanctity of the confessional, but his hands were shaking as he fingered the beads of his rosary. He didn't deny that Preston had confessed to killing Marilyn Baker.

Which wasn't the same as an admission or confession of guilt.

Flint squeezed his scratchy eyes together. His neck was tight. He felt the tension in his shoulders. He'd been staring at the screen too long. He closed the laptop.

He stripped and stepped into the steaming shower. The water didn't wash the details of Marilyn Baker's murder from his mind.

He had seen many witnesses confronted with horrible truths. While a priest might be expected to react differently from a lay witness, priests were human, too. This one seemed like a good man, and whatever Preston had told him had been upsetting, to say the very least.

Had Preston confessed what he'd done to Marilyn Baker? Possibly. But the priest had neither confirmed nor denied Preston's guilt.

Flint finished his shower and toweled off. He slid into jeans and a sweater and slipped comfortable loafers onto his feet.

Drake knocked on the door. “You ready?”

Flint had opened the laptop again to scan the time-sensitive file, marked “Urgent.” It still contained only one sentence.

James Preston. Scheduled to die by lethal injection at Huntsville, Texas. Thursday. The day after tomorrow.

Flint closed the laptop, ran a hand through his hair, and joined Drake in the hall.

As they walked toward the dining room, Flint said, “We’ll leave early tomorrow. Right after sunrise. We need to take a detour on the way back to Houston."

"Works for me. Where to?"

"Huntsville."

Drake raised his eyebrows and remained silent.

They'd been friends a long time. Worked together on some tough cases. Drake knew when not to ask questions.

Chapter Twenty

Red Maple Lake, California
Six Years Ago

After his shower, Josh donned Kevin's jeans and sweater and felt almost human again. He paced the bedroom while he waited.

Dan had hobbled into the shower a while ago. The water was still running. His ankle was swollen to twice its normal size and he was moving more slowly than usual. Kevin had brought him an office chair on wheels along with clean clothes.

He wanted to make a plan. But Skip was unconscious and Dan's behavior erratic. Probably due to his head injury, along with everything else that had happened. Whatever the reasons, both Skip and Dan were unreliable. It was up to him to get them all out.

Safely.

Soon.

His twisting gut told him he wasn't being overly fanciful, either. He looked outside. Mixed rain and sleet had turned to snow as the temperatures dropped with the arrival of darkness. The compound was beyond remote. No other people for miles. No cell signals. No way to communicate with anyone.

Yet the three of them just happened to be wandering in the woods close to where the Cessna went down? How likely was that? Not very.

They said they were hiking. But they'd been carrying no fishing or hunting gear. No hiking gear, either, for that matter.

There were acres and acres of empty land here. He shook his head.

No. Not believable. Not even remotely.

Still, trauma, exhaustion, and imagination had fueled his misgivings. No doubt. He stretched his sore muscles. The shower had warmed him and he was in reasonably good shape, but the day's events had worn down his reserves.

He didn't know what these men were involved with and he didn't want to know. But that Ruben guy looked downright menacing.

And Josh wasn't sure how to describe Mark. He resembled his wealthy brother in appearance, but he was familiar for another reason. Josh simply couldn't put his finger on it. Was it possible that he'd met Mark Wilcox before? He shook his head. Not likely. He didn't travel in those circles. Not even close.

Kevin was okay. Probably. At least, he had done nothing to arouse Josh's suspicions. Yet.

He heard the shower stop. Dan would be ready soon. They were expected in the dining room for dinner. His stomach growled. He was famished all of a sudden, and Dan must be, too.

Still, he'd have stolen the off-road vehicle Boyd Wilcox mentioned and driven to Red Maple Resort, even if it took him six hours to get there. He was that concerned.

But Skip couldn't take the rough ride and Josh couldn't take the chance that he'd make Skip's condition worse.

He didn't like it, but the only thing to do was get through the night and leave early in the morning on the helicopter, as planned.

Dan hobbled out of the steamy bathroom with a towel around his waist. He sat on the edge of the bed and awkwardly dressed in Kevin's clothes. "This guy has some nice stuff, doesn't he?"

Josh shrugged. "Cashmere and silk seem a little too much for this wilderness to me."

"Yeah, but his clean sweater and jeans are great." Dan slid his normal-sized foot into a sock and rewrapped the elastic bandage around his sprained one. "We should probably burn those clothes I took off. I'll never wear them again."

"I hear ya. Ready to go?" Josh pushed Dan into the dining room, the plastic wheels on the office chair traveling easily along the hardwood floors.

The others were already gathered at the dining table. The food smelled like something from a five-star restaurant. His stomach growled again and Dan joked, "Your stomach sounds like your throat's been cut."

The words were too close to Josh's misgivings. He shrugged and said nothing. With every passing hour, his desire to leave here grew. His gut said staying in this place was a mistake. As the shock of the crash and rescue receded and his head cleared, these people seemed more suspicious.

Ruben sat at one end of the table and Boyd at the other. Kevin and Mark sat diagonally across from each other. Places were laid next to each of them, one for Josh and one for Dan, effectively between two of the others. Which made Josh wonder whether they thought he and his friends needed watching.

After they were settled, Kevin said, "I just checked on Skip. He's still under. He won't be able to eat anything tonight."

Josh's appetite dulled as the guilt slammed his gut again, but the normally finicky Dan tucked into the beef stew in front of him as if he'd never eaten before. Which was odd. His behavior had been more than a little, well, off since the crash. One more thing for Josh to worry about.

Dinner conversation consisted mostly of small talk. Boyd was clearly the leader of the group. The others deferred to him. He started the conversations and kept them on track.

Josh noticed that the topics Boyd chose were all about Josh, Dan, and Skip. Where they lived. Why they were here. How long they planned to stay. The questions raised his internal radar, but Dan seemed oblivious to anything amiss.

Dan had been too chatty his whole life, but tonight he seemed to have no off switch. Maybe he was just nervous. Or maybe it was his head injury.

He blathered about his fiancée, Skip's wife, their kids, and how Josh was all alone in the world but looking for a good woman, if they knew of any, which got a laugh. He told where they lived, what kind of work they all did, how Josh was their pilot and they'd planned to stay at Red Maple Resort for a week to fish, and on and on.

Every time Josh tried to redirect the conversation, Dan took over again.

Josh noticed a few pointed looks between Ruben and Mark, and at least twice Boyd and Ruben locked gazes and nodded. But no one interrupted, and Dan kept talking all the way through the meal.

Mark left and came back with a tray of desserts and coffee. Dan had moved on to stories about Josh and Skip's more disastrous college exploits. The others seemed to be entertained while Josh became more and more uneasy.

"Now you know everything about us, down to our underwear preferences." Josh looked up when Dan finally paused a moment. "What are you guys doing out here?"

The question seemed harmless. But no one answered right away. Kevin looked down at his plate. Mark looked at Boyd.

"Same as you." Ruben was the one who replied. "We came for the fishing. Arrived yesterday."

"This is a beautiful home you have here, Boyd. Build it yourself?" Josh said, more to keep the conversational ball away from Dan than any desire to know.

“The property has been in our family for years. Our dad bought it when we were kids,” Mark replied. “Boyd rebuilt the house when StellarSoft became successful.”

Josh grabbed the opening and steered the talk to business topics. Superficial conversation of the kind men engage in when they don’t really want to share anything personal.

After dinner, Mark said, “You guys have got to be exhausted. Weather report is looking good over to Tahoe early in the morning.

We’ll take turns with Skip and I’ll wake you about five.” His words felt like orders more than suggestions.

"Sounds good." Josh pushed his chair away from the table and moved around to Dan's makeshift wheelchair.

Kevin handed Dan a couple of white caplets. "These will relieve the pain in your ankle and let you sleep."

Dan hated taking meds, but he swallowed both caplets without a murmur, which told Josh how much pain he was really feeling.

Kevin handed Josh a snifter of brandy. "This is Boyd's best. Take it to your room and you can sip it before you go to bed. It'll help you relax and get some sleep."

Josh nodded and took the snifter. "Smells amazing. Thank you."

He wheeled Dan back to the bedroom in the office chair and set the snifter on the bedside table while he washed up. When he came back to the bedroom, Dan was already in bed, deep into slumber. Within ten minutes, Dan's snoring rocked the rafters.

Josh intended to sit up for a while, but he only took one sip of the brandy before he crawled into bed and turned off the light, overwhelmed by exhaustion.

Just before he drifted off to sleep, in that twilight between consciousness and oblivion, Josh remembered where he'd seen Mark Wilcox before. On television. When his wife was kidnapped a few weeks ago from a casino in Las Vegas. The story had been on the TV news and all over the internet because she was Boyd Wilcox's sister-in-law. A ransom demand had been paid, but his wife wasn't returned.

Maybe that's why these guys acted so suspiciously interested in all of Dan's revealing conversation. Maybe they'd been worried that Josh and his friends were involved in the kidnapping somehow. Or maybe they were simply distraught over the missing woman.

That made sense. And was oddly reassuring. There was a good reason for their strange behavior. Josh was a practical man. He'd have been suspicious, too, under the circumstances.

Everything made sense. Finally. He relaxed and fell into a deep, exhausted oblivion.

Until a noise he couldn't quite place invaded his sleep. It sounded like a woman screaming. He opened his eyes briefly. He didn't know what time it was, but it was full dark. No ambient light of any kind entered the room. He closed his eyes and lay quietly, listening to Dan's heavy breathing caused by the chemically induced oblivion of the pain pills.

Josh waited a few seconds, listening for the woman's screams again, but he heard nothing. His eyes were still closed. His breathing even. Vaguely, his brain searched for reasonable causes. The screams had been an animal foraging in the woods.

Or he'd been dreaming something his subconscious dredged up. Frightening images of the Cessna crash flashed through his mind.

He listened hard. He heard the wind outside. Rain or sleet tapped the bedroom window.

When he heard nothing in the quiet house beyond Dan's snoring, he drifted back to sleep.

Chapter Twenty-One

Red Maple Lake, California
Six Years Ago

Later, Josh awakened again, still uneasy, for reasons he couldn't pinpoint. It was dark outside. He fumbled for his watch: 4:23 a.m. Mark would be coming for them at five, he'd said. Might as well get up now.

He tossed back the covers. The morning air hit him like a blow and stole his breath away. Man, it was cold in here.

He wrinkled his nose as he slipped into his pants and the blood, sweat, lake water, tears, and fears enveloped him, imbued with yesterday's nightmare. But he slid his arms into his sweater and jammed his feet into his boots. He patted his pockets and found his wallet and his phone where they should have been. He would buy new clothes in Tahoe. Until then, these would suffice.

Josh had been to Tahoe before. There were shops and restaurants and a good hospital there. The commercial airport was in Reno, thirty-five miles away. He could fly Skip's wife to Reno. As much as he dreaded facing Debbie, Skip would feel a thousand times better if she was here.

Dan was still snoring. Josh left him for a few more minutes. He'd check on Skip and confirm that the weather had cleared and get them all out of here.

He slipped out of the bedroom and pulled the door closed behind him. He walked quietly down the hallway to Skip's room. He opened the door.

Instantly, he sensed something was wrong.

His body began to thrum as if he'd been plugged into a high-voltage electrical tower.

Skip was alone. Mark and the others had promised to take shifts sitting with him all night, but no one was there.

Josh walked over to the bed and touched Skip's face. His skin was as cold as the room. Why had no one turned the heat on?

He placed three fingers on the side of Skip's neck to check his pulse. He felt nothing. He pushed harder against Skip's carotid artery. Nothing. He checked the other side. Still no pulse.

He bent down to put his ear close to Skip's face. He felt no breath emerge from Skip's nose or mouth. Instinctively, he pinched Skip's nose and opened his mouth to start CPR. He began the count. He put both hands flat on Skip's heart and pushed.

A deep part of his mind supplied the truth, but he ignored it.

He continued CPR for several minutes. Sweat formed on his brow. His arms fatigued. His breathing labored. He felt tears streaming from his eyes and still he kept going.

He began to accept that his efforts were failing. He continued to try for a long time before he gave up. He felt exhausted in spirit. He clamped his jaw, hard, to stop the screams that rose from his chest. He balled his fists instead of throwing something as hard as possible.

How could this happen? Skip was one of the best men on earth. He was young. He had a pregnant wife. A kid. He had the heart of a lion and yet he was kind and gentle. Josh didn't know how he would live with himself now.

Finally, he simply stood over his friend's body and sobbed until he'd used up all of his tears and then he stood a bit longer to let the truth sink deeper into his heart.

He'd killed Skip, his best friend since he was eighteen years old.

After a while, he went into the bathroom and pulled a long strand of toilet paper to blow his nose. He splashed cold water on his face and tried to get himself under control.

He squared his shoulders and took a few deep breaths to steady himself. Now what?

Kevin would know what to do. He was a doctor.

Josh left Skip's room and opened the next bedroom door. Kevin's bed was empty. He moved to the other rooms. Ruben's and Mark's beds were empty, too.

Josh hesitated, thinking about whether to wake Dan or keep looking for the others. He heard noises outside and was reminded of his nightmare. Was it possible that he'd actually heard a woman screaming? Had the others heard her as well? Is that where they were now?

Josh ran toward the front door and onto the porch. The wind and sleet had stopped during the night, as the weatherman had predicted. But the cold front had left a thin layer of frost covering the ground.

He paused to listen. Noises. Coming from the west side of the house. Definitely.

He dashed down the stairs and his boots crunched across the frost as he ran toward the noise.

He entered the woods where it was so dark he could barely see. He hadn't thought to grab a flashlight. He slowed his pace.

His feet slipped on the icy ground. Branches slapped his face and neck. He pushed them aside and slowed further. The last thing he needed was to fall and break something.

The air was so still. He continued to hear noises in the distance and navigated carefully toward them.

He rounded a bend and saw the faint light of a campfire ahead. Mark Wilcox was on the far side of the campfire. He was bent at the waist. He held a shovel in his hands.

Josh stopped. He controlled his rapid breathing. He allowed his eyes to adjust to the campfire light.

Now he could see that Mark was digging. He counted seven holes, each with a small pile of dirt next to it.

The scene made no sense. Why was Mark Wilcox digging holes in the darkness? Where were the others?

Near the campfire, not far from where Josh stood, was a red and white plastic cooler, the standard fifty-two-quart size. The kind Josh and his friends used to hold beer cans for tailgating during college football season.

The lid was open. Josh stood on his toes to peer over the rim.

He saw ice inside.

And something else.

The weak campfire's glow provided insufficient illumination. What was in that cooler?

The scene was surreal. Alarming. Josh blinked to refocus his eyes and turned his head slowly to examine everything he could see in the dim light.

Which was when he first noticed the other items.

A knife on the ground between the campfire and the cooler. Larger than a machete. More like a sword. He'd seen something like it in news reports. Swords like that were used in ritual killings in some parts of the world.

The blade was covered in something dark and gooey.

Two small piles snugged close to each of the holes Mark had dug. One pile was the dirt from the hole. But the second pile was something else.

Josh's grief-stricken mind finally grasped what he was seeing. Horrific images. He squeezed his eyes shut and shook his head as if to erase them from his corneas.

Surely what he saw here was nothing more than another nightmare. He was lying in the bed next to Dan's, back in their room. That's what this was.

He opened his eyes. The scene had not changed.

Beside each hole was a pile of fleshy stumps. Body parts. He could make out a forearm. A foot at the end of a short calf. A small woman's hand with fuchsia-pink polished fingernails.

Hacked expertly from a torso by that blade on the ground.

The blade splashed with dark, gooey blood.

His eyes widened and his mouth opened in horror. He slapped a palm across his lips to avoid crying out.

He raised up on his toes and peered into the cooler again. Now that his eyes had adjusted, he could see the severed head, face down inside the cooler. Long brown hair, starkly distinguishable from the ice upon which it rested.

His knees buckled. He fell to the ground and pushed himself upright. He backed away from the scene as quietly as he could, jaws clamped to keep the horror from spilling into the night.

He didn't know what was going on here, but it looked like Mark had killed this woman with a sword and dismembered her body. He seemed to be burying the parts. But that was insane.

Was he hallucinating? Had Kevin given him some kind of pills in that brandy that were making him see crazy things? Sleeping pills could do that. He knew a guy in college who sleepwalked right out of a third-story window because he thought it was a doorway. Sleeping pills made him do it.

That had to be what was going on here. Kevin had given him something like a sleeping pill. He'd wake up and everything would be normal again. Because any other explanation was too bizarre to contemplate.

As soon as he had put enough distance between himself and Mark, Josh turned and ran back to the house.

Chapter Twenty-Two

Red Maple Lake, California
Wednesday

An hour after sunrise, Flint had settled the bill at the resort. Neville drove them down to the lake in the Polaris. They'd stowed the gear and climbed aboard. Drake fired up the Cessna and executed a perfect takeoff.

"Fly around the perimeter of the lake one last time," Flint said. "I want to get some video and a better look at the area."

From the air, even in bright daylight, the trees were too dense to see through. The shoreline ebbed and flowed around the water.

According to the maps Flint had found online back in Houston, everything about the alpine lake was smaller than Tahoe.

Maple Lake was four point four miles long and two point four miles wide, with fourteen miles of unimproved shoreline and a surface area of thirty-two point two square miles. Maximum depth was reported at 329 feet.

Plenty of space for Hallman's trio to get into serious trouble.

The earliest recorded snowfall on the lake was September 13, which meant cold temperatures could invade the nine-thousand-to-eleven-thousand-foot peaks much earlier.

“Hallman probably followed the shoreline after the crash, heading toward the resort. Probably got in trouble in those woods,” Drake said when they reached the crash site. “Going the other direction would have been easier and faster, but counterintuitive.”

“Agreed. Can you see where that driveway up to the Wilcox place intersects with the path?”

“Not from this distance. But we know it’s there and we figure Hallman’s group was wandering around in the dark.” Drake cast a meaningful glance toward Flint. “They could have ended up anywhere.”

Flint nodded. "Let's take another look at that highway that runs along the mountainside before we head back to Reno."

Drake banked the Cessna and flew out of the basin, almost straight up from the lake until the ribbon of pavement came into view. The two-lane curved around the mountains and traveled into the valleys. Traffic was nonexistent.

But Flint saw two old farm trucks and one SUV along the eleven-mile stretch correlating with the distance between the Wilcox place and Red Maple Lake Resort.

One of the farm trucks turned off the road onto a long drive that led to an isolated ranch. He pointed the place out to Drake. “Can you land there?”

“Not in this boat.” Drake shook his head. “But we can come back with the Pilatus.”

“Next time.” Flint grimaced. “We don’t have time today.”

The Cessna’s flight path followed the road a while longer. Flint saw a small group of homes slightly north of the Wilcox place but no further signs of civilization for another twenty miles in any direction.

Drake turned the Cessna and headed north to the Reno airstrip where they’d left the Pilatus. He landed the Cessna and tied it to the dock.

Flint pulled out his laptop and tossed the rest of his gear into the back of the Pilatus. While Drake readied the jet, Flint walked to a quiet corner and fired up the satellite phone. He dialed the private number.

“It’s been a while,” his contact said, simply stating the fact without judgment. “How can I help you?”

“I need to get into Huntsville Unit. To meet with a death row inmate.” Flint cleared his throat. “It’s important.”

“When do you want to go inside?”

“He’s scheduled to be executed tomorrow.”

Flint knew the request was a problem. Visiting a death row inmate wasn’t a simple matter. There were protocols in place.

He'd have called the governor for intervention, but he detested the man and the feeling was mutual.

After a long pause, his contact said, "I'll do what I can."

"I'll owe you one," Flint replied.

The man laughed. "I'll add it to your bill."

Flint grinned and disconnected the call.

He carried the laptop inside the terminal building and found a place to sit. Using the encrypted hotspot, he connected to his secure server and sent an email in reply to the "time sensitive" one he'd received yesterday. "Acquire all available data on attached subject. One hour."

Her response pinged back immediately. “Acquired. Check server.”

He nodded. She’d continued working overnight, assuming he’d request the data when he had the chance.

He found the secure file, downloaded it, and replied, “Received. Anything more?”

“Still checking.”

He closed the laptop and bought coffee before he returned to the jet. He climbed aboard, handed one cup to Drake, and settled into one of the more comfortable back seats to read the files. He was absorbed by the materials long before takeoff.

The flight plan projected almost seven hours of travel time from the private airstrip near Reno to another private airstrip near Huntsville. The files were thin. He'd fully absorb everything in less than half the travel time.

He started with the most recent material.

James Preston was set for execution by lethal injection for the murder of June Pentwater tomorrow in the Texas State Prison at Huntsville.

Preston had been set to die five times before and received last minute reprieves each time. Last week, his lawyers had filed requests for additional DNA testing using current, more accurate techniques and a stay of execution until the results were returned.

Another last-minute reprieve could keep Preston alive until Flint completed the Hallman hunt, but Flint wouldn't risk what was likely to be his last chance to judge the man for himself.

Texas death row inmates are not allowed to have contact visits with anyone at any time, including prior to execution. Prisoners were sometimes allowed to use visiting cages outside death row and to talk to visitors via telephone from within the cage. It wasn't an ideal interview scenario, but Flint would take whatever he could get.

Preston's case had been argued by various anti-death-penalty groups over the years. Flint watched the video interviews his contact located before and after each loss.

Preston was always composed. He seemed to know that his case was hopeless, even if his lawyers refused to accept the obvious.

Photos of a young James Preston and Marilyn Baker were side by side in the file. That Flint might be looking at his mother and his mother's killer was an eerie feeling.

He wasn't sure what he thought of the situation or how he felt about it. There were too many unknowns. He'd examine his feelings later.

Over the years, Preston had repeatedly denied killing Marilyn Baker. Of course, he denied killing June Pentwater, too. Both denials could be true, but the Pentwater jury had found otherwise. He was only charged and convicted of killing Pentwater, not Baker.

Flint's contact pinged his secure server. The message said he'd made three phone calls and got lucky on the last one. Flint would be allowed to talk to James Preston using the visiting cage and telephone receiver for not more than thirty minutes.

Flint glanced at the time posted on his computer screen. He'd arrive early, with an hour to spare.

He closed his eyes and visualized the scene as he'd experienced it before. Preston would be in a visitation cage, holding the phone handset. Flint would be seated at a table outside the cage. He'd be able to see Preston and hear his voice.

He didn't know exactly what he expected to learn. Maybe he would get a feeling of some kind from this guy. Maybe he would simply know whether Preston killed Marilyn Baker. Sometimes, his gut check worked that way. More often, it did not.

What he needed was Marilyn's DNA. The evidence collected during her murder should be somewhere. Using newer techniques, DNA could be analyzed now. Maybe.

A better plan would be direct DNA testing from a fresh sample that hadn't been contaminated. Her body had been buried in a Mount Warren cemetery. He could get the body exhumed for fresh samples.

Yes, it could be done. But, as Scarlett had said, simply because he could make it so didn't mean he should.

If Baker was his mother, she was dead. Her killer could be dead tomorrow night. There was nowhere else for his personal heir hunt to go, even if he wanted it to.

Which he wasn't at all sure that he did.

He drained his coffee and lowered the lid to his laptop. He leaned back in the seat and closed his eyes for a nap.

Old habit he'd learned from his time with Uncle Sam. Sleep when you can.

Chapter Twenty-Three

Huntsville, Texas
Wednesday

He was alone when he pulled the rental into the Texas State Prison at Huntsville. He'd left Drake with the Pilatus to avoid answering a lot of questions.

He cleared the security gate, thanks to his contact's credentials, and parked where he was told. He cleared several other security checkpoints in the same way before being led to the visiting cage where he would meet James Preston for the first time.

He didn't know what he expected to find. He only knew he'd face his mother's killer one-on-one before the man was executed.

Assuming Marilyn Baker had been his mother.

And assuming Preston had killed her. Both assumptions seemed justified based on currently known facts.

After Flint walked into the visitor's room and took his place opposite the cage, a buzzer sounded and the door leading from the interior corridor to the cage opened automatically.

James Preston was already seated.

He was dressed in a white one-piece prison jumpsuit. The jumpsuit tied at the top of the V-neck. He wore a white T-shirt underneath.

The most recent photos Flint had seen were snapped at least five years before, but Preston looked the same. Paunchy. Round, bloated face. Pouch-size bags under his eyes. He hadn't shaved in a while.

He was sixty-four years old now and looked ninety-four. Long gone was the appealing young priest who might have caught Marilyn Baker's eye back then.

Preston settled heavily into the chair and picked up the telephone receiver. He waited for Flint to speak.

Flint had prepared no remarks or introductions. He picked up his receiver and held it to his ear. For a moment, they simply looked at each other across the chasm from free to caged.

Flint felt nothing.

No twinge of familiarity.

No spark of anger.

If Preston was connected to him in any way, no vibe of any kind jolted his awareness.

Flint cocked his head.

By the time Marilyn Baker was murdered, he was a toddler already entrusted to foster care by a woman who couldn't, or wouldn't, raise him.

She had attended the church where Father Preston was a visiting priest, and she'd offered him her heartfelt confession.

He had known her. He could have known she was pregnant. He could have met her child.

Shouldn't Flint have felt some twinge of something?

"My name is Michael Flint. I'm a private investigator."

Preston nodded but did not reply.

"I'm looking for information about Marilyn Baker. I'm told you knew her."

"I knew Marilyn. She was a nice girl." Preston nodded again. His eyes were dull. He didn't smile or offer any encouragement. "I didn't kill her."

"That's what you've said," Flint replied. "Her family is interested in finding her killer. They're hoping you might know something that you didn't share with investigators before."

"I thought Marilyn's family were all deceased." Preston shrugged.

When Flint offered no response, Preston said, "Like what?"

"This is a very cold case. At this point, I'm just looking for anything that might help."

"Do you believe I didn't kill her?" Preston narrowed his eyes and stared at Flint. "Because if you're trying to prove I killed her, I'm not interested in talking to you. I've got enough trouble already, if you hadn't noticed."

"I'm not with law enforcement. It's not my job to prove who killed her." Flint paused and took a deep breath. "She had a son. Did you know that?"

Preston shook his head. “I knew she had been in trouble, which is what we used to say back then when unmarried Catholic girls turned up pregnant.”

Flint nodded. One good assumption confirmed. “How did you know that?”

“She told me. She was very distraught. Her parents were quite strict. She was twenty-one years old and barely out of college. She was teaching at the parish school. She was a devout Catholic.” He shook his head. “An abortion was out of the question.”

“Was she seeking advice about the pregnancy from you, her priest?”

"Mostly, she cried a lot. She was very conflicted about what to do." He seemed to think about that for a moment. "As I said, her options were limited."

"What about the child's father? What did he want?"

"I asked her that. She said he couldn't marry her."

"Why not?"

"She wouldn't say. My guess at the time? He was married." Preston pushed his lips around under his bulbous nose. "I tried to console her as best I could, but as I say, it was mostly a lot of tears and incoherent babbling."

"She wasn't pregnant when she died. What happened with the child?"

"She went somewhere for the summer, while the school vacation took place. She was gone a few months. And when she came back, she wasn't pregnant and she didn't have a child with her. I never knew whether she delivered the child or aborted it." Preston shook his head again. "She died a couple of years later."

"Were you still around when she got back to town?"

"I was a visiting priest back in those days. I was moved around from one parish to another. I had been moved over to Paris for a year or so." He shrugged. "When I came back to Mount Warren, she was working at the school and still living at home, single, no kids."

"Did you continue as her confessor?"

Preston nodded. "She never mentioned a baby to me."

"Didn't you ask her?"

"Ask her? I was her priest, not her girlfriend."

"Seems like a natural question, though. You knew she was pregnant and you're gone when the baby comes and then you return." Flint narrowed his eyes. "Why wouldn't you ask about her child?"

Preston seemed to think about it for a while. Flint wasn't sure if he was creating some kind of story in his head or simply couldn't remember.

He didn't look healthy. Maybe he was mentally incompetent or something. He'd been in solitary confinement for the past fifteen years after a fight with a prison guard.

Fifteen years alone in his cell with no one to talk to but the cockroaches. Men had gone insane in those situations before.

Finally, Preston cleared his throat. "Marilyn and I were not friends. She was a teacher at the school and I was a priest in the church. From time to time, our paths would cross. Usually, she would look away. If she was embarrassed or simply shy, I don't know. But she never confessed anything else of consequence to me."

"The church takes a dim view of abortion, even now." Flint pressed on. "I'm surprised you wouldn't want to know what she had done with her pregnancy."

"It wasn't my place. It wasn't my problem." Preston shrugged and lowered his eyes. "I prayed for her, sure. I hoped she had done the right thing by her child. Since you said she had a son, sounds like she did."

Flint relaxed his tight grip on the receiver in his left hand. "Who was her boyfriend at the time?"

Preston shook his head and closed his eyes as if he was trying to think about it. "It was a long time ago. Marilyn was an attractive girl and there were a lot of men who were interested in her. I remember those two hellions, Crane and Shaw, were always hanging around. A few others.” He opened his eyes. “But whether she dated any of them in particular, I just don’t know. That was not my world. I was focused on the church. I’m sorry I can’t help you any further.”

“And you’re sure you were not the father of her child?”

“Certainly not.”

“Will you voluntarily give me a DNA sample to test against her son’s DNA?”

Preston shrugged. “Why not?”

Flint’s contact had made the arrangements in advance. The door behind Preston opened and a guard stood over him and he swabbed his cheek.

When the guard left, Preston said, "You can find my DNA results in the Marilyn Baker criminal file, you know. I gave them samples when they asked a couple of years ago. I didn't kill her. I didn't kill June Pentwater either, but nobody seems to care about that. I'll be executed this time, my lawyers say, so I have no reason to lie to you. I liked Marilyn. She wouldn't want her son to think his father killed her. No boy should carry that kind of weight around."

Flint's instincts finally seemed to kick in. Preston was telling the truth on both counts.

Preston wasn't the father of Marilyn Baker's child and he didn't kill her, either.

Flint would run the tests and confirm, but he felt the truth in his gut and he was glad about it.

Preston was right. No man should believe his father killed his mother. Even if he didn't know either one of them.

Flint glanced at his watch. Ten more minutes.

"Even if you aren't the father of her child, her son will want to know about her. You were her priest once. You might be one of the people who knew her best on this earth." This was the last time he'd ever talk to

James Preston, and he might never find anyone else to ask. "Tell me about Marilyn Baker."

Preston leaned back and closed his eyes. It was a long time ago. The world and his life had changed a great deal since then. He'd spent many hours in an empty cell with nothing to entertain him except his own mind. Flint figured much of his time was spent visualizing the life he'd lived outside this prison.

"Marilyn was beautiful. She had entered a beauty contest in college. Made it all the way to the finals. She didn't win, but she should have," Preston said, as if he was living the long ago.

Flint didn't interrupt.

"Several young men in town dated her. She was wholesome and funny and kind. Her students loved her. The whole town was shocked when she died. I think her death destroyed her parents' will to live, too," Preston continued.

He paused for a moment and sipped water from a paper cup.

"She was their only child. They were such lost souls without her. Her dad died a few months after Marilyn was killed, and her mother passed not long after that. She had no siblings. There may have been aunts and uncles and cousins. I'm not sure." He opened his eyes and looked frankly toward Flint.

"I think Marilyn was the only person ever murdered in Mount Warren up until then. It was a very sad situation," Preston said, finishing his memory.

The guard rapped on the door and opened it. "Time to go."

Preston looked at Flint with the kind of sincerity only psychopaths can manage. "Tell Marilyn's son I'm very sorry for his loss. May he find peace."

He hung up the phone receiver and left the cage. Flint returned his receiver to its cradle and watched him go.

He collected the DNA kit before he left the building.

The DNA would be tested and compared to his own, but Flint did not expect a match.

He had a particular talent for identifying lies and liars. Preston said he was not the father of Marilyn Baker's child and Flint believed him.

Marilyn Baker might have been his mother, but Preston's DNA sample wouldn't confirm that.

On the drive back to the airstrip, Flint reviewed Preston's description of Marilyn Baker. Everything Preston said dovetailed with what he already knew. There were no glaring differences to suggest she was not his mother. The more he thought about her, the more he believed he'd found the right woman.

If he was to have a mother, after all these years, he would be damned certain he'd found the right one. He would accept nothing less than a definitive answer.

Preston said Marilyn had many suitors. Finding a sperm donor was much more difficult than finding a mother, but he could do it. He could find anyone, anytime, anywhere. When he wanted to.

His personal phone rang. He looked at the caller ID. He could hear her crying even as he answered. "What's wrong with my best girl today, Maddy?"

She was always such a cheerful little imp. Her cries turned to sobs, which broke his heart.

"Honey, I can't help if you don't tell me what's wrong." He frowned and tried a different approach. "Is your mom there?"

"It's too late." She drew a ragged breath and pushed all the words out at once. "Jamie's dying, Michael."

She tried to explain but her sobs overwhelmed her voice until she disconnected.

Flint's mother would have to wait.

He dialed Veronica Beaumont as he pulled into the parking lot. Voice mail picked up. "Veronica, it's Flint. We need to talk."

He tossed the keys on the front seat of the rental and hustled over to the Pilatus. Drake was already in the pilot's seat. "Where to?"

"Houston." Flint pushed the number one button on his speed dial.

She'd occupied that place on his phone for years. He never stopped to think about it.

When Katie Scarlett answered, he said, "Meet me in your office in ninety minutes?"

"Not a problem. I'm already here." She paused. "Anything I can get started before you arrive?"

Flint grinned. Scarlett was almost as good at investigation of missing heirs as he was.

He'd promised Maddy not to tell her mother about the case, but he was a one-man show. He needed a team, and Scarlett had one of the best teams around.

“I’ll send you what I have on a missing man. Presumed dead.”

“But you think he’s what? Hiding in a cardboard box under the expressway?”

Flint shook his head. Prickly, as always. Situation normal. Which relaxed his tension. “Not exactly, but something like that, I’m afraid.”

“We’ll find out. I’ll get Gaspar on it, too.” She paused.

She sipped something. Coffee, probably. She mainlined the stuff almost around the clock. If the caffeine kept her awake at night, she never admitted as much.

"See you when I see you," she signed off.

He disconnected the call, opened his laptop, and sent her the files on Josh Hallman. He included a list of the men he'd met at the Wilcox house. She'd know what to do with them.

Chapter Twenty-Four

Red Maple Lake, California
Six Years Ago

Josh ran through the woods toward the house. He tripped and fell twice. The thick foliage blacked out dawn's weak light. He didn't hear anyone chasing him, but his blood pounded in his ears like an angry Japanese drummer.

By the time he reached the open green space, the morning sky had lightened enough to reveal the gravel driveway. Josh made no effort to approach the house with stealth. He dashed straight up the front steps, across the porch, and pushed through the front door. His pounding footsteps and ragged breathing would awaken everyone who might still be asleep, but he no longer cared. All he wanted was to find Dan and get away. And come back with the police.

He ran down the hallway to his room. He noticed that the house seemed too quiet. Where was everyone? He felt like the frightened victim in the kind of horror movies he'd consumed like popcorn as a teen. But he was acutely aware that he was living through an actual nightmare.

Josh reached his room, stormed inside, closed the door, locked it, and propped the straight chair under the doorknob for good measure.

Through it all, Dan snored. The painkillers Kevin had given him before bed must have buried him deep into oblivion.

“Dan. Wake up.” Josh shook Dan’s shoulder. Hard. “We have to get out of here. Now.”

Dan’s eyes fluttered open but he was not awake. He closed his eyes again and Josh shook him a second time. “Come on, Dan. Let’s go.”

Dan’s eyes remained closed. He frowned and mumbled, “Is the helicopter ready?”

At least he was semi-lucid. He remembered where they were and why they were here. Josh’s relief encouraged him to shake Dan again, but he didn’t move.

Josh jerked the warm covers away.

The cold morning air slapped Dan like an icy blow to his entire body. His eyes popped open. "What the hell are you doing?"

"We have to go. Right now." Josh reached out and grabbed Dan's arm and yanked him to a seated position on the edge of the bed.

"What the hell is wrong with you?" He shook Josh's grip away.

"Get dressed." Josh grabbed Dan's grimy clothes off the chair and threw them at him.

"What is your problem?" Dan was fully awake now. And angry. Good. He would need that adrenaline and the energy that came with it.

As Dan shoved one leg into his pants and slid the left one in a little more gingerly because of his sprained ankle, he continued to scowl. Josh saw the wince, though, when Dan's foot caught on his pant leg. The sprain was bad. They'd need to run through the woods like a three-legged race, with Dan leaning into him. They had no other options.

Josh lowered his voice to keep the quivering under control. He looked steadily into Dan's eyes, willing his friend to focus and process the insane situation.

"What I'm going to tell you is shocking. I don't have time to explain now. Just accept what I say. I'll explain more later. Okay?"

Dan's frown deepened as he nodded. Josh wondered how much Dan could absorb, but he had no time to soften the blow. "Skip is dead. I don't know what happened. He didn't make it through the night."

Dan's eyes widened and his mouth gaped. He shook his head and raised his hand to the cut on his scalp. Josh imagined that the hammering that must be going on inside his skull was overwhelming.

"These guys are dangerous. We have to get away. If I help you, do you think you can run?" Dan's eyes filled with confusion. He shook his head slowly. "Because I'm telling you, you've got no choice. If you stay here, they may kill you. Me, too."

"You're crazy. They rescued us. We had dinner with these guys." Dan frowned. He blinked. "We were talking about fishing and kids and college, for God's sake. And Kevin is a doctor. Why would they kill us?" He didn't believe the truth.

Josh bowed his head briefly. He wanted to avoid mentioning what he'd seen in the woods until they were safely away from the house. But Dan might not leave unless he knew. And there was no way Josh could carry him. Not as far as they had to travel. Not over that rocky terrain out there.

He lowered his voice, even though he thought they were alone in the house. "I saw something, Dan. Something bad. Something I wasn't meant to see." He paused. "I don't think they'll let me leave here, now that I know."

"What the **hell** are you talking about? What could you possibly have seen?" Dan was still sitting on the bed. He'd made no move to stand. "You know this is crazy, right?"

He nodded. "I saw Mark. Covered in blood. Standing near a woman's body." He paused again and gulped. This **was** hard to believe. He couldn't really blame Dan for doubting. "The woman. She was dismembered. He was burying her. In pieces. I don't think he saw me, but I'm not sure. If he did, he'll kill me. I know it, Dan, as well as I know anything." Dan looked at him now, head cocked, mouth agape.

"You can stay here if you want, but I have got to go."

"What about Skip?"

"Didn't you hear me?" Josh grabbed Dan's shoulder and shook him.

"Skip is dead. He died last night."

"Dead? Are you sure? Because Kevin said—"

"I don't care what Kevin said! Don't you get it? You could **die** here. **I** could die here." Josh ran his splayed fingers through his hair. "Get up and come with me, Dan. Otherwise, I'm leaving and you're on your own."

Dan wasn't convinced. He had not seen what Josh saw in the woods. But he must have believed that Josh would actually leave him, so he stood on his good right leg with his left bent at the knee. “I can’t walk on this foot. You’ll have to help me.”

Josh put his right arm under Dan’s left one and hugged his torso close. Dan threw his left arm over Josh’s shoulder. Josh walked and Dan hopped and they made it to the bedroom door. Progress was too slow, but he tried not to think about how easily they could be caught.

He threw the door open and they proceeded in the same three-legged hop down the hallway and out the front exit. When they reached the driveway, Dan was already sweating and trembling, but they kept going.

Josh glanced over his shoulder and saw no one coming after them. But morning had broken and dawn's light flooded the driveway and the green space. They would easily be seen running away unless they traveled through the woods, where the going would be even slower, rougher.

Speed was more important than stealth at the moment, but he was prepared to duck into the woods as soon as he heard or saw anyone coming after them.

They came much sooner than he'd hoped.

He heard the footsteps behind them before he was able to steer Dan off the driveway and into the shadows.

He glanced back to see Kevin hurrying in their direction with Mark close behind him.

Chapter Twenty-Five

Red Maple Lake, California
Six Years Ago

Josh moved in the opposite direction, dragging Dan along as fast as they could manage. They made it another ten feet before Ruben stepped out from the woods on the other side of the driveway. He must have circled around the back of the house.

Mark was still covered in mud and crusty dried blood. He had the sword in his left hand. He looked like a madman. Which he surely was.
But his alarming appearance finally broke through whatever denial Dan

had cloaked around himself. He hopped faster.

If they could make it into the cover of the woods, they might have a chance.

Josh looked around wildly for an opening between the trees wide enough for both he and Dan to slip through. Kevin and Ruben were too close. They seemed as normal as before, but given Mark's presence, their normal-like behavior horrified him.

Dan was breathing hard. Josh couldn't move him any faster. Three against one, best case. And Mark was both armed and dangerous. Hell, maybe the others were, too. Maybe they were all insane.

Josh stopped and turned to face Ruben as Kevin and Mark approached. Dan's eyes widened and he tugged on Josh's arm and hopped a couple more feet.

Josh had been in many a bar fight with Dan and Skip in their college days. He knew what was coming. He recognized the signs. Dan must have seen it coming, too.

And Josh knew he couldn't win. Not three against one. Not with Mark armed with that sword he was capable of wielding to lethal effect.

Yes. They were all crazy. For sure.

Briefly, he wondered what, exactly, he and his friends had stumbled into. If he hadn't seen the woman's dismembered body in the woods, he would never have believed any of this.

But he did see her. Denial was a deadly luxury.

“Dan, you can’t be walking on that ankle,” Kevin said reasonably, as any doctor might say to his patient. “Let’s go back inside and let me take a look at it. You might have made it worse with all this. As soon as the helicopter can take off, we’ll get you and Skip airlifted out of here.”

It was the mention of Skip that pushed Josh the short distance into panic. He’d thought Kevin, at least, could be counted on. He was a doctor. A healer. Not a killer.

But Kevin must have known that Skip died. No way he didn't know. Not a chance. Kevin was one of them, too.

Josh felt his heart pounding like he'd run a marathon uphill. Fear caused heart attacks. He could die, right here, without anyone laying a finger on him.

Ruben said, "Come on, Josh. It's damned cold out here. Let's go back inside. Get showers and breakfast and then Mark can fly you out to Tahoe. Just like we planned."

Josh tried a genuine smile and a friendly tone. "The weather seems to have passed. We'll find our own way." Kevin said, "What about Skip?"

"We'll come back for him," Josh said.

“What about Dan?” Ruben’s mouth split into a sneer. His tone snide. The pretending was over. “He’s already sweating. Weak. He’ll never make it hobbling on one leg. And you can’t carry him.”

“We’ll be fine.” Josh reached under Dan’s arm again and grabbed his torso. Dan hopped once.

Which was when Josh’s far peripheral vision picked up Mark raising his right arm and moving toward them. Mark was a big man. Powerful. Tall. He moved fast.

Dan hopped two more times before Mark reached them, arm in the air, the sharp sword raised to slash downward.

Josh jerked Dan away from the descending blade.

He lost his balance.

He hit the ground on his side and Dan landed on top of him. He rolled Dan off. They scrambled on their hands and knees in a desperate effort to get away.

Ruben changed position. In one smooth, practiced arc, he pulled a pistol from his belt. He pointed at Dan. And shot him in the back.

Dan screamed and fell face down onto the ground.

Josh darted away from the assailants. The shelter of the woods was close.

Dan continued to scream, but he didn't move.

Josh glanced over his shoulder just as Ruben shot Dan in the head.

Dan's screams stopped. His face fell into the mud. Blood spewed onto the ground. Dan remained silent.

Ruben looked toward Josh. His arm lifted, began the shooting arc again.

Josh dashed into the woods and hid behind a mammoth pine.

Ruben fired off two rounds. Somehow, he missed.

Josh sank against the big pine before he ran zigzagging between the trees, using the thick trunks as shields, putting distance behind him.

The three men came after him. They split up to cover more ground.

Josh could hear them yelling to each other.

Ruben yelled out. “You know who we are. You know we have limitless resources. Go ahead and run if you want. We will find you, Josh. I will find you. I will kill you. Just like Dan and Skip. You will never be safe. Never. You can count on that.”

He ran deeper into the darkness of the forest, moving as fast as he could on the uneven terrain, hiding behind the tree trunks, pushing himself up when he stumbled.

Adrenaline pumped through his body and increased his awareness of everything around him. The leaves had sharper edges. The tree bark was roughly etched. The muddy ground pebbled and squishy.

He ran forever. His breath tore from his chest. Raggedly painful.

His legs had never felt so fatigued.

He kept going.

He had no idea how far he'd traveled or in which direction. He ran blindly, seeking only to get far away.

The three voices fell farther and farther behind until he could no longer distinguish their words.

Ruben had stopped shooting a while back. Josh should've worried about that, but he just kept running.

There was nothing he could do for his friends now.

First, he had to get away. Then, he would try to make the police believe him. Even as he thought the words, he realized how unlikely his plan was. Boyd Wilcox was one of the most powerful men on the planet. Who would take Josh Hallman's word against his?

Chapter Twenty-Six

Red Maple Lake, California
Six Years Ago

Josh ran for quite a while. He wasn't sure how long. He was tired and stumbled too often. He had scratches and cuts on his hands and arms where he'd fallen several times. Once, he'd landed hard on his face and mashed his nose. He could feel blood mixed with sweat and grime on his skin.

But he kept going. Maybe he'd covered ten miles or so. He wasn't sure. All he knew was that Skip and Dan were dead and it was his fault and if he didn't keep moving, he'd be dead too, and no one would ever know what happened to any of them.

Maybe people would think they died in the plane crash. But surely when they were reported missing, someone would look for the plane. Red Maple Lake was deep and cold and spring-fed, but it wasn't the ocean. Bodies should be findable. The plane should be findable, too. It wasn't like a missing jetliner in a vast ocean.

Search and rescue would be called. He wondered how Ruben and the others would deal with that. They had three bodies to dispose of already, including the woman. And if Josh died out here, that would be four.

Surely even Wilcox's money wouldn't be enough to bury that news forever.

If Josh didn't die. If he escaped. He would bring down the wrath of God on them all. He'd go to the FBI and anybody else who would listen. Somebody would make those bastards pay. That somebody was Josh Hallman. No doubt about it.

He was so tired. He wanted to stop. He wanted to just stay here for a while. It would be getting even darker soon. Last night's temperature was below thirty degrees and tonight's forecast was colder.

He would survive because he had no choice. He owed it to Skip.

To Dan. And their families.

Brave words from a guy who also had no means of starting a fire.

He patted the cell phone in his pocket. When he could get a signal, he could call for help. He patted his pocket again, to be sure the phone was still there. Its presence was reassuringly normal.

In fact, he remembered that cell phones could be tracked. Yes. Of course. Skip had a cell phone and so did Dan. They had families who loved them, even if Josh did not. People who would be looking for them.

They could be tracked. They'd be found. His heart felt slightly lighter than it had for hours.

Did cell phone tracking work even after the phones had been submerged in lake water? He didn't know.

His phone had been in his pocket when they paddled the life raft from the sinking plane to shore. He remembered that he'd been submerged while he pulled Dan into the life raft. But his phone was waterproof. It was rated for diving. He'd been worried about losing it when they went fishing. Surely, his phone would still work, right?

But what about Dan and Skip? He hadn't seen their phones after the crash. He didn't know whether they still worked. Maybe their phones were at the bottom of the lake, with the Cessna.

Which was when he realized that Wilcox and the others would have taken care to eliminate any cell phone tracking. Boyd Wilcox was a tech genius. He knew what to do. When they disposed of the bodies, they would dispose of the phones as well. They'd probably done it already.

He pulled out his phone and fired it up as he ran. It still had battery life left but there was no cell signal. He couldn't connect to anyone in the outside world. At least, not yet.

He kept running, his feet pounding, heart beating hard in his chest, lungs gulping air faster than he could breathe.

His thinking was fuzzy. He was tired, hungry, cold. Not to mention horrified. He didn't have the luxury of treating himself for shock, although he'd be a cold bastard if he wasn't suffering from it.

He ran. He stumbled. He fell. He pushed himself up. He kept the phone in his hand for a few more steps before something he should have known all along reached his foggy thinking.

His phone could be tracked.

Once it reconnected to a cell tower somewhere, it could be found.

By anyone with the technology and the smarts to find it.

Which included Boyd Wilcox. StellarSoft was a tech company. StellarSoft had all kinds of tech equipment. Finding his phone would be no problem at all.

And as long as he had the phone on his body, finding **him** would be easy, too.

He stopped running. He put both hands on his thighs and bent his knees. He leaned over to rest and more clarity came.

That's why Ruben stopped following him. They could find him anytime. Using his cell phone to track him.

They didn't expect him to make it out of these woods alive. They had explained how far they were from the nearest neighbor to persuade him not to try.

But if he tried. If he made it out. If he found anyone who might help him. If he found any place where he could use his phone.

Wilcox could track it. Wilcox would find the phone and then they would find him. And it wouldn't take long because they were probably already looking and they knew where to look.

Josh removed the phone from the waterproof case. He bent down and found two large rocks amid the decaying undergrowth. Frantically, he pounded the case into pieces. Then he savagely destroyed the phone the same way.

He took a handful of pieces and tossed them into the woods to the east. A second handful he tossed west. He divided the remainder into three more handfuls and started jogging again. He flung the bits of technology as wide as he could throw.

When he'd tossed the last of the pieces, he swiped his palms together and kept running until the sun had crested and begun its slow westward descent.

He kept going. He was barely trotting now, but he felt he might have a chance as long as he didn't stop.

When he stopped, they would find him.

They would kill him.

Like they killed that woman.

Like they killed Dan.

And probably Skip, too.

His mind conjured disaster scenarios along the entire journey, to keep himself motivated when he would otherwise have stopped.

He was so tired. Adrenaline alone had fueled him for several hours, but now the full weight of his situation had begun to settle on his shoulders.

He was alone. He was on the run. He was responsible. He was the pilot. It was his job to fly and land safely. He had failed. His friends had died. The only reason he should live through this was to face their families.

He kept going.

When darkness fell and running became too treacherous, he found a big tree and collapsed at its foot. Exhausted in body and spirit.

If he made it through the night, he would run again tomorrow. But if he died, so be it.

He should have died back at that house, with Skip and Dan and that woman, whoever she was.

He'd sleep now for a few hours. If he didn't freeze to death, he'd wake up tomorrow to run again.

Chapter Twenty-Seven

Houston, Texas
Wednesday

Flint reached the offices of Scarlett Investigations in downtown Houston shortly after seven o'clock. The building was locked.

When he approached the front entrance, his face was captured on cameras at the door, which triggered the security system. The door clicked and he pushed it open. After he walked through, the door locked behind him.

His boots pounded the marble floors as he took the stairs to the fourth floor, two at a time. When he reached her office, he stepped through the open doorway without knocking.

Scarlett was behind the desk, staring at the computer screen. Black curly hair swirled wildly around her shoulders.

Readers perched on her nose magnified her eyes to the size of the boulder marbles he'd owned as a kid. The ones she'd stolen from him because she liked them. The ones he'd fought to get back, and still had the scars to prove she'd won.

He grinned and plopped down in one of her client chairs and picked up the square paperweight of brown boulders encased in glass from her desk. "Well?"

"Your missing guy, Joshua Hallman, is a dead man." She didn't look up.

"You found a death certificate?"

"No."

"Cremation records?"

"No."

"Cemetery plot?"

"No."

"A visit from the Ghost of Christmas Past?"

That made her laugh. She looked at him for the first time since he'd entered the room. "You look like hell. Where have you been?"

"Thanks. Nice to see you, too." But he felt weary and he wasn't surprised that she'd noticed. He could never get anything past her and he'd long ago stopped trying.

She nodded. "Okay. Keep things to yourself, then."

"Why do you say Hallman is dead?"

She hadn't mentioned the bank account, which meant she hadn't found it.

If Scarlett hadn't found it, then there was a chance no one else had found it, either.

"Because I can't find any paper trail anywhere on the guy. It's like he fell through a hole in the earth six years ago. Normally, I'd think witness protection in a case like that." She lifted her coffee cup and pointed to the pot on the sidebar. He walked over to fill a mug of the thick black sludge for himself. “But I checked. No dice.”

He raised his mug in a toast and drank the bitter brew. “That’ll put hair on your chest.”

She grinned again, looked down at her chest, and shook her head. “Not yet.”

He dumped the coffee and refilled the mug with water to wash the bitter taste from his mouth. He left the mug in the sink and paced the room to stretch his legs. He’d been sitting too much. He felt stiff and creaky.

“So the official story is that Hallman piloted a Cessna T206 into the cold waters of Red Maple Lake over in the California mountains six years ago. He had two buddies with him. They were headed for a fishing trip." She reported the facts like a robot would. "A week later, they didn't come back, and the families began looking for them. The plane was found. The men were not."

"Never?" He wasn't testing her. He wanted her to confirm his conclusions and to be sure she was up to speed.

"Well, this is where it gets interesting. Over the years, technology improved, and underwater search-and-rescue techniques improved, too. Hallman had no family. But the other two guys did. Someone hired a pricey crew to go down there with even pricier equipment. Like the stuff the navy uses for underwater research. Two of the men were found."

All of this dovetailed with the information Flint had already uncovered. Nothing new, which was reassuring.

He nodded. "And?"

"The bodies were well preserved. They think it was the cold water that kept them almost intact. They were snagged on the rocks on the lake bottom and tethered by junk down there. It was a struggle to bring them up, but when they resurfaced, autopsies were done."

He knew what was coming, so he nodded and kept quiet. When he said nothing, she kept talking, which was what she usually did. She could talk for hours without stopping. It was a gift.

“One guy had a serious leg fracture. The fish had gnawed away most of his right leg. Which was pretty grisly. But that’s not what killed him, according to the autopsy report. It was a morphine overdose.”

He nodded again. “And the other guy?”

“Even more curious. He was shot. Twice. Once in the back. That bullet pierced his lung and would have killed him eventually. But the second shot to the back of the head did the job faster.”

“So Hallman crashed the plane, killed his buddies, and hightailed it out of there?”

“That’s one possibility.” She drained her cup. “Another is that he died, too, and they just haven’t found his body yet.”

“Seems unlikely, but it’s been known to happen.” Flint nodded again. Her answers made his conclusions unassailable. “They might find him years from now, like that guy they found seventeen years later in that inland lake in northern Michigan.”

Scarlett folded her hands on her desk. “I don’t think that’s it, though. Do you?”

He cocked his head and watched her for a few moments. “I don’t know.”

"Why not?"

"Because of some other weird things that have been going on."

"Such as?"

"Such as, it's possible the tech tycoon Boyd Wilcox is involved. And his brother, Mark."

"That guy on TV? The one whose wife was kidnapped and murdered a while back?"

"That's the one."

"You worked on that case."

He nodded. "Not a great success. All we ever found was her head. We never found the rest of her body."

"Case was never solved, right?"

He scowled. “In the sense that we didn’t find the killers, if that’s what you mean. But my end of it was solved. We found her head. I got paid.”

She shook her head. “I’m guessing that wasn’t exactly what her husband had in mind when he hired you to find his wife.” Flint pursed his lips and said nothing.

“And you already knew all this about Hallman, didn’t you?” She arched her eyebrows. “So what is it that you need me for?”

“You’ve got a good grip on everything we know. I want all these loose ends nailed down. Quickly. I’ve got to find this guy in the next few days.”

"My team can handle that. I don't know what you expect to learn, though. The guy's been gone a long time. What are these people going to know that they haven't already told someone involved with the earlier investigations?"

"That's what I want your team to find out. We've already covered the records. We need personal contact now." He paused. "I'm especially interested in whether anyone even remotely connected with those four guys I found at Wilcox's house on Red Maple Lake have been in contact with the families or friends of Hallman's two passengers."

"You think the Wilcoxes are involved in this and you're looking for evidence to support your hunch?"

She cocked her head, like her daughter's little schnauzer, Whiskers.

Flint imagined that her ears might have pointed straight up like Whiskers' did, too.

"And I want to know what was said. Precisely." He paused. "If I'm right about the connection, it makes sense that they'd have covered all their bases and tried to find Hallman through the others."

"We can nail that down." She paused and settled back in her chair, hands folded over her flat stomach. She arched both eyebrows. "What do you think you're going to find here? Hallman and Jimmy Hoffa playing poker on some yacht in the Pacific?"

"More likely that Hallman has gone off the grid somewhere and some small fact will help us find him."

Flint ignored the sarcasm. "That's how it often works. A piece of information. Something that seems inconsequential. But it can hold the key to solving the case. You know that."

"Okay. We'll handle it. Let you know what we find."

Scarlett punched a button on a remote and a big-screen television came to life.

Two videos were cued up.

The left side was the Reno story on Hallman's plane crash that Flint had seen in Veronica Beaumont's office.

The right side was the final story on the kidnapping and murder of Mark Wilcox's wife.

"Notice anything similar about these two news stories, Flint?"

He said nothing. Of course he had noticed it. The second he'd learned that Wilcox owned the house that sat between the Cessna crash site and the Red Maple Lake Resort.

"Hallman disappeared a few weeks after Wilcox's wife." Scarlett pointed the laser to the date lines on each story.

"What do these two stories have in common? Several things." She tapped the laser pointer on her desk for emphasis.

"Timing. Wilcox." She gave him a pointed look. "You."

He nodded slowly.

"What do you make of that? Coincidence?" She shook her head. "Not a chance."

She put the pointer down, folded her hands on the desk again, and leaned forward. "Stop screwing around. Tell me what's really going on here."

He shrugged. "That's what I'm trying to find out."

"Let's say the original situation had nothing to do with you, but somehow concerned Wilcox. Making that assumption, seems to me there are three possible choices." She held up her index finger. "Hallman was a hit man. Somebody paid him. He killed the two passengers and Wilcox's wife. Then he disappeared with the cash."

"Possible. That story would answer a lot of open questions. A hit man could have created a false identity easily enough back then."

At the time, Flint had asked his inside contacts to find suspicious deaths that could have been assassinations, similar to Aludra Wilcox's murder.

Nothing had turned up, which made the theory unlikely.

But Hallman could be cleverer than most assassins.

Although nothing in Hallman's files suggested any particular expertise in execution techniques. His military service hadn't included deployments to countries where beheadings and honor killings were common.

"We could assume that Hallman was not involved with Wilcox at all." Scarlett held up a second finger. "Wrong place, wrong time, for Hallman and his friends. They saw something they shouldn't have out there and lost their lives for it. Which means that Hallman's body is most likely at the bottom of the lake. Or somewhere in that forest. All you have to do is find it."

"The place is remote. It's almost impossible to get in or out," Flint said. "Hallman's body would never be accidentally discovered if he died in the forest, or if he's in the lake. Searches have been restricted."

"Third option." Scarlett nodded and held up a third finger. "Hallman's crash was unlucky and his friends were killed by someone else, but he is somehow still alive and running from the killers. Probably living under an assumed identity and probably out of the country. It's damned near impossible for an average Joe to stay off the grid inside the US these days. Too little privacy. Too many ways he can be tripped up. But there are lots of places in the world with limited technology. He could be hiding in one of them."

This was the conclusion Flint had settled on. Not because he could prove it. But because he wanted Hallman to be alive. For Maddy.

“Got a favorite?”

“Of the three possibilities? They’re all good, but the third option is the least likely.”

“Agreed.” He grinned. “So I’ll take option number three. You rule out one and two.”

She scowled. “You still think you’re so damned smart, don’t you?”

“Maybe the guy is armed and dangerous, but I doubt it.” He shrugged.

Hallman’s short stint in the military included basic training, but he never saw action. Nothing turned up to suggest any serious combat training or covert ops or anything even remotely close to those skill levels.

Flint said, “If he got away and stayed below the radar all this time, we can assume he’s clever and resourceful. He’s got strong self-preservation skills. But he’s not a Mossad killing machine or anything like that.”

“You gonna tell me why we’re looking for this guy?”

“I will when I can. I promised the client confidentiality. It started out as a favor for a friend. But now that we suspect Mark Wilcox is involved in this thing, it feels like unfinished business. The guy hates me. Back then, I thought he’d get over it. And it’s been years. And I didn’t kill his wife. But he's not over it. Not even close." Flint paused and grinned again. "You know how I hate to leave loose ends. I need to find his wife's killer."

She wasn't amused. She cocked her head again and narrowed her eyes.

"Miles to go before I sleep. Drake's waiting for me outside." He stood and stretched. "How soon can you handle chasing down all of Hallman's contacts, including contacts for his two dead friends?"

"Not long." Her voice acquired a sharper edge. "What are you going to be doing while I'm handling your scut work?"

"Looking at the Wilcox case again."

She shook her head. “I don’t like it.”

“I’ll be fine, Mom. I promise,” he teased on his way out the door.

“Flint.” He turned at the threshold to hear the rest. “Maddy told me she asked you to find Jamie Beaumont’s father.”

He arched his eyebrows. “Is Maddy okay? She was too upset to talk when she called me.”

“She’s better, but her friend is really sick and she knows what that means. It’s not the sort of thing a kid simply gets over in a few hours.” Scarlett narrowed her eyes. “Is this missing guy, Josh Hallman, Jamie’s father?”

He took a deep breath and shrugged. “Veronica Beaumont says he is.”

"Let's say she's right," Scarlett said. "You think that barracuda hired you to find Hallman without knowing about your involvement in the old Wilcox case?"

He shrugged. "Wilcox's name never came up until I went out to the crash site. She never mentioned him. He didn't mention her."

"You know all these moguls hang out together. They belong to the same clubs, attend the charity balls and sporting events together, and all that crap. They talk."

"Meaning what?"

"You have a reputation in certain quarters as the best heir hunter in the world. You cultivate your rep to the point of being obnoxious about it.

But it's not like you're advertising on television." She paused. "You keep your skills quiet for good reasons. Your clients are referrals, usually unsolved cases from sophisticated investigators."

He knew what she was getting at. The situation felt like a setup to him now, too. But a setup by whom? And why?

"Somebody's feeding Beaumont information. And don't tell me she hired you because Maddy and Jamie are friends." Scarlett shook her head. "Veronica Beaumont isn't the kind of woman who makes life-and-death choices on the advice of a seven-year-old girl she barely knows. I don't like it. Something's off. There's more going on here."

She took a deep breath and dropped her voice a couple of octaves. “Watch yourself, Michael.”

“Yes, ma’am.” He grinned and lifted his hand to tip an imaginary hat to her before he strode through the building and outside to Drake’s limousine waiting at the curb.

Her point was well taken, though.

The Hallman case had become more complicated than a simple search for a missing bone marrow donor. He could have handled that in a single afternoon.

He agreed that Beaumont had used Maddy to get to him.

Scarlett was right, as she usually was.

But whoever was manipulating Beaumont had reasons for placing him in Mark Wilcox's path again.

Reasons that had nothing to do with Beaumont or her son or even her missing man.

There weren't that many people out there smart and resourceful enough to orchestrate the situation.

In fact, he could only think of one.

Chapter Twenty-Eight

Houston, Texas
Wednesday

Drake dropped him off at home. He showered to wash off the travel grime and dressed in black jeans, black turtleneck sweater, and black boots.

He found nothing edible in his refrigerator, which was fine. Houston wasn't a foodie haven, but there were places to eat along the way.

He grabbed his black leather jacket and his keys on the way out the back door.

He reached the hospital, parked in the visitor's lot, and made his way to Jamie Beaumont's room.Veronica Beaumont was there, by her son's bedside, as Flint had expected. She might be the wicked bitch of the west, as Scarlett insisted, but she loved her son. That much was obvious to any observer.

Jamie was sleeping. He looked even more frail than the first time Flint saw him at Daisy's Dairy Barn.

He knocked lightly on the doorframe.

Veronica looked up. She put a finger to her lips and stepped away from Jamie's bed, waving Flint into the corridor. She followed him out and pulled the door closed.

"Did you find Josh?"

Gone was the fashionable titan she'd been every other time he'd seen her. Her voice was raspy. Deep circles smudged under both eyes. She'd gnawed her lipstick off long ago. She looked exhausted.

"Not yet. We need to talk."

"I can't leave Jamie."

"We can do it here," Flint replied. "Who gave you my name?"

"What do you mean?" She blinked and shook her head as if she was confused by the question. "You know Maddy Scarlett told Jamie about you. After that, I did my research. I told you all of this before."

He watched her face carefully. “Tell me the truth this time. It’s important.”

She looked down at her shoes. He saw her shoulders rise and fall with deep breaths. He waited. When she looked up again, she pushed her lips around her teeth for a moment.

“Look, Veronica, here’s the thing. I’ll help you find Hallman. Maybe he’ll be the donor Jamie needs. I hope he will. But we’re running short on time. I’ve got to make some decisions here and I can’t do it blindfolded.” He ran a palm over his face. “You need to be straight with me. Last chance. Who gave you my name?”

“He told me not to tell you.” She closed her eyes for a moment.

"Of course he did. Tell me anyway."

She did the thing with her lips again, stalling. She narrowed her eyes and gazed into his face, searching for something that she didn't find. She shook her head.

Her reluctance told him more than a blurted answer would have.

She was afraid of the man.

Not many people had the capacity to frighten her. She was tough as nails and she did exactly as she pleased. He admired those qualities in a woman. Usually.

"Let's do it this way, then. I'll suggest a few names. You tell me if I get one right."

She cocked her head. He took that as consent.

He'd narrowed the options to one real possibility, but he didn't start there. She'd be more likely to tell him if he warmed her up first, so he began with a man her age.

In her orbit.

Financially, close to her equal, although he'd acquired his money the old-fashioned way—his daddy gave it to him—and she'd earned hers.

According to the gossip rags, it was a man she'd dated as recently as six months ago and might be dating still. "Jasper Crane."

Her eyes widened. “You’ve worked for Jasper? He never mentioned it.”

He’d never even met Jasper Crane and he’d certainly never worked for the man. He wouldn’t even consider it.

It was Crane’s father Flint had crossed. But he’d let her find that out on her own.

“Mark Wilcox.”

“Don’t know him and don’t want to.” She shook her head and trembled with something resembling revulsion. “Word is, he’s rich and famous, but jealous and controlling. Hot temper, too. A total asshole.”

Flint didn’t argue, although he wondered who’d supplied her with that assessment. “Boyd Wilcox.”

She shook her head again. “You do get around, don’t you?”

He’d never worked for Boyd Wilcox. Nor would he, given the way things had ended with his brother. “Sebastian Shaw.”

Her eyes widened involuntarily and her lips formed a little O before a frown crossed her face and she pursed her lips as if to hold her comments in check.

Flint nodded. Bingo. Exactly what he’d thought.

“What did Shaw tell you about me?”

She shook her head again. Whatever Shaw had said, the words had been strong enough to keep her quiet.

"Okay. I'll ask him myself."

She shrugged, and her usual defiance was back.

He'd confirmed that neither Jasper Crane nor Mark Wilcox had sent her his way. Baz Shaw was another matter.

Shaw was one of the wealthiest oil tycoons in Texas and a client of Scarlett Investigations. Flint had been coerced into handling an heir hunt for him. It had ended in disaster and he'd vowed never to work with the man again.

He'd found Shaw to be every inch the ambitious, wealthy, manipulative, controlling snake his reputation claimed. Veronica Beaumont was smart to be wary of him.

Shaw had pushed Beaumont to hire Flint for his own reasons. Which probably had nothing to do with Veronica or Josh Hallman.

Shaw played a long game. Whatever his motives were, they could wait.

Flint moved on to his second goal. "I've been out to Red Maple Lake. Boyd Wilcox owns acreage and a house there. Near the site of Hallman's plane crash. Did you know that?"

She nodded. "It came up when I hired an investigator to find Josh a while back. Why? Is that relevant?"

"Probably. Wilcox hasn't been in touch with you?"

"As I said, I've never met the man. Or his brother."

"I found three men out there with Mark Wilcox yesterday. They might have been the ones who came to your home looking for Josh."

He pulled his phone out of his jeans and found the headshots he'd looked up online.

Ruben Vega from an old company profile.

Kevin Hayes from his medical practice.

The pilot, Larry Cole, from the California DMV.

He showed Cole first. "Is this the man?"

"No." She didn't even have to think about it.

He showed her Hayes next. "Is this the man?"

She took the phone and looked carefully at the photo. She enlarged it and cocked her head for a slightly different view. "He could have been the one behind the wheel of the SUV. I'm not sure. I didn't get a good look at him and it was a long time ago."

He took the phone back and showed her the photo of Ruben Vega. "What about this guy?"

Almost instantly, she said, "Yes. That's him."

Her voice quivered. She handed the phone back. "I'll never forget his face. Never."

"Okay." He slipped the phone back into his pocket. "Maddy's upset about Jamie. How's he doing?"

She looked away. When she returned her gaze to his face, her eyes were glassy with unshed tears.

"The doctors say he could be cured completely if we can find a donor." She paused and wiped one of the tears away. "If you find Josh, please make him understand that he could cure Jamie. The whole thing can be done anonymously. He doesn't need to meet Jamie or ever see us again afterward. We certainly don't need his money, if that's an issue. We'll leave him alone."

"You never explained why Hallman has never met Jamie." Flint frowned.

"Jamie's a good kid. Maddy likes him. That makes him worthy, in my book. Why wouldn't Hallman want to meet him?"

"It's complicated. Josh doesn't know Jamie exists. Let's leave it at that." She looked down at her feet and swiped her palms down the sides of her pants. She cleared her throat before she looked up again. "Show Josh that video of Jamie that I gave you. He'll see how special Jamie is. Just tell him it's **really** important and I wouldn't ask if we had any other options, okay?"

"I will. Sure. But—"

She cleared her throat again and pushed Jamie's door open with her hip. "I've got to go."

"Okay. But I'm going to need extra expense money to find Hallman."

She pulled her phone out of her pocket, and after a few clicks she said, "Done. Keep me posted."

She slipped inside and the door closed behind her. A moment later, it opened again and a nurse stepped out.

Flint walked a few feet along the corridor with the nurse. "How's Jamie doing?"

"Not good, I'm afraid. If we don't find a donor soon . . ." Her voice drifted off.

"Can you check me? To see if I can be a donor?" Flint had donated blood before. He'd never registered to be a bone marrow donor, but better late than never.

“Not here, but you can do it on the fourth floor. It’s a simple cheek swab to start.” One of her colleagues called to her and she gestured that she’d come along in a moment. “Are you a blood relative?”

He shook his head. “I’m not. But I could still be a match, right?”

“Yes, you could. There’s a lot of variation in tissue types, which means we can’t predict whether or not you’ll be a match until we do the testing.”

“I understand.”

Her colleague called again, urgently this time. She pointed behind him.

"Take the elevator. Fourth floor. Follow the signs. They'll explain everything." She hurried away toward the nurse's station.

He took the elevator. When the doors opened on the fourth floor, Jasper Crane was waiting to board.

He was as smarmy looking in person as he was in photos. But the resemblance to his father was like looking at Felix Crane through a time machine.

Flint remained inside the elevator car. Crane stepped in and pushed the button for Jamie Beaumont's floor. Like hospital elevators everywhere, this one was slow to move. The doors closed about a decade later and the car began its glacial descent.

When the car reached the space between floors, Flint hit the emergency stop button with the flat of his hand. The car lurched to a bouncing halt.

Crane glared at Flint. “What the hell are you doing?”

“Jasper Crane, right? We’ve never met.” He cocked his head. “Michael Flint. I knew your father.”

“I know who you are.” Crane’s eyes narrowed.

A dark cloud covered Crane’s features. If he’d been a different sort of man, he might have started a fight. Too bad he didn’t.

As it was, he glared and demanded, “What do you want?”

Flint stayed ready, just in case. “I heard about your dad. I’m sorry for your loss.”

Jasper barely blinked. “When they pulled him out of ten feet of snow under that avalanche in the spring, he had two bullet holes in him. Best guess is that you put them there.”

Flint controlled the shudder that ran through his body from head to foot.

He’d been buried in that avalanche, too. Only luck, and his avalanche beacon and Recco transponder nestled in a special pocket of his snowsuit, brought rescuers to him soon enough to keep him alive.

Rescuers searched for Crane well into the night, long past the time when he might have been saved alive. They found his body only after the snow melted, months later.

“Let’s discuss this outside.” Flint reached over and pushed the alarm button again to restart the car’s downward movement.

Crane squared his shoulders and shoved his chin forward. “I have nothing to say to you.”

“I saw the autopsy report. He died of suffocation, not gunshot wounds.” Flint’s words were measured.

“Tells me what kind of man you are. You shot him in the back. Twice. Otherwise, he might have made it out. Like you did.” Crane’s fists clenched at his sides.

Flint braced his weight over both feet, just in case Crane had a change of heart about starting a fight.

Crane punched the second-floor button with the side of his fist instead. When the door opened, he stalked out.

Flint watched him march down the corridor to Jamie Beaumont's room and push the door open so hard that it bounced against the wall and came back to slap him in the face.

Under different circumstances, Flint might have laughed. As it was, he figured Crane had a right to be pissed.

There would be a better time and place to deal with Jasper Crane.

When his search for Josh Hallman was over. Crane could wait. Jamie Beaumont could not.

Flint went back up to the fourth floor and found the testing center. He filled out the forms and left the cheek swab.

Thirty minutes later, he was on his way.

He fished his phone out of his pocket and made the first of several phone calls.

The plan was more than a little crazy, but it could work.

At least it had the virtue of never having been tried.

Chapter Twenty-Nine

Red Maple Lake, California
Six Years Ago

Josh shivered with cold and shock throughout the night. He had no food, no water, and no weapon of any kind. He'd become disoriented. He didn't know how far he'd run through the woods or even if he'd succeeded in traveling southwest. He huddled into himself as much as possible and tried to stay invisible and warm. He failed at both.

Several times during the long, dark night he was awakened by sounds from the forest. Each time he was startled into consciousness, he listened hard for hunters. If they found him, they would kill him. He was sure of that. As soon as daylight made it safe to move, he would go.

Exhaustion overtook him and he fell deep into oblivion for several hours. His eyes fluttered open when he heard something larger than a bird crackling through the undergrowth nearby. He didn't know whether to stay or run again, so he waited until he could identify the threat.

The first thing he noticed was the smell. The overwhelmingly disgusting odor of a large animal that had probably never bathed in its life. He remained motionless, and prayed the smell was not announcing the approach of a bear. After five minutes, or perhaps ten, he spied three deer rooting through the decaying underbrush for food. Relief washed over him like the warm Hawaiian waterfalls he'd enjoyed in Maui. And then he smiled when he realized he probably smelled no better than the deer, and maybe worse.

"Okay, Josh. Use your head." When the deer heard him talking, they flipped up their tails and bounded away, which was fine with him.

With the morning light and the gnawing hunger in his stomach came a bit of clarity and logic. There was a driveway on Wilcox's compound, leading to the house. There must have been some kind of a two track or fire trail or something at the end of the driveway. The two-track must've led somewhere. Eventually, there must be a road.

"Find a road, you can hitchhike. You can get out of this. All you have to do is be smart about it."

Of course, Ruben and Mark had access to the off-road vehicle Boyd had mentioned. Josh had not seen nor heard a motor vehicle since he ran from the compound. But he should be able to hear one approach in the woods. He listened carefully, but the only sounds that reached him were leaves blown by the sturdy wind.

He could continue walking west. Eventually, he'd reach the Pacific Ocean. Miles and miles away. But it was there. He should find some sort of road where maybe he could flag down a truck or a car. As long as he moved south and west, he'd be putting distance between himself and Wilcox's compound. Without a cell phone emitting a constant tracking beacon, he might get away. Possibly.

He pushed his wobbly legs into a standing position and steadied himself, emptied his bladder, and headed away from what he could see of the rising sun. His progress was glacial. He walked a jagged path because of trees and undergrowth and holes in the ground. He looked back a few times and couldn't see his own boot prints. Which he hoped meant no one else could see them, either.

He slept another night in the woods. By this time, his gnawing hunger had become a constant companion. He ignored the pain because he had no food and no way to get any. No point in focusing on juicy steaks and bulky potatoes.

On the third day, late in the afternoon, he saw the first signs of civilization. In the distance, he noticed smoke from a chimney. Then a second chimney, followed by a third. When he saw a truck driving past, he almost wept.

A road. He'd found a road.

He stayed in the woods behind the village, moving parallel to the two-lane highway. It was too dangerous to approach the homes. This could be the closest town to the Wilcox compound, and if it was, Wilcox's men would be looking for him here.

He snuck around through the backyards and maneuvered outside visual range until he was south of the cluster of buildings. He continued walking in the woods, within sight of the road, until he reached an area where he thought it might be safe to try hitchhiking. A few vehicles had passed. Not many. But it was afternoon again and soon it would be dark. He'd never get a ride after dark. Now was the time.

The village was far in the distance behind him. He had to take the chance that he might be seen and returned to the Wilcoxes.

For the first time since he'd run from Ruben's gun, he left the cover of the dense woods and made his way to the road. He glanced around him, staying aware of his surroundings, but he saw no one.

He crossed the road to the southbound shoulder and, hunched into his jacket, continued walking. He could hear the traffic before the vehicles approached. So far, every vehicle had been traveling northbound, and there was no way he was heading back toward Red Maple Lake. Not on a bet.

Eventually, a farm truck came by, traveling south. Josh turned and held out his right thumb in the classic hitchhiker's gesture. The truck slowed and pulled up next to

Josh. The old man said, "Hop in the back. Save you a few miles of shoe leather."

"Thank you," Josh croaked from his dry throat. He put his foot on the bumper and tossed his left leg over the tailgate and settled into the back of the truck. He slumped onto the cold metal bed and relaxed his back against the side wall. He'd give about anything for a cup of hot coffee or even a bottle of water at this point. The old guy didn't offer him any. For now, Josh was simply beyond grateful for the ride.

The farm truck traveled south about fifteen miles until it approached an intersection and slowed to turn west. The sun had long ago settled low in the horizon, but it wasn't quite dark. The old man pulled over to the shoulder and slid the back window open.

“You got anywhere to stay tonight?” he asked. His voice was dry and gravelly, but he seemed safe enough. Josh shook his head. “You running from the law? I don’t want no trouble with the law.”

“No, sir, I’m not.” Josh shook his head more firmly this time. Quite the opposite. If he saw an actual lawman, he might embrace him instead.

The old man nodded, seemed to decide something. “I’ll give you some supper and you can sleep in my barn tonight if you don’t have anywhere else to go.”

Tears sprouted in the corners of Josh's eyes. Pressure. Stress. Pure fright leaked out with the saline that streaked through the grime on his face. He nodded. "I'd be very grateful."

The old man said, "It's settled then." He pushed the window closed and returned to his driving. About five more miles down the road, he pulled into a long driveway that led farther south. Josh figured he was still going in the right direction, and anyway, what alternative did he have? Every mile the truck covered was a mile he didn't have to walk.

Chapter Thirty

Younge Farm, California
Six Years Ago

When they reached the barn, the old man parked the truck. He showed Josh to a room in the barn with a bed, a sink, and a toilet. He told Josh to wash up and come to the house for a bite of dinner.

As soon as the old man left, Josh did the best he could to wash up at the sink. He stuck his entire head under the running water and let the pungent odors of sweat, blood, and tears wash away. He must've looked pretty scary out there on the road. He wondered briefly what kind of person would actually stop for him, but he shrugged. The old man couldn't be any worse than the people he was running from.

All he had to do now was find a way to get home. He had his wallet. As soon as he could find a place to use his credit cards, he would rent a car and find an airport and take a commercial flight back to Chicago.

Josh did the best he could to knock the grime off his clothes, but that was a losing battle. Then he followed the old man's footpath to the back of the house. He knocked on the screen and went inside, led by the heavenly scents of coffee and fried food.

Fried bologna, fried potatoes, plain white bread, black coffee. Josh's stomach was queasy but hunger won out. He ate like a famished bear.

Like this was the best meal he'd ever eaten. He tried not to shovel in more than his share of the food, but the old man ate very little and didn't seem to mind Josh's appetite.

They talked a bit across the table.

The old man's name was Sam Younge. He'd inherited the ranch from his father and lived alone here since his wife died. He had a few head of cattle, a few pigs, and some chickens. "My wife used to have a little vegetable garden, but I don't bother with that anymore."

Josh told him he had been dropped off in the woods by a tour company for a two-week wilderness survival trip. He said he'd lost all his equipment somehow and needed to figure out how to get home. He said he lived in Denver. The story wasn't so far from the truth, and the old man seemed to accept it.

"I'm afraid I'm not going to be able to help you much. I don't have a telephone or any kind of computer equipment out here. We do have a television. Gets broadcast signals when the weather cooperates. No cable or internet or nothing like that."

Sam poured more coffee. Josh sat back in the straight chair and crossed his ankles. He was starting to feel almost human although he shuddered to think how he must look.

“You want to wash those clothes? Be dry in a couple hours. You could wear mine while you’re waiting.” Sam was shorter and wider than Josh. But clean clothes sounded like a luxury beyond his wildest dreams right at the moment. Sam looked him over. “Maybe you want to get a shower and shave, too.”

Josh closed his eyes to keep them from leaking again. “That would be great, Sam.”

The old man showed him to the laundry and the shower. He handed Josh a disposable razor, a pair of old work jeans, and a scratchy old T-shirt.

Sam went back to the kitchen while Josh peeled off his dirty cargo pants, shirt, and everything else down to his bare skin. He set up the washer and got it going and then slipped across the hallway and into Sam's shower.

He stayed under the hot spray until he drained the tank and the water ran cool. When he stepped out and dried off, he felt as close to normal as he had since the Cessna crashed.

He rummaged in Sam's medicine chest and found a stick deodorant and swiped it under his arms. Sam's old T-shirt was okay, but the jeans hit him midcalf. They were stiff and scratchy denim, but they were clean.

Josh went back into the kitchen. Sam was washing the dishes. Josh pitched in to help.

Sam said, "I generally watch the nightly news. You interested in that?"

"I like to know what's going on in the world."

Sam moved to the refrigerator's freezer and stuck his head inside.

"I got ice cream for dessert. Vanilla. You want some?"

"Sounds great."

After Sam dished out the ice cream and handed a bowl to Josh, he led the way to the living room. The space was a bit old-fashioned, but clean and tidy. Probably the decorating had been done by Sam's wife.

A flat-screen TV took up most of one wall. Across from it, two floral-print upholstered chairs were positioned for perfect viewing.

Sam took one chair and waved Josh to the other. Sam picked up the remote and found the broadcast news station he wanted.

It was Monday night. Josh was startled to realize how long he'd been running and how many days had passed since he'd left Chicago.

The local news came from Reno. After a few national and local stories, a reporter who would never make it in a top-fifteen market mentioned that a small floatplane was thought to have crashed in Red Maple Lake four days ago. He showed video from a drone of the area where they believed the plane went into the lake. Divers were in the water.

The reporter said there had been three men aboard, but neither the plane nor the bodies had been recovered. He said divers would continue looking, but reminded viewers that bodies should eventually float to the surface. He ended with a plea for information and a phone number for a tip line.

“Do you know where that place is?” Josh asked Sam.

“North of here. South of Lake Tahoe. Hard place to get to. Never been there.”

Josh watched as the short news story unfolded. And then Boyd Wilcox’s face filled the screen. An off-camera reporter held a microphone and asked Wilcox questions. He claimed not to know much. He said he didn't know about the plane crash and he had not seen the three men. And then he said, "Red Maple Lake is deep and cold. If those guys went down in the plane, you might never find them."

Josh asked Sam, "Is that possible? That they might never find those guys? I mean, isn't that an inland lake? They'll find them eventually, right?"

Sam shrugged. "Hard to say. There's all kinds of folklore about people going into those lakes up there and never coming out again. A few years ago they found a guy who had drowned about sixteen years earlier. But, yeah. If they keep looking, it's likely they'll find the bodies eventually. Might take a while, though."

Josh said, "I don't understand that. Don't they have equipment that can just search the bottom?"

"Usually, the bodies float up after a while. They don't have to go looking for them very often. But I guess it's not as easy as you say. Otherwise, they'd have already found those guys, right?"

Josh had not considered the possibility that Dan and Skip would not be found. If they weren't, it would be because the Wilcoxes did something with them. Something like what Wilcox had done to that woman.

And if that had happened, then the Wilcoxes would be looking for him, too.

Briefly, he considered calling the authorities and telling his story. Could he be protected? Ruben had been very clear when Josh was trying to get away. The promises were stamped in Josh's memory.

"You know who we are. You know we have limitless resources. Go ahead and run if you want. We will find you, Josh. I will find you. I will kill you. Just like Dan and Skip. You will never be safe. Never. You can count on that."

Was it true? Could Ruben find him anywhere, everywhere? Because if Ruben found him, Josh was certain Ruben would kill him.

He realized Sam was looking at him strangely. “Are you in some kind of trouble, son?”

Yes, he was. He was in serious trouble. But it wasn’t the kind of trouble Sam could help with. So he replied, “Other than being out in the middle of nowhere with no car and no way to get back home, you mean?”

Sam said, “I can help you with that. Tomorrow, I can give you a ride to the bus station. You can take the bus until you reach a city. Catch a plane home.”

Josh nodded. A ride to the bus station. And where would he go? How far would he have to go to escape Ruben’s reach?

"That would be great, Sam. I'd be happy to pay you. I have a little bit of cash on me."

Sam shook his head. "I don't need nothing. You don't owe me nothing. We'll head out tomorrow morning after breakfast. How's that?"

Josh nodded. "That'll be just fine. Thank you." Sam found an old John Wayne Western on TV and they watched it while Josh's clothes finished in the washer. He moved them over to the dryer, and once they were done and the movie was over, he went back to the barn.

He lay awake on his bunk for longer than he'd expected. He was thinking about where he would go and how he would get there. Not back to Chicago. That much was certain. Ruben would easily find him there.

No, he'd go somewhere else. He'd become someone else. And he'd spend the rest of his life looking over his shoulder. But at least he'd be alive.

Chapter Thirty-One

Younge Farm, California
Thursday

The next morning, Flint met Drake at the airstrip and they flew back to Red Maple Lake. The closest town to Red Maple Lake Resort was Layton. Tahoe was in the opposite direction.

Flint figured Hallman wouldn't have run to Tahoe. Too easy to find him there. Of course, if he wasn't running from anything, then Tahoe would be the logical choice. Somehow it didn't feel right to Flint, though.

Drake flew over the two-lane highway again. This time, Flint identified a few houses and a couple of storefronts clustered together a couple of miles north of the Wilcox place. Hallman could have stopped in there. But if he was running away, he'd have steered clear of people likely to know about the Wilcoxes and about the crash. Homes closer to the crash site were more likely to know about it.

Flint sent Scarlett an encrypted message asking her to find contact information for those homeowners and everyone who lived there. He also asked for a list of residents six years ago. They'd go there next.

Drake circled the farm they'd seen on their last flyover. He set the Pilatus down easily on the long drive and taxied closer to the house. The old truck he'd seen on the road two days ago was still parked in the side drive. By the time Drake shut the Pilatus down, Flint had pulled off his headset, lowered the stairs, and climbed to the ground.

An old man came out of the side door. He watched as Flint walked toward him. He was medium height and reed thin and wore an old-fashioned ribbed tank-style T-shirt.

He approached the man directly, right hand extended. "I'm Michael Flint. I'm sorry to bother you."

The old guy shook hands. "Sam Younge. Nice plane. You lost?" He shoved both hands into the back pockets of worn work jeans that had probably served him for a couple of decades.

Flint grinned. “No, we’re not lost.”

“Nothing out here except me, and I don’t know you, do I?” He had a wooden toothpick held between his teeth and it bobbed when he talked.

“I’m looking for a guy. I thought you might be able to help me find him. It’s important, or I wouldn’t be here.” Flint fished a card from his pocket and handed it to Younge. He squinted to read the large black print.

“Not many folks wander out this way,” Younge shrugged, stashing the card in his jeans.

“He’s been missing for more than six years. His plane crashed over in Red Maple Lake. I thought maybe he’d found his way here, looking for a ride or something.” Flint paused, removed his sunglasses, and focused an earnest look on Younge. “His family has hired me to find him. They’ve already tried everything else. He could have been hurt. Hit his head or something. Maybe lost his memory. They aren’t sure.” Younge squinted in the sunlight. He chewed the toothpick. Thinking things through, maybe. “Red Maple Lake is a long way from here. Hard to walk that far, especially with any kind of injury.”

Flint nodded. “We’re not sure whether he was walking or might have hitched a ride. Anything at all you could offer could be helpful.”

He stared at Flint for a few seconds before he said, “We can talk inside.” He turned and limped toward the house, favoring his left knee.

Flint followed the old man into the house. “You live here alone?” The kitchen table was set for one. He’d finished his meal moments before.

“Since my wife died. Coffee?” Younge picked up his mug and walked to the pot.

“That would be great. Black,” Flint replied. Younge poured the coffee and handed a full mug to Flint. He sat at the table and waved Flint to a chair.

“I remember when that plane went down. It was all over the news for days. And when they pulled out the bodies years later, it was heart-wrenching.” He shook his head and blinked away tears. He drank the coffee to conceal his sentimentality.

"I guess when a man gets to be my age, people think we've seen everything and we're pretty jaded. But that young man's wife, the pregnant one? I felt sorry for her."

"Of course." Flint nodded. "They never found the pilot's body. He could be down there in the lake, too, I guess. But his family hopes he escaped whoever killed his friends."

Younge's eyes widened. "His friends were killed?"

"Murdered," Flint said. "One had two gunshot wounds in his body. Autopsy says the gunshots were the cause of death. It's pretty clear the guy didn't shoot himself in the back."

"You think the pilot killed him?"

Flint shrugged. “Hard to say. But it doesn’t make a lot of sense that Hallman would have flown the guy all the way out here to shoot him.”

“That was his name? The pilot?”

Flint nodded. “Josh Hallman.”

Younge studied his coffee like a gypsy studied tea leaves, as if he might find the answer somewhere in the black liquid.

“I’m not the law, Sam. I’m a private investigator.” Flint lowered his voice. The old man was sentimental. He’d be moved by the facts, maybe. “I’m looking for Hallman because his son needs a bone marrow transplant.”

Younge looked up. “He had a son?”

"Good kid, too." Flint nodded, pulled out his phone, and found the video of Jamie. He passed it across to Younge, who stared intently at the images. "The boy's mother thinks Josh could be a suitable donor."

Younge kept looking at the video. "Is that true? Could he save the boy's life?"

"I won't lie to you. It's a long shot. But Hallman's his father. He has a better chance. I need to find him and do it soon." Flint leaned closer and spoke earnestly. "If you know anything at all, it could really help his son. Everything I've learned about Hallman says he'd want to help the boy, if he knew."

Younge stood and paced the room, obviously agitated. After he'd done a few laps, Flint said, "Look, Sam, I'm running out of time here. If you know something, now's the time to say it."

Younge nodded. He leaned his back against the sink and folded his arms over his scrawny chest. "I was driving home. It was late in the day. I saw him staggering along the road, his thumb held out, kind of half-heartedly. Like he didn't expect anybody to stop, you know?"

"So you picked him up."

Younge shrugged. "He seemed harmless enough. I've done some hitching in my day. It's hard. Thought maybe I could help."

"You brought him back here?" Younge nodded. "How long did he stay?"

"Couple of days. I took him to the bus station in Layton, few miles south, and dropped him off."

"Where was he going?"

"He didn't say. I figured he'd head back to Denver. That's where he lived."

Hallman had lived in Chicago. So he'd lied to the old man about that much. Flint figured he'd lied about heading to Denver, too, but he'd ask Scarlett's team to follow up, just in case. "And you never heard from him again?"

"I did, actually. A few months later, he sent me some cash. Repaid what I gave him for the bus ticket."

"Do you still have the envelope?"

Younge shook his head. "That was years back."

"Any return address?"

Younge shook his head again and scrunched up his face, as if he was visualizing something that happened a long time ago. "But the stamps were interesting. Lots of them. Colorful. And the postmarks. Quite a few of those. The envelope had traveled a long way. Pretty beat up, but the cash was all there."

"Did he include a note?"

"Yeah. Short one. It said thanks for the loan. That's all." He shrugged. "Sorry, but I threw it away, too."

"How long had Hallman been out there on the road when you picked him up?"

"Maybe a few days, from the look of him."

"Did he tell you anything about what had happened?"

"I didn't know for sure about the plane crash at that point. The plane hadn't been found and the men hadn't been reported missing.

Josh was already gone before all of that came to light."

"You didn't call the police? Later? Once you knew what had happened?" Younge wiped his face with both palms. He cleared his throat. "Look, I didn't know what happened. I still don't. At that point, I thought Josh had gone back home. Later, when they pulled up the bodies and started talking about him being missing . . ." He shrugged. "I don't know what I was thinking. Except I guess I had a feeling that Josh could be in trouble and I didn't want to add to that. He seemed like a decent guy to me."

Flint didn't buy that part of the story. Younge was a cantankerous old man. He didn't tell anyone about Josh Hallman for a better reason than sentiment.

At least he'd confirmed that Hallman had made it out alive. He'd sent money through the mail a while later, which meant he'd been alive at that point, too. But why didn't he collect that $50,000 from his bank account? That much money would go a long way in many countries. There was only one reason Flint could think of. He was afraid to make the withdrawal. Afraid someone was watching.

Younge said the envelope Hallman sent had come from someplace far away, where they used brightly colored stamps. Flint had found other people with less information than that. This thing might be looking up. "You know anybody living in that village up the road?"

"Geraldine?" Younge shook his head. "Josh didn't stop off there."

"How do you know?"

"Because if he had, he would have told me. And if he'd stopped there, wouldn't he have stayed instead of walking on down the road? He was dog tired. Barely putting one foot in front of the other. He looked like he'd been chased by the hounds of hell, you know?" Younge shrugged. "Nice people up in Geraldine. Somebody would have taken him in for the night. Given him a meal. When I found him, he hadn't eaten in days. No. He didn't go there."

Flint nodded. Made sense. And would save him some time. But he'd have Scarlett's team check with the residents of Geraldine anyway.

"I've got to get going, Sam. You've been helpful. Thank you." He pulled out another card and wrote his satellite phone number on the back. "If you think of anything else, call me, okay?"

Younge looked at the floor for a few seconds. When he looked up, he was frowning. "People came looking for Josh before. Right after they pulled the bodies out of the lake."

"What kind of people? Police?"

"Two men. One stayed out in the SUV. Expensive one. I never saw one like it before. The other guy came to the door." Younge shook his head. "He asked me if Josh had been here and I said no. I didn't like the guy. Mean-looking SOB."

Flint pulled out his phone. He found the photo of Ruben Vega and held it out. “Was this the guy?”

He squinted at the photo. “Yeah. That’s him.” He handed the phone back. Flint showed him the photo of Kevin Hayes and Younge squinted, nodded, and returned the phone. “He was the one driving.

How did you know about them?”

“They threatened the boy’s mother. What did they say to you?”

“They said they were looking for Josh, and they told me some crap about him being dangerous and to watch out for him.” Younge cleared his throat and his voice was much stronger. “I knew that was a lie. Hell, he’d stayed overnight. Slept in my barn. Ate my dinner. He washed his clothes here. I'd talked to him a lot. He wasn't the least bit dangerous. I told them nothing. They never came back. Good thing, too. I'm pretty handy with a shotgun."

"I'll bet you are." Flint grinned. Younge had to be ninety-five years old, at least. But he looked like he could shoot pretty straight. "I've got to go. Please call me if you remember anything else that might help Jamie."

"Not likely to happen," Younge said. "Josh wasn't here that long and it was too many years ago. And he didn't tell me about the boy when he was here. Must have been a good reason why he didn't mention his son. Do you know?"

It was a valid point, but Flint declined to engage the old man. He shrugged. "Maybe he was just exhausted, like you said."

"Maybe." The old man's tone was doubtful. "I'll call if I think of anything. I hope the boy's gonna be okay."

They shook hands again and Flint hustled out to the Pilatus.

Drake said, "Now what?"

"Great question. Wish I had a great answer." He strapped into the copilot's seat. "There's a bus station about twenty miles southwest of here. Let's start there."

Chapter Thirty-Two

Layton, California
Thursday

Layton, California, was an old mining town that time had forgotten. From the air, Flint saw a central business district with half a dozen buildings. A few rows of wood-framed homes clustered behind the main road. Not many vehicles parked on the streets, mostly pickup trucks and SUVs. On the east side, Drake found a patch of grassy field where the Pilatus could land.

"You stay here," Flint said from the co-pilot's seat when they hit the ground. He removed his headset. "I won't be long. Thirty minutes, tops."

He opened the door and pushed the steps down and deplaned. He jogged to the south end of town, where the quick internet search he'd done from the plane had located the bus station.

The building was at the end of a row of storefronts on the south end of the street. A driveway on the side was for loading and unloading the bus as it came through. From the looks of the setup, they never had more than one bus at a time. There was no bus around now. Only two vehicles parked in the lot, a faded red sedan and a shiny black SUV.

The bus station looked like it had been built in the 1920s. Flint pulled the glass door open and stepped inside the dim interior. The furnishings were the same vintage as the building. There were eight wooden pews lining the walls and two back-to-back in the center of the open room. On one end was a ticket booth with a woman sitting on a stool behind the glass window.

A schedule was posted on a letter board next to the ticket window, and a map was plastered to the wall next to the letter board. The letter board was an old-fashioned contraption that could be changed manually, but this one didn't seem to have been changed lately. Even the letters were dusty.

The letter board proclaimed arrivals and departures. There were two of each posted. The bus arrived on Tuesday and Friday at 1:00 p.m. It departed on Tuesday and Friday at 4:00 p.m. There was only one destination listed: Stockton, California.

Flint and the ticket agent were the only two inside. He approached the window and waited. The frumpy woman seated behind the counter pulled her attention from her tattered paperback and looked up.

“No bus today,” she said. “Come back tomorrow.”

Which answered his first question. The letter board schedule was accurate.

“So you only have one bus every three days, then?” He smiled, friendly like.

“That’s right. To and from Stockton twice a week. You can catch a bus or rent a car from there, if you need to.”

“I guess I thought you’d have more options.”

She shook her head. “Sorry. Only one bus to Stockton since Methuselah was a pup. Twice a week. There and back. That’s it.”

“I see.” When he didn’t say anything else immediately, she returned to her paperback. “How long have you been the station agent here?”

“All my life,” she said, without looking up again. Must have been an exciting book.

"I'm trying to find a friend of mine. I think he came through here a while back."

"How long ago?"

"Six years, I think."

"He'd have gone on to Stockton, then, and changed there." Her eyes kept scanning her book, left to right. She flipped a page.

"Do you take passenger names when you sell the tickets? Keep any records?"

"If they pay with a credit card, I guess the bank would have a record. Cash or check, we give them the ticket and they ride the bus." She looked up. Her eyes narrowed. "That your SUV outside or do you need a ticket?"

"I don't need a ticket, thanks."

She nodded and returned to her book. He left the ticket window and moved to study the route map on the wall next to the letter board. The map was stained where travelers had run their fingers over the lines, checking their routes and destinations. The line representing the road from Layton to Stockton was marked by more black grime than the others.

Stockton was located near Interstate 5, which ran north and south along the western United States. Hallman could have hitchhiked along I-5 from there. Not a bad choice, given his circumstances.

From Stockton, Hallman could have traveled I-5 to Canada or Mexico. He might have made his way to a US airport, but even six years ago, air travel required government-issued ID. Plane travel would have left a paper trail, too. But no such paper trail existed for Hallman.

Flint studied the map, checking the places Hallman might have disappeared to and how he might have managed to slip off the grid. From Stockton, he could have traveled into Central and South America. Or he could have reached the Pacific and crossed. “It’s a big world out there. Lots of places to hide.”

“It certainly is,” the ticket agent said. Her voice startled him. He hadn’t realized he’d voiced his thoughts aloud. Or that she’d been listening.

He smiled, bowed his head, and turned to leave. The black SUV was still in the lot. He'd assumed the vehicle belonged to an employee at the bus station. But the ticket agent would have known that. She wouldn't have asked if he owned it.

He walked over to the back of the SUV and snapped a quick photo of the California license plate. Not likely to be related to him. But he sent the photo to Scarlett with a text asking her to trace it, just in case.

He walked the length of the main street, to get a feel for the place, wondering how Hallman had spent his time here. He wasn't still here, for sure. Layton wasn't the kind of place anyone would go to hide from the world. For one thing, a newcomer would stick out like a red rose on a snowy grave.

Flint made his way back to the Pilatus. Drake was ready to go. "San Diego next?"

"Works for me," Flint replied. "But let's fly over Stockton. That's the origin and destination for the bus."

"Works for me," Drake echoed, cheekily. "Looks like about an hour and a half to San Diego, assuming all goes well over LA."

Flint grinned. "When does that ever happen?"

He moved into the back of the plane, found his laptop, and went to work.

Chapter Thirty-Three

San Diego, California
Thursday

San Diego's waterfront glistened in the sunlight. From the cockpit of the Pilatus, Flint could see across San Diego Bay to Coronado Island, which was as impressive as ever. The ribbon of I-5 stretched up the California coast for miles on its way to Canada and beyond. Tijuana, Mexico, in Baja, was an hour straight down the I-5 in the opposite direction.

Had he chosen to go north, Hallman would likely still be living in Canada. Leaving Canada would have required connections that he simply didn't have. But from Baja, Hallman could have traveled anywhere in the world, and probably did.

Where are you now?

Flint could find Hallman by tracing all the possible options, but that was a tedious process. Heir hunting the old-fashioned way was grunt work and burned through a lot of shoe leather. Nothing but trial and error. Hide and seek.

A simple matter of chasing down all the possible leads until he found the missing man. He'd done the job many times before and he'd do it many times again.

There was no magic to it.

He was successful for one reason only: he knew what to look for and he never gave up, even when everyone else did.

But for Jamie Beaumont, time was running out. He couldn't wait long enough for Flint to exhaust all the options. Jamie needed to find his father now, not two years from now.

"So what are we going to do about all of this?" Drake asked when they were about halfway to San Diego.

"Let's hash it out."

They discussed Flint's plan for the rest of the flight. There were some holes in it, but every operation carried risk. For this one, the risks of failure were high, but the potential success was worth the effort.

The plan Flint concocted was simple, but not easy. Still, it should work. And that was the only thing that mattered.

He'd use his connections, Drake's expertise, and Veronica Beaumont's money to gather what he needed and set the trap.

Once everything was in place, he'd begin with the weakest link.

When they landed, Flint left Drake to finish up preparations at the airstrip and called a taxi.

Dr. Kevin Hayes's office was located in a medical building he shared with several renowned pediatricians near the University of California Medical

Center, not far from Old Town. Flint had called ahead to confirm his office hours today.

The taxi dropped him off at the front entrance of a three-story building set back from the street and surrounded by a dedicated parking lot. An eight-foot chain-link fence surrounded the perimeter of the property, presumably to keep wayward children from running into the street.

He expected Hayes to behave professionally around his patients, employees, and colleagues. But Hayes would also be constrained by the large parking lot and the fence, which could be helpful if he didn't live up to Flint's expectations.

Flint paid the taxi driver in cash and moved to the front of the building. The doors opened automatically, to avoid germ transfer from the hands of dozens of sick kids every day.

A large oval reception pavilion filled the space inside. The center of the pavilion opened to reveal a spacious waiting room full of noisy children and frazzled adults. A pleasant-looking middle-aged woman worked at a keyboard facing the entrance doors. Two more women were seated behind her inside the oval, facing the interior reception area.

Flint turned left to walk around the desk. He didn't get far before the woman looked up. “May I help you?”

He flashed a megawatt smile in her direction and kept walking. He was well aware of the impact of that smile on most of the women he met. "I'm here to see Dr. Hayes."

"Do you have an appointment, sir?" She frowned, less than enthralled with his flashy good looks. Hayes was a pediatrician. No doubt most adults who entered here were tagging kids along and stopped at the desk to check in for their appointments.

"Kevin is a friend of mine. He asked me to stop by." He smiled again and waved as he continued around the big desk and into the open waiting room. He saw her pick up a phone receiver and push a button.

Security was no doubt on the way. He didn't have much time.

Several office doors led off the big open waiting room, and an entryway to a corridor on his left appeared to run the length of the building. He ducked through the entrance and hurried toward the opposite end, glancing into open exam rooms and offices along the way, looking for Dr. Kevin Hayes.

About halfway down the corridor, he saw an elevator with a sign that listed physician offices on the higher floors. Hayes was listed on the second floor. He ignored the elevator and took the stairs two at a time.

He followed the signs to the left. At the end of the corridor, he reached a wooden door with Hayes's name on it. He turned the handle and pushed his way inside.

The door opened to a small waiting area. This one featured a saltwater aquarium in one corner. Another corner held a kid-size table and chairs with a few toys scattered about. Two doors led from the room.

Behind one, he heard a toilet flush immediately before a mom and daughter walked in.

Flint crossed the waiting area in four strides to reach the second door. He turned the knob and slipped inside. Straight ahead, at the end of another short hallway was an open door. Dr. Hayes sat behind a small desk, head bent, pen in hand, making notes on a patient chart.

Flint reached the doorway before Hayes looked up. His eyes widened and his head pushed back.

Flint stepped inside and closed the door and leaned against it. Hayes rolled his chair away and stood. "How did you get in here?"

"Call your front desk and apologize for the inconvenience. Say I'm an old friend." Kevin continued to stare, slack-jawed, as if he couldn't believe his eyes. Flint barked out the order like a drill sergeant. "Do it now!"

The shouting made Hayes blink, but he didn't move toward the phone. He took a deep breath and his chest puffed out. "Absolutely not. We have San Diego PD on-site. Unless you intend to shoot me, you will be arrested very shortly."

"Won't be the first time." Flint cocked his head. "When I explain why I'm here, I'll be released. Too bad that you can't say the same."

"Meaning what?"

"Frankly, I don't think you're a killer. But I doubt San Diego PD detectives will take my word for it, even if I was inclined to vouch for you. Which I'm not." Flint relaxed against the door. "Murder investigations take a while to complete. I'm sure this one will be extremely inconvenient for you and your friends for months. Not to mention what the media will make of it all. Probably devastate your practice. Parents don't want their children treated by an accused felon."

“What the hell are you talking about?” His words were indignant, but beads of sweat had popped out on his forehead.

“Happy to explain. But first,” Flint reached over and picked up the handset on the desk phone, “make the call.”

Hayes punched a button and reassured his staff that he had no need for San Diego PD. After he hung up, he said, “You have five minutes.”

Flint ignored the threat. He opened the office door again. “Come with me.”

Hayes arched his eyebrows. “I’ve got patients. I’m not going anywhere,” he said, still aggrieved.

Flint simply waited until Hayes walked around his desk.

“Are you armed?” Flint asked.

“Of course I’m not armed. This is a **medical** facility. For **children.**” Hayes’s chest puffed up again.

Flint opened the door and waved Hayes through.

“Where are we going?”

“Outside.”

Hayes shook his head, but he walked through the open door. He preceded Flint down the short corridor to the outer office and straight through to the main corridor, down the stairs to the first floor.

“Where is the exit to the back parking lot?”

Hayes led the way to the door. Flint gestured toward a keypad. Hayes punched a four-digit code and the door clicked open. He walked outside and Flint followed.

The covered parking area was much smaller than the flat lot in the front of the building. Closest to the exit were reserved parking spaces for the doctors. Flint gestured toward the sporty silver convertible parked in the space labeled "Kevin Hayes, MD."

Flint held out his hand. "Keys." Hayes fished around in his front pocket, pulled out an electronic key, and held it out. Flint pressed the button to open the door locks. "Get in."

Hayes took the passenger seat and Flint settled into the driver's side. He started the car and rolled through the parking lot and out into the flow of traffic.

"Where are we going? I left a room full of patients back there." Hayes was starting to sound less belligerent and more whiny. Good.

Flint suppressed a grin. He had pegged Hayes for the entry point to whatever was going on with the Wilcox crew, and his assessment had already proved accurate. Neither Vega nor Wilcox would have been whining already.

Flint drove in silence until they reached the landing strip where Drake was waiting in the pilot's seat of an old Sikorsky helicopter. An identical Sikorsky was tied down next to it. The helos were painted electric neon yellow with bold red stripes on both sides. They would be unmistakable from any distance. Even a child could identify them.

He parked the convertible. “Let’s go.” When Hayes looked like he might object, Flint said, “Get out.”

Hayes shrugged and exited the car. Flint pushed the door lock button and gestured toward Drake’s helo.

“Are you crazy? I can’t fly anywhere. Didn’t you see all those sick kids in my office?” Hayes became more agitated with every unexplained moment. “I have responsibilities. I’m a doctor, for God’s sake.”

"So you said." Flint shrugged and gave him a little push in the center of his back toward the helo. "You should have thought of that before you and your friends killed Dan Shafer and Skip Evans. Was it your idea to dump their bodies in Red Maple Lake?"

Hayes's eyes widened to the size of silver dollars, but he didn't say anything at all. Innocent men could be counted on to object when they were wrongly accused. The guilty ones held their silence. Which was all the confirmation Flint needed.

"That's what I thought." His gut said he was right and that was more than enough for him. What he needed was evidence. As soon as he had what Jamie Beaumont needed, he would turn this trio of murderers over to the authorities.

He gave Hayes a harder shove between the shoulder blades to get him moving. Without further comment, Hayes put one foot in front of the other and climbed the stairs into the Sikorsky.

“Give me your phone.” Hayes fished around in his pocket and pulled the phone out. He handed it to Flint without comment.

“Sit over there.” Flint gestured to the passenger seat behind Drake and settled himself into the passenger seat across the aisle. “Buckle up.” He nodded toward Drake. “Everything ready?”

"All set." Drake spooled up the Sikorsky and lifted off the ground.

Flint searched Hayes's phone for contacts until he found the one he needed. He sent a quick message, turned the phone off, and dropped it into his pocket.

After the helo was airborne, Hayes said, "What's the point of this, Flint?"

"The point? I'm looking for Josh Hallman. You're going to help me find him."

Hayes stared. "You think we know where he is?"

"No." Flint shook his head. "If you knew where he was, he'd be dead. Like the others. Why did you kill them, Kevin?"

"I didn't kill anyone! I already told you that!" he screamed while his eyes bugged and spittle landed on his chin. Kevin Hayes was coming unglued. Predictably. Flint resisted the urge to laugh.

He found the medical kit he'd stowed earlier. He unzipped it and removed a prefilled syringe and a rubber tourniquet. He tore open an alcohol swab pack. "Give me your arm." Hayes shook his head wildly.

"I'm not going to kill you. At least, not yet." Flint removed the plastic cover from the syringe and squirted a bit of clear liquid from the needle. "Give me your arm."

Hayes gripped the armrests on his seat. His fingers turned white with the pressure.

Flint smiled. So predictable. He grabbed the syringe in his fist with his thumb on the plunger. Before Hayes could jerk away, Flint shoved the needle into the side of his neck and pressed the plunger all the way down. The fluid slid smoothly from the syringe into Hayes's body, and Flint pulled the needle out.

"What the hell?" Hayes raised a palm to the puncture spot.

"We've arranged a little party with your friends," Flint said. "Don't worry. We'll wake you up before the fun starts."

Before Hayes could say anything more, his head lolled as if it was too heavy for his neck and his chin dropped onto his chest. Flint closed a pair of handcuffs around his wrists and left him to sleep it off.

Chapter Thirty-Four

San Diego, California
Thursday

Flint used Hayes's phone to send a second text five minutes before Drake flew over Petco Park and landed the Sikorsky on the helipad at Stellar Towers in San Diego's downtown financial district. Boyd Wilcox owned the building, which housed the StellarSoft executive offices. Mark Wilcox's **The First Two Days** studio was located on the top floor.

Also inside the multiuse towers were offices, a symphony hall, and an upscale restaurant with a spectacular view overlooking the helipad. A dozen witnesses watched Ruben Vega step out to greet the Sikorsky while Drake landed.

Flint pulled his Glock and held it concealed at his side. He opened the helo door and lowered the stairs. He kept his face turned from view of the diners in the restaurant and walked down to where Ruben Vega stood, buffeted by the rotor wash from the big helicopter.

Flint glanced around the rooftop area. Ruben Vega worked here, directly reporting to Boyd Wilcox. No doubt there were patrons and employees inside the restaurant who recognized him on sight. People were watching. Behavior would be noticed. Reported. Perhaps even recorded on cell phone video.

Vega said, “Kevin’s meeting me for lunch. He said nothing about bringing you along.”

“We’re not dining here.” Flint nodded his head up the stairs, toward the Sikorsky. “Hayes is inside. Let’s go.”

Vega paused and seemed to be considering the setup. He shook his head once and turned his back, prepared to walk into the building. Before he could move, Flint grabbed his arm and pushed the Glock to his side, careful to hide the gun from the audience.

“Let’s go this way,” Flint said, close to his ear. He pushed the Glock firmly and tugged him toward the stairs.

“What are you going to do? In front of all these witnesses?” Vega cocked his head and refused to move. “I think not.” He jerked his arm, but Flint tightened his grip.

The door from the restaurant opened. Mark Wilcox walked through and closed it behind him. Good. Both texts he’d sent from Hayes’s phone had reached their recipients. “What’s going on here, Flint?”

“We’re headed out for lunch. Please join us.” Flint’s tone was friendly, because others could be listening, but he didn’t release his grip on Vega or move the Glock from his ribs. The restaurant patrons were beginning to stare and nod and talk about what was happening on the helipad.

Wilcox had closed half the distance between them. “We have a good restaurant inside. Let’s eat here.”

Flint waited until Wilcox’s hulking body partially obscured the sightline between Vega and the restaurant and limited the view for the diners inside. It would be said that he’d acted strangely by some. Others wouldn’t know.

Quickly, behind the cover of the helo door, Flint raised the Glock and landed a solid blow to Vega’s left temple. Vega crumpled almost to his knees on the concrete.

Flint pointed the gun toward Wilcox's belly. "Act concerned about your friend. Help him up the stairs." The scene would play out perfectly as planned on the news.

Wilcox paused, looked at Vega on his knees on the pavement and up into the Sikorsky. He looked back toward the gawkers on the other side of the windows. He shrugged. He helped Vega to his feet and guided him up the stairs.

Flint concealed his weapon and climbed quickly behind them. Inside the Sikorsky, he shoved Wilcox toward a seat, pulled the stairs up, and closed the door. "Let's go!" he shouted to Drake.

The Sikorsky began to rise from the helipad. The riskiest part of the plan was done. Flint had been careful to shield his identity from the diners. It was possible that someone saw Flint's face and might identify him later, but not likely. When presented with a situation like this, eyewitnesses were notoriously fallible. They'd have focused on the famous faces they recognized. He'd deal with any blowback later, if he had to.

He pointed the Glock at Wilcox. "Buckle up." He patted Vega down and removed two handguns, one from his shoulder holster and one from an ankle holster. He jerked Vega into one of the passenger seats and strapped him in.

"What about you, Wilcox? Are you armed? Because you don't want to shoot off a gun in here, believe me."

Wilcox shrugged and stuck out his right leg. Flint pushed his pant leg up and removed the pistol from its holster.

"Got another one?" Wilcox shook his head and held his suit coat open to prove he wasn't wearing a shoulder holster.

Flint held his gun steadily pointed at Wilcox while he pulled out the second syringe and plunged it into a dazed Vega's neck. The third syringe was in his fist. He turned to Wilcox. Wilcox shrugged again, but didn't bother to resist. Flint repeated the sedative administration.

Flint's heart pounded with exertion and adrenaline. When Wilcox's chin fell to his chest, Flint found the two sets of handcuffs he'd brought along and shackled their wrists. Then he moved to the copilot's seat and donned his headset.

Drake said, "Everybody comfortable back there?"

"They'll be out for a few hours." Flint made the call on his satellite phone. "Execute."

Drake watched the air traffic. Using visual flight rules, he'd filed no flight plan and was not in touch with local towers. He flew up and out toward the Pacific to give the patrons a clear view of the helo's path, but once he was out of view, he immediately turned away, effectively hiding the helo.

From this altitude, they could see the decoy helicopter flying over the Pacific. The second Sikorsky from the airstrip. An old training helicopter. Painted exactly like the one Drake piloted, electric neon yellow with bold red stripes on both sides. Remotely controlled from the ground.

They watched the decoy break up and plunge into the ocean.

The decoy bird went down hard. Witnesses would have seen its destruction. Rescue teams would be on the way in minutes.

The plan was like a magic trick. Sleight of hand. Draw attention to the fake while the real one slips away.

The restaurant patrons would quickly report that Wilcox and Vega were in the helicopter. Connection to the crashed Sikorsky would be established with a few phone calls. Flint's contacts were happy to have the old bird as a water rescue training exercise. They'd be on the way now to collect the dummies from inside the downed helo.

There would be negative fallout when authorities learned about the hoax. But by then, if all went according to plan, he'd have found Josh Hallman. Veronica Beaumont's money, and the lack of any actual harm to anyone, would take care of any problems. The real Sikorsky would return, its passengers would exit unharmed. All would be forgiven. Or, should lingering issues arise, they would be resolved with a few well-placed phone calls to the right people.

It wasn't a perfect plan, but what plan was?

When Drake turned east toward Red Maple Lake, Flint relaxed a bit in the co-pilot's seat. "What's our ETA?"

"On schedule and under budget," Drake replied.

Chapter Thirty-Five

Red Maple Lake, California
Thursday

The reports of the Sikorsky crash began almost immediately after it went into the water. Rescue efforts to retrieve the five bodies presumed aboard were doomed from the start because the decoy helo was piloted remotely and no bodies would be found inside.

As expected, Mark Wilcox's celebrity status, both on his own and as Boyd Wilcox's brother, drove the story to trending everywhere around the world in less than thirty minutes.

The deception was an expensive ploy, but Veronica Beaumont had the money and she was willing to use it. Cooperation from Flint's covert ops contacts was stellar.

The entire world would believe Mark Wilcox had died in that crash within a couple of hours.

Unless Josh Hallman was living in a cave, he'd hear about the crash.

And when he heard, would he withdraw his money from the bank account that he hadn't touched in almost seven years, before his hard-earned cash landed in government coffers?

Flint had set the traps. His contacts monitored the traps.

If Hallman came out of hiding and took the bait, Flint would know it immediately.

From there, Hallman would be traceable.

The ruse was a very long shot with significant downside potential. But it **could** work.

Maybe.

With luck.

Wilcox might be temporarily outraged, but the publicity would only improve his TV ratings. He'd get over his anger pretty fast.

Or he wouldn't, and Flint would deal with that, too.

Flint watched the reports on his satellite phone until the signals stopped as they neared Red Maple Lake. Cell phone videos of the Sikorsky landing on the top of Stellar Tower and Mark Wilcox boarding the helo were already posted online and making the rounds of the broadcast stations.

The plan was working as intended.

Drake set the helo down expertly on the helipad behind Wilcox Lodge. The three passengers were still out cold. Flint broke into the house. The locks on the back door were easily breached. No need for state-of-the-art security systems in the middle of nowhere.

He walked through the empty house and found bedrooms for his passengers. There were eight guestrooms and a master suite in the house.

Plenty of space.

Lugging the unconscious Mark Wilcox into the house was a two-man job. He was big and heavy. Drake and Flint settled him onto one of the beds and handcuffed him to the bedpost before they brought the other two inside. They put Vega in one room and Hayes in another and secured them to the bedpost with handcuffs, as well.

Once the hostages were settled, he and Drake went back to the helo, unloaded their gear, and lugged it inside. While Drake tied the Sikorsky down for the night, Flint set up the long-range satellite hotspot and found a newsfeed for the laptop.

He tested the satellite phone with a quick call to his source. “Any movement on that bank account yet?”

“I’ll use this number to notify you and confirm with an encrypted text.”

“Perfect.”

“How long are you going to wait?”

“As long as it takes,” he said, and disconnected the call.

Drake had been poking around in the kitchen. The night lights flickered on. He’d found the generator outside and the circuit breakers inside. He'd turned on the electricity. He'd also turned on the water, located coffee, and started the brew. The aroma wafted through the lodge, drawing Flint from the dining room into the kitchen for a mugful.

Drake stood with the refrigerator door open. "Looks like they weren't planning to come back for a while. Bottled water, beer, and not much else in here, and none of it's cold."

Flint rummaged through the pantry and found a few staples. The choices were limited, to say the least. He closed the door and frowned. "If we don't find something to cook, we're looking at the MREs we brought along. Unless you want to go out and shoot a squirrel or something."

Drake could fly out for supplies, but every trip in and out presented a risk that they'd be discovered before the ruse had a chance to reach Hallman and spur him to action. Success depended on keeping the three hostages out of sight and presumed dead.

"Hunting is a possibility. We can catch some fish, too, if we have to." Flint had finished his coffee and set the mug down in the sink. "I'll go see what I can find. Hayes said the freezers in the equipment cabin were well stocked. Maybe we'll get lucky."

"I'll keep looking around. We should have things like rice and canned goods somewhere," Drake replied.

Flint left by the back door. He walked across the patio and ducked into the cottage where Wilcox's helo pilot had bunked. The cottage was exactly what Hayes had said. A studio apartment. One bed, a couple of sitting chairs, a small kitchen, and a bathroom. Nothing unusual. He looked quickly through the cabinets for food. No luck.

He continued to the larger second building, the one that Hayes said stored the generator and freezers and other equipment for maintaining the lodge. He turned the doorknob and pushed the door, but it was stuck. Humidity had swelled the wood. He leaned his shoulder into the task. With his body weight behind it, the second shove pushed the door free. It creaked on its hinges as it opened and he stumbled inside.

This building was twice the size of the guest cottage. There were two generators, a smaller one to power the freezers and a heater inside the cabin, and a big generator for everything else on the compound. Both were probably fueled by a propane tank, most likely behind the building. Both generators were running now because Drake had fired them up.

The walls of the cabin were lined with floor-to-ceiling wood cabinets. He opened the doors and glanced inside. Two of the cabinets contained shelves of food. Canned goods and anything that might freeze when the heat was off in the big house were stored here. He'd carry an armload back with him. At least they wouldn't be eating freeze-dried MREs tonight.

He looked inside the other cabinets. He found chemicals for the hot tub, lawn equipment, water hoses, flower pots, and the like. Hanging from hooks on the interior walls were pruning shears, hatchets, hammers and other small tools, and several long blades, probably for dealing with the overgrown vegetation around the property. At the very back of the last cabinet, hanging from hooks by leather thongs, were several rakes and shovels, and a sword with a leather-wrapped handle. The kind he'd seen commonly in the Middle East when he'd served there.

There were two big chest freezers. Each was at least sixty inches wide and thirty inches deep. He guessed each was about twenty cubic feet in capacity and would hold big game like deer and elk that hunters might find around here. One freezer was propped open and empty, cleaned out for the season, he supposed.

He pushed the lid up on the second freezer. A blast of air hit his face, so cold that it drew tears from his eyes. He stepped back for his vision to clear and then looked through the frosty air swirling inside the big open cavern.

Packages wrapped in white freezer paper were stacked neatly along the interior walls of the freezer. On the left side was a wire basket that held smaller packages, also wrapped in white paper. Everything about the freezer was white. Inside, outside, and contents. It resembled an igloo.

The packages were labeled with heavy black letters to identify the contents. Meats, grouped together by type, filled two-thirds of the space. Potatoes and other vegetables filled the last third. The basket held a few prepared dishes, labeled “Pasta—Mark,” “Eggplant—Boyd,” and the like.

At the bottom of the basket was the smallest package. It was labeled simply “Aludra.” Seeing the name, black on white, jarred him. He remembered the grisly severed head found in the Las Vegas dumpster. Why would Mark Wilcox have kept this package all these years? He’d never seemed that sentimental to Flint.

Flint pulled packages labeled “Steaks” and “Potatoes” from the freezer. He grabbed the one marked “Aludra” and added it to the pile.

He closed the lid on the freezer and left the building, pulling the swollen door firmly into place behind him to keep nocturnal animals outside. He returned to the main house with the frozen food to find Drake still foraging in the kitchen.

Flint held up two of the wrapped packages, one at a time. “Steaks.

Potatoes. According to the labels.”

“Sounds good. What’s the third one?”

“That’s where it gets interesting.” He held the small package to display the label.

“Aludra?” Drake frowned. “I don’t get it.”

“Mark Wilcox’s dead wife.”

Drake's eyes widened. "What's inside? Not food, surely, after all this time."

Flint pulled out a drawer looking for a sharp knife to open the package without damaging it. "We're about to find out. You don't have a pair of latex gloves in your pocket, do you?"

"In the emergency kit in the helo. Want me to get them?"

Flint nodded. "While you're gone, I'll check on our guests."

Drake went out the back door toward the helipad and Flint went down the hallway to the bedrooms.

When Flint reached Vega's door, he turned the knob and pushed the door open wide enough to see inside.

Vega's bed was empty. The bedpost to which he'd been handcuffed was broken off at the base, leaving a jagged stump.

Flint reached for his Glock with his right hand. With his left, he pushed the door open wider. He stepped over the threshold into the room.

Out of the corner of his left eye, he saw movement. He whipped his head left.

Vega stood behind the door, arms raised over his head, holding the bedpost like a club, prepared to strike.

Vega screamed and brought the club down hard and fast.

Flint feinted right.

Half a moment too late.

Vega's heavy bedpost arced down. It missed Flint's head, but landed a solid strike on his left shoulder.

Sharp pain seared through his shoulder toward his chest and his back and down his arm all the way to the fingers of his left hand. But Flint was still standing and he heard no sickening splinter of bones.

Vega screamed again, a look of pure fury on his face, as he lifted the club for another blow.

Flint pivoted on his left foot, raised the Glock in his right hand. "Stop! Ruben, I'll shoot!"

Vega didn't even blink. Momentum carried him forward and before Flint could squeeze the trigger, Vega swung the club hard and fast again.

The blow landed across Flint's back on the left side. Flint staggered and fell to the floor. He landed almost face down and rolled to the right, lifting his gun in his right hand as he moved.

Vega stepped forward. He raised his arms overhead for the third time. He aimed to bash Flint's head in with the next blow.

"Stop!" Flint yelled again, but Vega was enraged beyond rational thought. He started his downward strike.

Flint fired twice.

Both rounds landed solidly in Vega's torso. The impact pushed him away as his arms fell downward.

He plopped onto the floor on his ass, back resting against the wall, club still held in both hands, resting between his legs.

Dead in that instant.

Flint rolled over on the floor and winced as his weight pressed against his back. Searing pain in his left shoulder stole his breath. He raised his right hand to feel the bedpost's point of impact.

Nerves in his left arm and hand still pulsed shooting pains from fingertips to shoulder, but the sensation had subsided. He'd have a hell of a bruise on his shoulder and another on his back. He'd be sore for a good long while. But nothing was broken. No blood to mix with Vega's.

Drake came running into the room, weapon drawn. He slipped through the partially open doorway. In one glance, he took the situation in. Vega was dead on the floor. Blood pooled around his body. The silence was all-consuming.

He reached out a hand and pulled Flint to his feet.

"What the hell?" Drake asked, lowering his gun.

"He came at me. My left arm's almost useless." Flint grimaced as he felt around the shoulder, pressing the pain point, confirming the bones were still in place. “Let’s check Hayes and Wilcox.”

Weapons drawn, Flint in the lead, they raced down the corridor to the two bedrooms where they’d left Hayes and Wilcox unconscious two hours before.

“No one in here,” Drake said, coming out of Hayes’s bathroom.

Flint checked Wilcox’s bathroom to be thorough, but he knew he’d find nothing. He met up with Drake in the hallway. “Check the rest of the guestrooms. I’ll take the common rooms.”

Flint returned to the great room and made his way to the kitchen. From the window, he saw Hayes struggling to open the quick-release mechanism on the Sikorsky's webbed tie-downs. He'd already removed the wheel chocks.

"Outside!" Flint yelled back to Drake before he ran to the back door and rounded the corner to the helipad.

Chapter Thirty-Six

Red Maple Lake, California
Thursday

Wilcox was inside the Sikorsky, seated in the pilot's seat. His attention was focused on the cockpit and he'd begun preflight procedures.

The sedative Flint had pumped into his system would have lingering effects. His reaction times would be slowed. Thinking processes and vision impaired.

He wasn't fit to pilot the Sikorsky now, and probably hadn't been qualified in the past several years. He'd hired a pilot to fly in and out of this place, which was a good indication that he knew he couldn't do it himself, when he was thinking clearly.

Now that he was closer, he saw that Hayes was carrying a weapon. It looked like a Glock 19 Gen4 from this distance. The same reliable pistol Flint carried.

He shouted, "Hayes! Come on, man! You can't fly out of here until that sedative wears off. You'll crash and burn. You know I'm right. Mark's in no shape to fly."

"Stay back, Flint. I'll shoot you if I have to." Hayes waved the Glock in Flint's general direction, but he was crouched under the tail section of the

Sikorsky, struggling with the tie-down release. He was unsteady on his feet.

Drake ran up behind Flint. Quietly, he said, “That tie-down lever was tough to close when I engaged it. He won’t get that one open without a tool of some kind to move the lever.”

“Will it break when the Sikorsky takes off?”

“If they get enough torque on it, it’ll break. I could break it on takeoff. You could do it.” Drake shrugged. “But we’ve got at least two to three minutes before that can happen. He needs to get the other tiedowns off, for sure.”

Flint lowered his voice so that only Drake could hear. “They’re both still drugged and unstable. Physically and mentally.”

He nodded toward Hayes. “Get his gun. I’ll handle Wilcox.”

“Roger that,” Drake replied.

“I’ll cover you.”

They watched Hayes until he dropped his right arm and turned his gaze back to the tie-down. Drake used that moment to rush forward.

By the time Hayes saw him, it was too late.

Drake tackled Hayes to the ground.

Flint used the distraction to run forward and hop into the Sikorsky.

Wilcox's attention was focused on the dozens of levers, buttons, and dials on the instrument panel. He'd never flown this particular helo before. In his impaired state, he seemed more confused than the situation demanded.

"Wilcox. Come on. You can't pilot this bird right now. Let's go back inside." Wilcox didn't move his gaze from the instruments.

Flint brandished his Glock.

"Maybe you're right. Maybe I can't think straight right now." Wilcox shook his head. "But you're not going to shoot me, Flint. We both know that. You'd never get this bird out of here if you start a gunfight. You'll damage the helo. Then what?"

He smirked before he reached up and pressed the starter and the engine came to life. The rotors began to turn. The ear-piercing whine drowned all conversation. He turned his gaze back to the instruments.

Flint balanced his weight and changed his hold on the Glock. The grip was slightly exposed from the flat of his right fist. In one smooth motion, he raised his right fist, pushed hard, and lunged with all of his body weight providing momentum. He slammed his fist and the gun butt as hard as possible into Wilcox's left temple at his skull's most vulnerable spot.

The blow pushed Wilcox's head like a bobble doll, hard and fast, against the Sikorsky's side window.

Wilcox was stunned, but the blow didn't render him unconscious. The engine had spooled up and the rotors were turning at a speed sufficient to support takeoff. Wilcox pulled on the yoke and the nose of the big helo began to rise.

"Wilcox!" Flint raised his Glock, pointed it, and yelled, "I will shoot you."

Wilcox turned to stare at Flint, smiled, and shook his head. Quickly, he reached down on his right side and fumbled with something on the floor. He bent his arm at the elbow, raised a pistol, and held it across his stomach, pointed directly at Flint, ready to fire.

Flint's instincts kicked in. **Kill or be killed.**

He fired his weapon into Wilcox's head. The bullet went through his skull and shattered the Sikorsky's side window. Blood and bone and the gray matter of Wilcox's brain splattered from the exit wound.

Flint hustled into the copilot's seat and set the Sikorsky down. He shut the engine down and slumped in his seat.

He looked across the cockpit. Wilcox's body slumped into the pilot side door. The irony hit Flint's gut like a blow. The entire world believed Wilcox had died in this helicopter. Now, in truth, he had.

Flint stood and walked to the still-open door in the back. He looked out to the tail section of the Sikorsky. Drake had Hayes on the ground, right arm bent behind his back, but all the fight had gone out of him.

Drake pulled Hayes up and pushed him ahead as they walked back to the house. "Now what?"

Flint stuck his gun in his belt and used his right hand to massage his sore shoulder. "I'm gonna need some time in that hot tub."

Chapter Thirty-Seven

Red Maple Lake, California
Thursday

When they returned to the kitchen, Hayes saw the package marked "Aludra" on the counter. His eyes widened and his breathing quickened. His voice quivered when he asked, "Where did you get that?"

"Why? What's in it?" Flint picked up the package in his right hand and felt the smooth paper.

Hayes stared at the package and shook his head rapidly.

It was flat, maybe five-by-seven inches, and two inches deep. About the size of a single rib-eye steak. It weighed less than a pound. The freezer paper was heavy and the contents of the package were well wrapped against freezer burn, like a steak would be.

Drake reached into his pocket and pulled out the latex gloves he'd retrieved from the first aid kit in the Sikorsky. He handed the gloves to Flint, who pulled them onto his hands one at a time.

Flint picked up the sharp knife he'd removed from the drawer earlier and used the knifepoint to gently lift the label from the paper at the seam.

He placed the package on the counter to unwrap it. After the label was lifted, the thick paper unfolded easily. Inside was a sealed plastic bag and inside the bag was a hinged purple satin jewelry box.

"Don't open that. Please don't." Hayes began to cry. He blubbered like a baby. Snot ran from his nose and tears from his eyes. He collapsed onto a kitchen stool.

Drake exchanged a puzzled look with Flint. He tore a paper towel from the rack and handed it to Hayes. "Clean yourself up, man."

Flint opened the plastic bag and carefully pulled out the purple box. He rested it on the plastic bag.

Using both thumbs, he lifted the hinged lid and opened the box.

Hayes stared, mesmerized, but he'd stopped blubbering.

The contents rested on the same purple satin that enclosed the outside of the box.

Sparkling on the satin bed was a tangled pile of gold and diamond jewelry.

Flint pushed the pieces apart with one gloved finger to separate them. He lifted the largest piece from the box.

A wedding crown with an attached bridal headdress frontlet. The frontlet was meant to rest in the center of the bride's forehead. The crown was not a tiara but three strands of diamonds that fanned from the frontlet and anchored into an elaborate hairstyle.

He visualized the crown and frontlet worn by the ravishingly beautiful Aludra Wilcox on her wedding day. The day she'd married Mark Wilcox.

Flint had seen her wedding photos when she'd been kidnapped. Her jet-black hair had been the perfect foil for the light dancing from these jewels.

He returned the crown to the box. These pieces must have been valuable. They also had significant sentimental value to her family. Storing them in the freezer was odd, but not necessarily sinister.

The other items in the box supplied the answers.

He lifted her distinctive diamond nose ring from its resting place.

The one her parents gave her when she became an adult. She'd worn it constantly, her husband had told Flint all those years ago. She'd been wearing it when she was reported kidnapped.

But when her head was found in that Las Vegas dumpster, the nose ring was gone, presumed stolen.

Also in the box were six gold bangle bracelets that she never took off, even to sleep.

The last item was her gold-and-diamond wedding band.

The band that matched her husband's.

It had never turned up after she died. Or so Wilcox had said at the time and in many interviews since. She was sentimental, he'd said. She had never removed it from her finger with her favorite fuchsia-pink nail polish since her marriage. Not once.

He hadn't lied.

Flint moved the partially thawed finger around gently on its purple satin bed as Hayes and Drake stared.

Flint reached into his pocket for his phone and snapped a few photos of the contents, the box, the plastic bag, and the white paper. He slid the phone back into his pocket. He closed the box, slipped it into the plastic bag, and zipped it shut. He wrapped the paper around the box and pressed the label firmly to reseal.

He put the box into the kitchen freezer, which had already begun to chill.

Flint looked at Hayes. “Let’s go.”

“Go where?”

“Into the dining room. You’re going to tell me everything you know.”

Hayes sniffled and blew his nose. “And then what?”

Flint said nothing, but what he thought was, **And then what, indeed.**

Drake started another pot of coffee. Hayes slid off the stool and walked ahead of Flint into the dining room. Flint’s laptop and satellite phone were still on the table. He glanced at both quickly. Nothing on Hallman's bank account yet.

The news story about the helicopter crash and Wilcox's death had gone viral on social media. If Hallman was getting broadcast or internet news, he should know about the crash by now. Flint was counting on the deadline for removing his money from the bank, added to the sense of safety that having Wilcox dead would give him, to encourage him to come out of hiding.

If it didn't work, he'd be back to pounding the pavement and the keyboard, hoping Jamie Beaumont would make it until he found Hallman.

Drake brought the coffee pot and three mugs into the room. He poured the coffee. Flint recognized the effort to return to normalcy for what it was. The sunlight was gone and the cold crept down from the mountains. There were two bodies that needed to be dealt with and authorities to notify. They could deal with the bodies tonight, but everything else would need to wait.

But first, Hayes had answers and Flint had questions.

Drake settled into the chair at Flint's left elbow and stretched his legs out. Hayes leaned on his forearms on the table, both hands around his coffee mug, shivering, although the inside temperature was at least seventy-five degrees. Vega's body would soon begin to stink.

“Start with what happened to Josh Hallman.”

Hayes glanced down at the table and then met Flint’s gaze. “I already told you. I don’t know where he is. None of us knew. We tried to find him for a good long while. But we never had any luck. He could be dead. Because if he’s hiding, he’s done a damned good job of it.”

“Okay.” Flint nodded. That story rang true. “What happened to his friends?”

“Skip was injured badly in the crash. He’d lost a lot of blood by the time we found him. I did the best I could with his leg and then gave him a sedative and some painkillers to help him get through the night until we could take him to Tahoe the next day. But he died during the night." Hayes shrugged. "Nothing I could do."

"Were you with him when he died?"

"We were taking turns with him." Hayes cleared his throat.

"So who was with him when he died?"

"Mark was."

Flint nodded. "You're sure Mark didn't kill him?"

Hayes looked away again. "We didn't plan any of this. When they crashed their plane, we tried to help them. I feel responsible for Skip. I did the best I could with his leg. I must have given him too much morphine."

"Kevin? Are you sure Mark or Ruben didn't kill Skip?"

Hayes shook his head. "How would I know? I wasn't in the room." Flint narrowed his eyes. "You believe Mark killed him, don't you?"

Hayes cleared his throat and took a swig of the coffee. "Maybe I did, at first. But I've seen the autopsy report. I know he died of morphine overdose."

Drake said, "What made you think Mark might have done it?"

"Because," his voice squeaked and he took another swig of coffee, "because of Aludra."

Flint said, "Yeah, we'll get to that. What about Dan? Who shot him?"

“Ruben. He didn’t have much choice. I gave Dan painkillers and I put some in brandy for Josh. They should have slept through the whole thing. But Josh woke up.” His voice dropped to a near whisper. “Ruben couldn’t let Dan and Josh get away.”

“What did you do with the bodies?” Drake asked.

“You put them in that extra freezer out there,” Flint said. “And then, after the families had stopped looking for them, you came back here and took the frozen bodies out and dropped them into the deepest part of the lake, weighted down, believing they’d never be found.” Hayes blanched, and then nodded.

“And Josh? What happened to him?”

Hayes shook his head. “He got away. We looked for him. We tried to find him.”

Drake said, “But you never did.” Hayes shook his head again.

“What about Aludra?”

“I had nothing to do with that. Nothing.” Hayes’s eyes widened and he shook his head.

“She was never kidnapped, was she?” Flint asked. He’d suspected as much back when he’d been investigating her disappearance, but he’d never found any evidence to support his hunch. “She came here willingly. She died here.”

Hayes swallowed hard before he whispered, “Yes.”

“So Wilcox made up the kidnapping story to cover up the murder?” Drake asked.

Hayes looked down and shook his head. “Mark believed Aludra was kidnapped. He hired Flint to find her. That was all real.”

Flint pushed back. “Mark believed she’d been kidnapped, but it wasn’t true?”

Hayes nodded miserably. “She came here with Boyd. They were having an affair. We didn’t know until we found her here with him that weekend.”

Flint shook his head. Mark Wilcox had a hell of a temper. He could just imagine how Mark had reacted to finding Aludra here with Boyd. Flint had often wondered who killed Aludra. After the ransom was paid, there was no reason for the kidnappers to kill her.

"You didn't know about that purple box, either?" Drake asked.

Kevin shook his head again, more violently than before. His hands gripped the ceramic mug as if he might squeeze it to shards.

"Mark killed Aludra, didn't he?" Drake asked. "He did it here, in this house. That's why her jewelry was in that freezer. He took it off her body here."

Kevin inhaled sharply. "Mark's dead now. Can't you let him alone?"

“Why did he do it when he could have just divorced her?” Drake pressed.

Kevin picked up the mug and slammed it down on the table. Hot coffee splashed onto his hands and he didn’t seem to care.

His nostrils flared. His eyes narrowed. “I told you. I. Don’t. Know.”

Flint’s satellite phone pinged.

Chapter Thirty-Eight

Red Maple Lake, California
Thursday

The satellite phone alerted Flint to one text message. He picked it up and opened the text. **10–18. Repeat. 10–18.**

Assignment completed.

Hallman had taken the bait. He'd accessed his bank account and withdrawn the money.

He texted back. **Copy that. Location encryption requested.**

She would send an encrypted message to his laptop.

He paused a moment and then texted a second request.

10–6. This location at 0900. Send civilian police tomorrow morning.

She replied, **Copy that.**

He closed the satellite phone and turned to Drake.

“Looks like Hallman must have had some sort of trigger set up to move his money. I figured it would take him a few days, but he’s already transferred the balance,” Flint said. “The guy is as smart as we gave him credit for. He’s been watching, waiting for his chance. He must have seen the news. Which means that he’s connected to the outside world.”

Drake nodded. “I wasn’t looking forward to sleeping with Ruben’s corpse in the house.”

Flint winced as he used his left arm to push away from the table. “Can we take the Sikorsky out of here tonight?”

“Weather’s good enough. We should be okay.” Drake nodded. “We’ve got to get Wilcox out of it first, though.”

“Hayes and I will take care of that. We’ll bring him inside with Vega.” He looked at Hayes. “Come on. You can help me.”

Hayes shook his head and looked like he might start wailing again.

Flint had already had as much of that as he could take.

He walked around the table and walked behind Hayes's chair. He lifted Hayes up and hit him hard in the solar plexus. Hayes crumpled to the floor, unconscious.

Drake grinned. "He's gonna have a hell of a tummy ache when he wakes up."

"That's not all he's gonna have when the locals come out here and see two dead bodies and Aludra's finger in the freezer."

Drake grinned again. "Right."

"He'll come around after we've gone. Let's get Wilcox out of the helo and get the hell back to civilization." Flint collected his laptop and his satellite phone and followed Drake to the helipad.

They opened the pilot-side door and let Wilcox's body fall to the ground. Flint found his gun and stuffed it into his pocket. They picked him up and muscled his body into Vega's room and closed the door.

Flint rummaged around in the kitchen until he found the keys to the Range Rover. It was the only transportation Hayes could use to get away before the locals arrived in the morning. He took the keys with him, and before he joined Drake in the Sikorsky, he tossed the keys into the forest. If Hayes could find them, he could be long gone before the cops started asking him questions. But what was the chance of that?

He settled into the copilot's seat as Drake finished his preflight check and started the engine. In less than five minutes, they were airborne. The broken window made the interior of the Sikorsky even louder and colder than usual, like riding in a convertible with the top down in the winter. "Where to?"

"LAX. You can leave this helo there and fly commercial back to Houston." When they were far enough away from Wilcox Lodge to get a consistent signal, he fired up the laptop and downloaded the encrypted file. He scanned it quickly.

Hallman had transferred the entire balance of his bank account by wire to Plantain Bank. There were branches of Plantain Bank around the world, but this particular branch was the only one in Fiji.

Flint grinned. “Gotcha.”

He picked up the satellite phone and made a call. When she answered, he said, “What time is my flight to Fiji?”

“You’re on the eleven forty. We’ve located your target. You’ll need a private plane for the final leg. We’ve booked an operative at Nadi Airport.”

He nodded. “Send me whatever you can find about Hallman’s life in Fiji. I’ll read it on the plane.”

“Copy that.”

Chapter Thirty-Nine

Republic of Fiji
Saturday

The flight time from LAX was more than eleven hours, but Flint had slept and ate and watched television for a while.

He'd read through the research files on Joshua Hallman again, looking for anything he might use to persuade Hallman to help his son.

Perhaps he wouldn't need persuading. But the man had disappeared for a reason and stayed away for almost seven years. It was pretty clear that he wouldn't be all that excited to be found.

Flint wasn't exactly sure how he would change Hallman's mind.

The new materials were likely to be more helpful. Flint had reviewed those and committed the salient facts to memory.

When he deplaned at Nadi International Airport, halfway around the world and a day later, he still didn't have a solid plan.

Which wasn't the way he preferred to operate.

He grabbed his bag and stretched his legs on the way to the terminal exit.

The operative was waiting for him outside, leaning against a black sedan parked at the curb, arms folded across his chest. A big man, black. Close-cropped hair. Dressed in jeans and a tight-fitting T-shirt that left nothing about his punishing fitness routine to the imagination.

“Flint?” He pulled off his sunglasses as a courtesy, so that Flint could see his eyes. He extended his hand. “Charles Bell.”

Flint shook hands. The man was strong. He’d be an asset, should they meet trouble.

“Thanks for coming on short notice. Where are we headed?”

Bell looked up at the terminal and nodded toward visible surveillance cameras. “Fill you in on the way.”

He took the passenger's seat while Bell slipped his sunglasses on and walked around to the driver's side. Bell started the sedan and merged into traffic, which was surprisingly heavy.

"We'll need to fly to another island to find your man." Bell glanced into the rear view mirror, perhaps to confirm no one was following. "Helo is the best way to get there. Any problem with that?"

Flint shook his head. Helicopter travel was as normal as breathing to him. "Tell me what I need to know about this place."

"The Republic of Fiji has had a tortured history." Bell shrugged. "These days, it's mostly a tourist mecca. Resorts, sand, sea, sunshine. Fijians are good people. What's not to like?"

"How many islands?"

"Three hundred and thirty, I've been told. But don't worry. Only a hundred and ten of those are inhabited." Bell flashed a smile as he turned the sedan onto the main highway. "Piece of cake to search. If you don't move on to the more than five hundred islets."

Flint nodded. Hallman had chosen a perfect place to disappear.

Not many investigators would be dogged enough to pound that much ground to find him. He could easily have lived in anonymity for the remainder of his life.

If.

If Jamie Beaumont wasn't sick.

If Veronica Beaumont wasn't rich enough to pay for Flint's inspired methods.

No doubt, Flint might have searched for Hallman forever, success nowhere close to guaranteed.

Hallman might have been the one to spoil Flint's perfect record.

Might have been.

If Flint hadn't discovered the bank account and devised a plan to lure Hallman to withdraw his money.

If the plan had failed.

Which it had not. He grinned.

"While you were in the air, we followed the money, like you asked. Located your man. We didn't approach him. Left that for you."

When they'd boarded the helicopter, Bell grinned again. He ran through the start-up procedures expertly. The helo was ready to fly in less than five minutes.

"As the pilots say, sit back and enjoy the ride."

"How long before we reach the island?"

Bell said, "Thirty minutes, tops. But it's early here. Joshua Hallman's not likely to be awake yet. Bet fifty bucks we'll find him home in bed."

Flint nodded. "You're on."

The helo flight over the country was enough to entice any tourist to stay forever.

A group of islands with rugged landscapes, clear lagoons, and sandy beaches as far as the eye could see. He didn't know how Hallman had made his way here, but this island paradise would be hard to leave.

Bell pointed out the small town where Hallman had been living for five years. "Your man's got a wife and two kids. They live in a modest house on a smaller lot in the interior."

"Find any photos of the wife or kids?"

"Not yet. She's a Fijian native. Kids, too. They seem happy enough, based on what we've found so far. No domestic violence reports in the local blotter, anyway." Bell paused to make an adjustment to the flight path. "He uses a different name now. Or he did. He had to provide proof of his identity to transfer the money."

Flint nodded.

Fifty thousand American dollars would go a long way here, and replacing those savings would have been near impossible. No wonder Hallman took Flint's bait.

Maybe he'd thought it romantic to leave the money when he ran from Wilcox Lodge. But after a few years, the romantic glow had been worn off by the reality of grinding poverty.

He'd had plenty of time to figure out how to get his money. Flint wondered briefly what Hallman had planned to do to get his cash if Wilcox hadn't died.

Bell landed the helo in a parking lot and shut the engine down near a green army Jeep. "Borrowed our wheels from a mate. Bumpy ride out to the Hallman place."

Flint shrugged. Of course it was. This entire case had been a bumpy ride, and he was glad to be wrapping it up, one way or another.

They secured the helo, and Flint stowed his laptop in the backseat of the Jeep. Bell set up a GPS connected to a US military satellite, and they left the business district, such as it was, for the interior.

Bell drove through the little town, past a school and the bank, along a dirt road, and turned onto a poorly marked path that led to a dilapidated house with a rusty metal roof. The board siding had been painted bright pink once, but that was long ago.

Bell parked the Jeep.

Flint stepped out. “Wait here. If I need help, I’ll let you know.”

“Got it.”

Flint walked through the dusty front yard strewn with broken toys and an old satellite dish. Flint smiled. Hallman wasn’t totally disconnected from the world after all.

He heard chickens in the back and a rooster crowing. The grass, such as it was, might have been mowed by lazy goats a while back.

He knocked on the doorframe while he looked through a crack between the frame and the wall. The house was quiet. He knocked again. A cat roamed the kitchen, meowing for breakfast, or cat litter.

Flint knocked again, louder, and the screen door banged against the frame. A man came through an open doorway wearing boxers and a holey T-shirt, roused from sleep. He rubbed his face with one hand and scratched his crotch with the other. His eyes were half closed and he yawned.

He opened the inside door and slipped outside. “Keep it down, okay? The kids had a late night. They need to sleep.”

Flint moved back off the stoop. “I’m Michael Flint. I need to talk to you, Josh.”

Hallman’s eyes rounded and he came wide awake in an instant. He looked like he might rabbit. “What?”

“I know all about what happened to you at Red Maple Lake six years ago. I’m not here to harm you.” Flint prepared to give chase. “What I have to say is important. A matter of life or death. Seriously. Veronica Beaumont sent me.”

"Veronica?" Hallman's wide-eyed fear turned to something Flint couldn't read in his body language well enough to define. "I haven't seen Veronica in years. Is she okay? What could she possibly want with me?"

"Let's find a place to sit. Got any coffee?"

Hallman ran a hand through his hair again. "Uh, coffee? Yeah. Sure." He looked over his shoulder toward the house. "Can you wait out here? I'll bring it out. Everybody's asleep inside."

Flint nodded. He found two plastic chairs under a tree in the front yard, turned upside down to keep the rain off. He righted the chairs and sat in one to wait.

He figured there was a fifty-fifty chance that Hallman would run out the back. But after a while, he emerged with two plastic mugs. He hadn't dressed or donned shoes. He carried the mugs over to the tree and sat in the second chair.

The silence between them lingered a few minutes. Flint tried to sip the strong black coffee, but it was scalding hot. He was waiting for inspiration. None came. So he just laid it out.

"Veronica Beaumont has a son. She says you're his father. The boy's sick. He needs your help."

"What? How can that be?" Hallman fell back into the chair with his mouth open. He blinked several times.

He wiped a palm over his face and through his hair and shook his head. “How old is this boy?”

“He’s almost eight. His name is Jamie. I’ve got a video. Would you like to see it?”

Hallman nodded. Flint pulled out his cell phone and found the video. He queued it up and pressed the “Play” button and handed the phone to Hallman.

The video was two minutes long. Flint had watched it several times.

It began in the delivery room right after Veronica gave birth and continued through four random birthdays and three school events. The final thirty seconds was Jamie in the hospital, asking his doctor if he would get better. The doctor looked down and didn't respond for a moment. When he looked up, he told Jamie what every patient wants to hear, but the certainty didn't reach his eyes.

Hallman's face crumpled. He watched the video again and returned the phone to Flint. He sipped the coffee and leaned his forearms on both thighs and looked at his house, with his family sleeping inside.

"Veronica says I'm this boy's father?"

"You doubt it?"

Hallman shook his head. His voice was raspy. "I don't know."

"Why?"

"Before we broke up she told me she was getting an abortion. I believed her. I never knew." Hallman's shoulders shook. Flint looked away from his pain, giving him a chance to pull himself together.

Hallman cleared his throat and wiped his nose with the back of his hand. "Have you met him? Jamie?"

"He's a good kid. My niece has a crush on him and she's got great taste," Flint teased to lighten the mood.

"Yeah? That's good. Is Veronica a good mom?"

"She is. Believe it or not." Flint smiled and Hallman gave a weak smile in return.

Hallman cleared his throat again. “What does she need me to do?”

“It’s for Jamie. He needs a bone marrow transplant. Veronica knows there’s only a thirty percent chance that you can be a donor. But she’s desperate.”

Hallman looked toward his house again. “I can’t leave here. My family doesn’t know anything about”—he stopped to compose himself—“what happened. I can’t mess this up, Flint. Don’t ask me to do that.”

“We need a cheek swab. I brought the kit with me. If you’re a match, we’ll contact you. It means a quick trip to a good hospital.” Flint paused and cleared his throat.

Damn, this was harder than he'd expected. "Veronica told me you can do the whole thing anonymously if you want. You don't have to see him or have any contact with either of them."

Hallman nodded, slowly. "You got the cheek swab kit on you?"

Flint pulled it out of his pocket and administered the test. He knew what to do. He'd done it himself. When Hallman had completed the test, Flint sealed it and stuffed the baggie into his pocket.

"Thanks for doing this, Josh. We'll let you know in the next couple of days."

Hallman simply nodded, too emotional to speak. He cleared his throat and changed the subject. “How’d you find me? The money?”

Flint nodded. People would reveal more than they should, as long as he didn’t interrupt. It was a lesson he’d learned long ago. So he said nothing.

“I worried about that for years.” Hallman grimaced. “But you see how we live. I’ve got a wife and two kids. I have an obligation to them, too. When I saw that Wilcox, Vega, and Hayes were killed in that helicopter crash . . . Well, the money would go to the state, and they don’t need it. We do.”

Flint didn’t reply.

"It was a risk, I know. Boyd wasn't on the helicopter. He didn't die. And he had more power than any of them. He pulled all the strings. He'll come after me one day, won't he?"

Flint cocked his head, trying to make sense of the question. "Why would Boyd come after you?"

"I've had a lot of time to think about this. That night, I thought I had a nightmare. I heard a woman screaming."

"You think now it was really Aludra Wilcox you heard," Flint said, nodding because that theory dovetailed with what Kevin Hayes had said before he'd stopped cooperating. "Do you know what happened to her?"

"I didn't see it happen, but if Aludra Wilcox was murdered that night, everything that happened to us makes more sense." Hallman cleared his throat. "It's the only way any of it does make sense."

"What do you mean?"

Hallman said, quietly, "I think Boyd Wilcox killed her."

Flint raised both eyebrows. "Boyd? Not Mark?" Boyd was about as hot-blooded as a cold fish in Alaska. Hard to believe he could muster enough emotional energy to kill anyone.

Hallman reached over for Flint's empty mug. "Let me get more coffee."

Chapter Forty

Houston, Texas
Monday

Sebastian Shaw Tower dominated downtown Houston in the same way its namesake dominated the entire state of Texas. It jutted from the pavement as a monument to modern engineering. The reflective bronze glass sparkled in the sunlight, twisting from the center of the earth into the stratosphere like oil gushing to the sky.

Baz Shaw said his first oil gusher, the one he'd found when he was a wildcatter decades ago, looked just like the tower. He exaggerated, of course, because that's what men like Shaw do. But the gusher had been impressive and both his reputation and his wealth were built on its liquid foundation.

Shaw was a man used to getting everything he wanted, every time. He'd taken an unwelcome interest in Flint a while back and Flint had been unable to shake him. Not for lack of trying.

Had he known that Shaw manipulated Veronica Beaumont to hire him, would Flint have refused to help her and her son? He'd like to believe the answer was yes, that he'd absolutely have sent Beaumont to someone else.

But then, Jamie might not have made it.

Flint's feelings on the issue were unsettled, so he left them alone.

The elevator shot like a bullet, eighty stories up from the lobby. Flint stepped into the sky high above Houston. On the penthouse floor, there were few obstructions to Shaw's breathtaking view of the city. From the elevator lobby, Flint's sight line was straight across the cavernous building to Shaw's open office, where he stood with a drink and a cigar in his hand, waiting.

Flint had last seen Shaw a year ago, but it might have been yesterday. He hadn't changed so much as a fine line around the eyes. His body was fit and his mind, no doubt, as sharp as ever. He'd been a lady-killer in his youth and he was blessed with movie-star handsome looks even now. He wore the luxury surrounding him as comfortably as Flint wore sweats on weekends.

Shaw simply stood, relaxed, waiting for Flint to complete the journey across the divide. Flint walked straight and true and stopped twenty feet short. Shaw grinned and stuffed the cigar in his mouth for a quick puff before he said, "How can I help you today, Michael?"

"If you want to talk to me, all you have to do is pick up the phone. I know you can make a phone call because you've done it before."

Shaw sipped his booze. scotch, probably. His tastes in everything ran to the best that money could buy. He didn't offer to share. "I hear your search for Ms. Beaumont's missing ex was successful. Congratulations."

Flint nodded and watched him carefully. "Why do you care about Jamie Beaumont?"

"What makes you think I do?" Shaw puffed and sipped and lied. "She asked me for help. I gave her your name. Nothing more."

"You know she's dating Jasper Crane."

Jasper's father, Felix Crane, had been Shaw's biggest rival for decades. They'd come up in the same small town in West Texas. Both sons of oil wildcatters.

Before Crane died, he and Shaw had been locked in a blood feud without end. Jasper now owned his father's business interests. With Crane dead, keeping closer tabs on Crane's offspring was second nature to Shaw.

Shaw's eyes narrowed. "For such a beautiful woman, Veronica has appalling taste in men."

"Before he died, Crane told me you two had agreed to a cessation of hostilities. He said you'd settled your differences. Was that true?"

"More or less." Shaw shrugged. "Hard to maintain a war against a dead man and Jasper's not half the man his father was. Very little pleasure in fighting things out with him. No challenge, you know?"

Flint straightened his shoulders. The left one was still sore as hell. “So it wasn’t the kid and it wasn’t Jasper. Why did you give my name to Veronica Beaumont?”

Shaw moved to his drink cart for a refill. With his back to Flint, he said, “I told you. She asked me for a recommendation. She said she’d tried everything. She said her kid would die if she didn’t find her ex.”

“Right.”

He turned, backlit by the Houston sunshine so that Flint couldn’t see his face. “What was I supposed to do? She needed the best. And whatever else you are, Michael, you most definitely are the best heir hunter money can buy.”

"Except that you know it takes more than money to buy me. That's why you used Katie Scarlett's daughter to hook me in. And that's a lot more effort than simply passing my name along."

"Look. I've got business to do. I answered your question." Shaw raised his glass in farewell and nodded toward the elevator. "If there's nothing else."

"You and Boyd Wilcox have known each other for decades. You knew I'd handled the Mark Wilcox case six years ago. You knew how that ended. Why didn't you tell Beaumont all that?"

Shaw shrugged. "Didn't seem relevant."

Flint shook his head. Whatever game Shaw had been playing at the time was over now that Wilcox was dead. And whatever game he'd been playing with Beaumont was done, too.

"What about James Preston?"

Shaw frowned and his eyes narrowed. His nostrils flared. "What about him?"

"So you know who he was, then."

The phone on his desk buzzed. He ignored it. "A rapist and a killer, according to the jury. He was put to death last week."

"He was. But I talked to him first. He had some interesting things to say."

“About what?” The phone buzzed again.

“About Marilyn Baker.”

Shaw continued to stare, chin out, like a pugilist assessing his next jab. But his arms weren’t long enough to reach from across the room. He said nothing.

“You knew Marilyn Baker. She lived and was murdered in your old hometown. You and Crane offered a reward for information that would lead to her killer’s arrest.” Flint moved to get a better look at Shaw’s face. “Why?”

Shaw did not reply. The phone buzzed again. And again. He walked over to the desk and picked up the receiver. "Yes . . . I see . . . Five minutes." He replaced the receiver and said, "I'm afraid I have another meeting. You can find your way out."

Flint didn't move. "What was Marilyn Baker to you?"

"A murder victim. Mount Warren is a small town. Crane and I were both living there. Up and coming at the time. We contributed money to a reward fund. That's it." Shaw nodded his head toward the elevator. "Nothing sinister. We contributed to all kinds of causes. I still do."

"I don't believe you. I think you or Crane killed Marilyn Baker. Then you offered up the reward as a cover-up." He could be stubborn, too, even if he preferred to think of himself as tenacious. “And you sent Veronica Beaumont to me to keep me out of the way until James Preston was executed so I wouldn’t find out what you did.”

“What you think is not my problem.” Shaw scowled and picked up the phone again. “Do I need to call security, or are you on your way out?”

Shaw would make good on his threat to have him escorted from the building, but that’s not why Flint let him win today’s contest of wills.

Shaw had already confirmed enough.

He’d known James Preston. He’d known Marilyn Baker. He’d paid money to help find her killer. And he’d wanted Flint out of the way to be sure Flint didn't keep Preston alive.

Those facts were enough for Flint to work with for now.

Without another word, he turned on his heel and walked to the elevator. When the doors opened, Shaw's visitor was not inside. Flint entered and turned to watch Shaw, still talking on the phone, until the doors slid shut.

What the hell was he up to?

Chapter Forty-One

Houston, Texas
Three Months Later

Katie Scarlett arrived after midnight. She let herself in through the back door and collected a crystal tumbler on the way to his den. He offered her the bottle of scotch. She poured a healthy shot.

She removed her jacket and tossed it on the sofa and sat across from his favorite chair.

“Jamie Beaumont’s eighth birthday party was today. Maddy and I went. He’s doing so much better, thanks to you.” She stretched her long legs onto the ottoman between them.

"I heard from Veronica that Josh was a match and they did the transplant a few weeks ago. I'm glad. Jamie's a good kid." He grinned. "How do you feel about having Veronica Beaumont as Maddy's mother-in-law?"

"That was so last month, Flint." She laughed and lifted her Scotch in a toast across the divide. "Maddy's moved on."

"Thank God." Flint smiled and raised his glass toward hers. "Can you imagine countless Thanksgiving dinners with Veronica Beaumont? What a barracuda."

"So what's keeping you up tonight?" She sipped and smiled with pleasure as the smooth taste lingered on her tongue. "Boyd Wilcox?"

Flint nodded. She knew he'd been ruminating on Boyd Wilcox for several weeks. He'd invited her for a fresh look at the problem, he'd said. But he already had a plan and he needed backup.

"Want to talk it through? See if something sparks?" Scarlett asked.

He stretched out in his chair. He wasn't dressed in comfortable sweats. Scarlett would have noticed. He'd get to that in a minute.

Flint said, "Josh Hallman said Boyd was at Wilcox Lodge the night his friends were killed."

"The same night he saw Mark Wilcox bury his wife, and saw Aludra's decapitated head in the plastic ice chest, right?"

He nodded again.

"You're thinking it's extremely long odds that Boyd Wilcox is innocent in all of this," Scarlett said slowly.

"Kevin Hayes said Aludra wasn't really kidnapped. But she went missing weeks before Hallman's plane crash, and her husband absolutely believed she'd been taken. I could tell."

Flint didn't refill his own glass. He'd be leaving in a couple of hours. No time to get buzzed. "Hallman said Boyd was inside the lodge the whole time. He also said he was awakened during the night by a woman's screams. He believes Aludra was murdered that night and maybe inside the house."

"You think Boyd killed her?" Scarlett stared.

"Hallman thinks so. Boyd Wilcox is used to being in charge. Telling everyone what to do." Flint paused, waiting for her to walk through the logic and confirm his theory.

"And didn't you say that Ruben Vega worked directly for Boyd?" Scarlett pushed her lips around as she thought about the problem. "No question Brainy Boy Boyd is in this up to his eyeballs. But that doesn't make him a killer."

Exactly what Flint had concluded.

No way Boyd Wilcox could have been isolated from what was going on. That lodge house in the woods was large, but not large enough to insulate him from the murder and mayhem.

“Here’s what I think,” Flint began to lay it out. “The autopsy report said Aludra had sex just before she died, and she was strangled, remember?”

“So she was decapitated after death.”

Flint nodded. “Her body had been frozen, according to the medical examiner.”

“It could have been angry makeup sex with Mark gone wrong, I guess.”

“Possibly. But I’ve been digging around, and it turns out that Boyd has some kinky appetites. Complaints from women have been hushed up and the women paid off." Flint paused and let her think about it. "If Boyd killed Aludra, I don't think he meant to. I think the sex simply went too far."

"Meaning that after she died, the rest was a cover-up," Scarlett said thoughtfully. "So the whole kidnapping thing was what, a ruse?"

"Hayes said Mark reported her missing and said that she'd been kidnapped because he believed it. That's when he hired me." Flint shook his head. "Boyd had to play along because I'd made sure the story got out when I was trying to find her."

"And she was never missing at all?"

"As far as her husband was concerned, she did go missing. But that's because she left with Boyd. Like Hayes said." Flint nodded again. "That's why the whole Wilcox group was acting so strangely the day Hallman's plane crashed. They knew Aludra was there, at the lodge, when the world believed she'd been kidnapped."

"So their plan was simply to release her?" She cocked her head and her eyes unfocused.

"Remember that Boyd had paid the ransom demand and someone had collected the money. So yeah, I think they were just going to release her and claim that the kidnappers had let her go," Flint said.

“That’s pretty messed up, don’t you think?” Scarlett asked.

“I think they were making a plan that weekend at the lodge. And that night, Boyd accidentally killed her. When she died, they probably panicked and concocted the cover-up.” Flint paused and they both considered the theory for a while.

Scarlett was still thinking it through.

Flint couldn’t see any flaws in the timeline. Everything he knew fit together like a complicated puzzle. “If Josh Hallman hadn’t seen Mark burying the body, the plan might have worked.”

Scarlett paused a lot longer, as if she was trying to decode another answer from the data.

"Boyd won't be brought down by accusations alone," Scarlett finally warned. "You'll need proof. Do you have any?"

"Not enough to satisfy a prosecutor." Flint shook his head and clasped his hands across his flat stomach.

"No witnesses."

Flint nodded. "Neither Veronica Beaumont nor Josh Hallman wants more trouble. She paid me already and made it clear that she won't finance what she called my Don Quixote quest to nail Boyd."

"Not that you need her money, but that sounds like something Veronica would say." Scarlett frowned and stared at the brown liquid refracting lamplight from the crystal glass. "She's solved her problem. Everybody else can fend for themselves."

"Hallman will never testify against Wilcox, either." Flint ignored the barb. He wanted to stay on track. "He went back to his life on Fiji and plans to stay out of sight."

"That's smart, don't you think? Boyd can reach him anywhere in the world. He's right about that much." She cocked her head. "What about Kevin Hayes? We know people. Maybe we can get him some sort of deal if he testifies against Boyd, shorten his sentence by a few years?"

Flint shook his head. He had rejected that possibility a while back. “Too many ways Boyd can reach him inside, make Hayes’s life even worse.”

“Or end his life completely.” She inhaled deeply and tapped a knuckle against her lips, thinking things through. He recognized the signs of her process.

“Boyd is unfinished business. I want him finished,” Flint said sourly. “Simple as that.”

“I get that.” She nodded. “He left the country right before Hayes was arrested. Nobody can find him. I put the word out, like you asked. Nothing yet. You have any luck with your contacts?”

She drained her scotch and rolled the empty glass between her palms. He raised the bottle in a silent offer to refill, but she shook her head.

“He’ll turn up. Soon.” Flint narrowed his eyes and stared straight ahead.

“I know that look, Flint.” She scowled from across the room. “What are you planning to do?”

“Depends.”

“On what?”

“What he does first.” Flint shrugged. “Look, I killed his brother. And his right-hand man. Self-defense, sure. But Boyd won’t accept that as an excuse.”

"Watch your back. He's no match for you or anybody else, physically. Brainy boys rarely are. But Boyd Wilcox travels with a lot of protection." Scarlett didn't try to persuade him to give up. She had to know that would be a waste of breath. "I'll keep looking. Gaspar will help me and he's damned good at finding people and things when others can't."

"But?"

"But the entire world is Boyd Wilcox's oyster. Don't forget that. He's got a lot of resources you don't have access to."

Flint had never been afraid of powerful people. He didn't intend to change now. Scarlett had to know how he felt about that.

"I have no affection for Veronica Beaumont, but she may be right about this," Scarlett said. "Can't you let it go? Just this once?"

"I know where he is. I'm going after him. Tonight."

She looked at him as if he'd lost his mind. Which he probably had.

"Boyd is a big astronomy buff. So I've been following that trail." Flint nodded. "He owns a home in the Atacama Desert. In Chile. Solely because it's one of the best places on earth for observing celestial events. He's installed one of the most expensive telescopes in the world down there."

She cocked her head. "And there's some sort of rare celestial event happening soon?"

"Extremely rare, I'm told. The transit of Mercury across the sun."

Her face screwed up into a question.

He grinned. "Yeah, I didn't know what it was, either. Turns out the planet Mercury will move directly between Earth and the sun, and if you're in the right place, at the right time, with the right equipment, you'll be able to see it."

"Rich men have the craziest hobbies, don't they?" She shrugged. "So when is this transit supposed to happen?"

He grinned. "Best viewing is Wednesday, just before sunrise. In the Atacama Desert."

"I've heard about Atacama. Six hundred miles of absolute desert. The driest place on earth." She paused, thinking. "You don't know for sure that he'll be there. He could just catch this transit the next time."

"Not likely. Happens only thirteen times every century. The last time was 2019. Won't happen again until until 2039. Hell, the North Koreans could blow up the world by then. Who knows?" Flint grinned again and nodded firmly. "He'll be there."

"Your contacts have already confirmed this somehow." She took a deep breath. "He's already there, isn't he?"

"You know me too well." Flint smirked. "Yeah, I asked Gaspar to help me. He owed me a couple of favors. So he's been working on it. Like you said, Gaspar's good at finding things when others can't."

She gave up the fight. "What do you want me to do?"

"What you always do. Come to my rescue if I get in over my head." He pointed his chin toward the table beside her seat where he'd placed a small manila envelope. "There's a thumb drive in there. It contains the specifics of my plan. Satellite shots of Wilcox's Oasis, which is what he calls his place there. Looks like he's got a small staff when he's on-site. A security team and some domestics."

She picked up the envelope and felt the thumb drive inside. She said nothing.

“You should hear from me that the job is done and I’m on my way back before Wednesday, zero three hundred hours. Otherwise, you know who to call.”

“If you die out there in that wasteland, Maddy will never forgive you.” Her voice was quiet.

He knew what she was saying. To be careful. Not to take crazy risks. To come back safely because he was the only family she and Maddy had.

He nodded and said nothing because there was no acceptable response he could make.

“Meanwhile, we’ll keep at it. Gaspar, too. There could be some trace evidence against him they haven’t found yet." Scarlett stood, empty glass in hand. She slipped the envelope into the pocket of her jacket. "When you bring him back here, we'll still need evidence to lock him up forever."

"Maybe so."

But he wasn't counting on it.

Crime techs had been sifting through the evidence for weeks. They'd found nothing incriminating Boyd for Aludra's murder yet.

No reason to believe they ever would.

If there had been positive proof at one time, it was likely destroyed long ago.

She placed a hand on his shoulder and squeezed as she walked past him on the way out. He heard the back door close and lock behind her.

Briefly, he second-guessed his decision not to tell her about Marilyn Baker. About how he believed Baker was his biological mother. About her murder and the man who was accused of killing her.

He shoved the thoughts aside. There would be time to deal with all that when he came back.

He thought again about the Romanov pendant and his client who had risked lives to retrieve it.

He shook his head. The only family he really had was Katie and Maddy

Scarlett. He liked it that way. He didn't need to know anything more about Marilyn Baker. No reason to dredge up a dead woman's past.

He glanced at his watch. He had a few minutes yet before Drake arrived. He pressed the remote to turn up the volume on his music, closed his eyes, and let his head loll back on the chair.

He did some of his best thinking when he was relaxed like this.

He visualized Wilcox Lodge at Red Maple Lake.

The patio, the one with the newer pavers, had been torn up when authorities searched for Aludra Wilcox. They'd found the body parts in several small holes under the foundation, like Hayes had said they would.

They'd matched the body parts and the finger in the purple satin box to her DNA.

No doubt, the woman Mark Wilcox buried was his wife. Which didn't mean he'd killed her.

Hallman thought Boyd Wilcox killed Aludra, and from what he knew of the two Wilcox brothers, Flint was inclined to agree.

They were still processing the crime scene, even after all these weeks. They might find forensic evidence against Boyd Wilcox somewhere.

Maybe he'd handled that sword his brother had used to hack up the body. The one Flint had seen in the shed. Which wouldn't mean much, either.

Hayes took care of the loose ends to get the plea deal.

He'd admitted nothing incriminating about Boyd Wilcox.

He'd said Mark beheaded Aludra. Hayes and Vega helped him conceal the crime. They would have succeeded, too, if Josh Hallman had been a better pilot, Hayes said. He'd been pissed off about that, as if Hallman was the cause of all their troubles.

Of course, none of this would have happened if Hallman hadn't crashed the Cessna. His friends would be alive. Flint wouldn't be on his way to Atacama.

But none of that mattered.

Flint had spent his entire life accepting everything as it came, when it came. He dealt with reality, here and now. He spent no time wishing for events to be different from what they were.

If Flint failed, Boyd Wilcox would keep walking around as if he were untouchable. He'd keep doing exactly what he pleased, when he pleased.

He'd get away with murder.

Simple as that.

And Flint would never let that happen.

Chapter Forty-Two

Atacama Desert, Chile
Tuesday

Sixteen hours of travel time from Houston south to Antofagasta, Chile, which was on the Pacific coast. During the flight, he and Drake slept six hours and spent the rest of the flight reviewing the location and his plan of attack.

Preparation was key.

He had one chance to make this work and no room for error.

The satellite images Flint had obtained showed Wilcox's Oasis built into the side of a mountain. He'd used the famous ESO Hotel at Paranal as inspiration.

Wilcox's Oasis was much more luxurious than the ESO housing for scientists, but it borrowed the design elements intended to eliminate light pollution. Scientists required absolute darkness.

From the east side, the roof looked like a dome buried in the sand.

The dome was a huge skylight with a retractable shade that, when deployed, held all interior light inside the building.

On the west side, the wall of the house was exposed. Windows were fitted with blackout shades. The entire residence was enclosed from the inside to completely eliminate exterior light at night.

Small trees and greenery surrounded the exterior, irrigated as only unlimited wealth could afford. There was an indoor swimming pool for recreation and to provide much-needed humidity. Water was trucked in and recycled.

A few hundred feet up the mountain from the house was Wilcox's private state-of-the-art observatory, equipped with his own VBT, or "very big telescope."

He alone used the VBT and spent his nights in the observatory without interruption.

They landed in Antofagasta midmorning. Flint preferred to attack in the dark hours before dawn.

The approach had worked well for legions of armies and clandestine operations.

But it wouldn't work here. All serious astronomers and scientists were awake all night for the celestial show.

When Wilcox slept, his staff slept. Only one man on his security detail would be standing watch in the video room as a precaution.

No one seriously expected to be attacked in the Atacama Desert.

Two hours' drive time from the airport to Wilcox's Oasis would have been the easiest means of approach.

But any degree of stealth was impossible using a land vehicle.

Nothing but a few outbuildings, his observatory, and miles of sand surrounded Wilcox's house. A land vehicle would kick up dust and be seen on the long-distance closed circuit cameras monitored by Wilcox's security.

Which made the decision to approach by air using a steerable parachute the only option.

At the terminal, they collected their gear.

Drake drove the rental to the private airstrip where he'd reserved the skydive aircraft.

There were several popular jump planes. The Cessna 182 Drake located was common and familiar. It would take him up to ten thousand feet in twenty minutes, which served Flint's purposes.

More important today, this one was painted gray, like a fighter plane. It would be tough to spot from the ground.

Flint dressed in the gray jumpsuit and checked his steerable gray parachute again while Drake readied the Cessna. Soon they were airborne, flying east from the coastal town into the desert.

The plane was loud, as all plane engines were. But at ten thousand feet and a radius of three miles from Wilcox's Oasis, occupants of the house should not hear the Cessna.

Drake flew wide of the target. Flint lifted the binoculars to his eyes to get his first real look at Wilcox's Oasis.

The house and grounds seemed unoccupied from this vantage point. No vehicles outside. No people, either.

Flint saw the glass dome reflecting sunlight even though its shade was deployed inside.

The two outbuildings that housed vehicles and supplies were closed up tight. The observatory's VBT had been covered for the daylight hours, too.

All was as Flint had expected.

He gave Drake a thumbs-up from the back.

He checked his parachute again as Drake flew to the jump point, east of Wilcox's Oasis as the sun was nearing its apex. The surveillance cameras would be looking into the sun. In his gray suit with the gray parachute, ten thousand feet up and three miles away, Flint should be effectively invisible.

In theory.

He opened the door of the Cessna. When Drake had the plane in position, Flint jumped into a brief free fall and then deployed the chute for a long, slow glide.

The outbuildings surrounding Wilcox's Oasis came into view.

He steered the chute to land behind. His feet hit the ground and he ran and tumbled to a safe stop.

Quickly, he released his harness and stepped away from the chute. He gathered it up in his arms and found a place to stash it behind the building.

He stripped off the gray suit, revealing desert camo garb beneath, which would visually blend his body with the terrain. He settled his small equipment pack around his waist and moved his gun to his belt where he could grab it easily.

He crouched close to the ground and ran from the cover of the building to the cover of the trees, careful to avoid the security cameras, until he reached the exposed side of the house.

The side where Wilcox's master suite was located.

Wilcox's windows were covered by blackout shades.

Gaspar's best intel said he was inside and he was alone. All Flint had to do was breach the bedroom's security.

Flint made his way to the bedroom window farthest from the bed. He opened his equipment pack and pulled out the specialized glass cutter and a roll of heavy duct tape.

He stuck two long strips of the tape, corner to corner, in a big X across the window glass, leaving enough slack in the center to form a handle for his gloved hand.

He cut a large rectangle around the X and, using both hands on the center of the X, pulled the glass free. He set the glass against the side of the house.

He dropped his work gloves beside the roll of duct tape and the glass cutter.

The blackout shade was now the only barrier between Flint and Boyd Wilcox.

The shade was on a track attached to the wall, like a second window. It opened and closed electronically.

It provided not only a light barrier but also a heat and humidity barrier, and sound deadening as well.

He was close enough to hear Wilcox breathing. He listened for snoring inside the bedroom but heard none. Probably because of the shade.

Moving quickly, Flint pulled his specialized utility knife from his belt and slashed the blackout shade in the same big X pattern he'd used on the window.

He tossed the knife to the ground and gripped his gun in his right hand and a Maglite in his left. He pushed aside the heavy shade with his left arm as he stepped over the window's threshold into the room.

The brief flash of light when he stepped through the X was almost immediately shuttered when the X snapped back into place, as if it had never been sliced.

Flint stood in near-total darkness inside the bedroom.

He waited a moment for his eyes to adjust.

He pointed the Maglite to the floor and turned it on.

The bed was to his left in the drawings he'd seen. Quickly, he brought his hands together, right over left, and raised both light and gun at the same time, pointed straight ahead.

The light illuminated the king-size bed in a solid beam, leaving the rest of the room in darkness.

The covers were thrown back. The bed was unoccupied.

"You're later than I expected, Flint." Wilcox said. He had heard Flint coming.

From ten feet ahead, on his left, in the near-total silence, Flint heard the unmistakable rack of a gun slide. A pistol.

It was exactly the kind of sound that Flint had trained his whole life never to miss. A precise set of movements, one following the other. The magazine spring, the brass-cased shell clicking home, the return of the slide. Fast, sure, solid.

Less than half a second, even for an amateur like Wilcox to accomplish.

Less than a tenth of a second for Flint to process.

Wilcox was seated. The pistol was small. The magazine held not more than thirteen rounds.

Which was more than enough to do the job, in the hands of a man who knew how to use them.

In one smooth motion, Flint pushed his light and his gun to the left and down to meet the attack's origin.

He squeezed the trigger on his pistol and fell onto his left side and away.

He felt Wilcox's bullet pass through the void where Flint's body had been half a moment before.

He was in that zone where his mind raced and his body slowed.

Like slow-motion in films, he saw his shot hit Wilcox's chest and red blood spurt onto his naked torso.

The blood pumped out and darkened when it hit the room's oxygen and covered his body, running down to his lap and pooling there in the chair.

Flint was barely breathing heavy. "You thought you'd get away with murder, didn't you?"

Wilcox grimaced. He lifted his left hand to cover the wound. His voice wheezed. "Aludra was a cheap slut, Flint. You didn't know her."

"So you killed her."

"In the moment just before orgasm. Too much pressure on her throat." Wilcox coughed a bit and blood seeped from the corner of his mouth. He shrugged. "It happens."

"You've done the same thing to other women, then," Flint said coldly.

Wilcox shrugged again. "Like I said, it happens."

Flint's Maglite illuminated Wilcox, but Flint and everything in the room was still cloaked in darkness. Even as he watched Wilcox through narrowed eyes, Flint listened intently for footsteps in the corridor outside.

Wilcox's right arm lifted his gun and pointed at Flint.

This time, Flint shot first.

The second bullet slammed into his heart.

Blood pulsed once, twice.

Wilcox's arm fell to the side, eyes wide open.

His blood stopped spurting. His heart quit pumping.

The world regained normal speed.

Flint could hear his own breathing, blood pulsing in his ears in syncopation with his pounding heartbeat.

He nodded. Now he knew for sure.

All the dominos fell into place.

Boyd Wilcox had faked Aludra's kidnapping and then killed her.

Everything that flowed from Aludra's death was on Boyd Wilcox's conscience. If he'd had one.

The gunshots had awakened the household.

Flint heard footfalls in the corridor outside the bedroom.

Gaspar's intel said there were four security guards on-site, along with three male staff members trained in combat. He couldn't outrun them all, but he hadn't planned to kill them, either.

He pushed up from the floor and ran to flatten himself against the wall. The door burst open. Weak illumination filtered through the hallway.

The security guard flipped the light switch and flooded the bedroom with blinding light.

The room was decorated like a desert hideaway.

Sand colors permeated the modern furnishings. The floor was cool brown tiles. The walls looked like blocks of sandstone, as if the building had been carved out of the mountain, one room at a time.

The guard looked at Wilcox. The damage to his torso from the close-range gunshot was spectacular. No one who saw Wilcox would believe he still lived.

The guard swiveled his head. Took one look at the outline of light from the giant X in the blackout shade. Should he pursue the attacker? He was gripped by indecision for half a second too long.

Flint raised his gun and pressed it to the back of the guard's neck. "Drop your weapon."

The guard didn't respond.

Flint pushed his gun harder. "You want to join Wilcox?"

The guard dropped his weapon.

Flint closed the door to Wilcox's bedroom and locked it from the inside.

"On your knees. Hands on your head."

The guard dropped to the floor.

Flint pushed him onto his face and pulled out a plastic cable tie from his pocket. He secured the tie to the guard's wrists and then pushed him over onto his back.

The man's nose flared and his eyes narrowed into slits.

Flint crouched down and stuck the barrel of his gun under the guard's chin. He put one knee on the guard's chest and leaned his weight onto him.

While he was immobilized, Flint reached into his pocket and pulled out the fast-acting sedative he'd intended for Wilcox.

The guard struggled to break free, but Flint pulled the cap off the needle with his teeth and jabbed fast, dosing the guard with about half the contents of the syringe.

When the guard's eyes fell closed, Flint rolled him under the bed.

He picked up the guard's gun and put his own weapon into his pocket.

The entire exchange lasted less than two minutes.

This was the guard on duty, but the others would be on the prowl now, too. Three more guards and three combat-trained staff, Gaspar had warned

Six against one. He hesitated for a moment before he ducked out the window into the blinding sunlight.

Flint left Wilcox's room the same way he'd entered. He stayed out of sight of the cameras and made his way to the outbuilding that served as a garage.

He collected his parachute from behind the building and stuffed it into the back of Wilcox's SUV.

He pulled the starter fuse and the fuel pump fuse on the second SUV and slipped them into his pocket.

He saw the electronic key fob resting in the cup holder. He pushed the ignition button to start Wilcox's armored SUV and reversed fast out of the garage.

Two guards came running out of the front of the house, brandishing handguns.

He sped faster, reversing down the driveway.

He took evasive maneuvers, serpentine driving, toward the road, increasing speed, putting distance between the vehicle and the shooters.

Two shots at the SUV went wide. Another hit the left front side and bounced off.

A fourth shot hit the windshield. The round screamed through the bullet-resistant glass and embedded into the rear seat.

When he reached the road, instead of slowing Flint floored the accelerator into a fast J-turn.

The top-heavy SUV wobbled and the left tires threatened to leave the road. He removed his foot from the accelerator, and the left side slammed hard onto the gravel roadway, facing the right direction.

The tires gripped the gravel and he accelerated again and the SUV leapt forward.

He glanced into the rearview mirror.

The two guards ran around the house to the garage. He patted the fuses in his pocket and smiled.

They wouldn't be able to start the second SUV, but they might have access to transportation from somewhere else. He drove away from the house as fast as the heavy SUV would travel down the straight road along the desert.

He kept the pedal on the floor until he reached the extraction site where Drake was waiting with the helo. He jumped out of the SUV and left it running.

With luck, no one would find it before it ran out of gas.

He dashed to the waiting Bell 407, stepped inside, and closed the door. “Let’s go!”

The helo lifted off the ground and headed west, toward the airport.

Which would be the first place Wilcox’s team would look for him.

“How far can we go in this bird before we need to stop for fuel?”

“Without using the reserve, about two hundred and fifty miles.” Drake glanced at Flint and raised his eyebrows.

When Flint offered no comment, Drake said, “I’ll find a private airstrip within that distance. And we’re going to need a jet to get home.”

Flint watched the never-ending desert and felt as if he were on Mars. Hazy mountains in the distance looked purple against the perfectly cloudless blue sky above and the miles of desert below.

“Copy that,” Flint replied. “I’ll get Gaspar on it. The jet will be waiting when we get there.”

In every direction, the land was parched and lifeless. Not a blade of grass or a cactus stump as far as the eye could see.

Author's Note

Every new book begins with a spark that leads to an idea I can turn into an exciting story. In the case of **Trace Evidence**, the idea was sparked by an unusual true story.

Years ago, when I was a practicing lawyer in Detroit, one of my clients disappeared. He had been vacationing with his family at an inland lake in northern Michigan. He went out fishing alone, early in the morning, and didn't come back. His boat was found, with all of his gear inside. He was never seen again.

The story stuck with me for several reasons. Because I knew him. And because it was a shock to learn that drowning victims could disappear from small inland lakes. When there is no outlet to a river or ocean, logically, the bodies should eventually be located, and the families deserve closure.

A decade later, I read about an unusual case at another inland lake. A young man, nineteen years old, went out alone on a jet ski in the afternoon. Later, the jet ski and his life jacket turned up, but the young man did not. A search was undertaken immediately, but he was not found. Ten years after he disappeared, new technology in use for underwater search and recovery had been developed. Using that technology and cadaver dogs, his body was found, lying peacefully and intact on the sandy lake bottom, about one hundred feet from the surface.

Thus, my research for **Trace Evidence** began. What I learned along the way forms the foundation for this story featuring Michael Flint.

A real-life heir hunter is a forensic genealogist, someone who researches ancestry by means of standard records and more, for profit. It was the “and more, for profit” piece that I’ve used to create the Michael Flint novels. The “and more, for profit” opens all sorts of story possibilities, doesn’t it? My writer’s mind went to work, furiously plotting.

For **Trace Evidence**, my research revealed that what happened to my client, and to the young jet skier, is only one of many unusual circumstances related to the thousands of lakes in North America and around the world.

ABOUT THE AUTHOR

Diane Capri is an award-winning **New York Times**, **USA Today**, and worldwide bestselling author. She's a recovering lawyer and snowbird who divides her time between Florida and Michigan. An active member of Mystery Writers of America, Author's Guild, International Thriller Writers, Alliance of Independent Authors, Novelists, Inc., and Sisters in Crime, she loves to hear from readers. She is hard at work on her next novel.

Please connect with her online:

DianeCapri.com
Twitter.com/DianeCapri
Facebook.com/Diane.Capri1
Facebook.com/DianeCapriBooks

www.ingramcontent.com/pod-product-compliance
Lightning Source LLC
Chambersburg PA
CBHW020346310726
48979CB00015B/2526/J

* 9 7 8 1 9 6 2 7 6 9 3 1 0 *